OFF PLAN

by

Nick Pope

**Grosvenor House
Publishing Limited**

This book is published by
Grosvenor House Publishing Ltd
28-30 High Street, Guildford, Surrey, GU1 3EL.
www.grosvenorhousepublishing.co.uk

A CIP record for this book
is available from the British Library

ISBN 978-1-78148-534-7

*Thank you for buying my first published
book and helping a great cause with
my proceeds going to help find new treatments
and cures for Lung Cancer, a terrible disease
that I have been fighting since 2009*

*Writer's proceeds from the first 1,000 copies
sold are going to the Roy Castle Lung Cancer
Foundation, which is the only U.K charity
devoted solely to raising funds to fight the
commonest cancer in this country*

Disclaimer

'Off Plan' is a work of fiction. Names, characters, businesses, places, events and incidents that are referred to are either the products of the author's imagination or used in a completely fictitious manner. Any resemblance to actual persons, living or dead, or actual events is purely coincidental

About the Author

Nick Pope was born in West Kirby on October 26th 1954. He now lives in Cheshire with his devoted and gorgeous second wife, Sue. Apart from writing he enjoys playing golf, walking and cycling.

Following a period of nearly thirty years working for large Global organisations he became disillusioned with all the politics and bureaucracy so decided to set up his own consultancy business back in 2009, with the aim of helping small businesses. This would also free some valuable time to pursue his passion for writing.

Some six weeks after starting the company he was diagnosed with both Cancer of the throat and lung cancer. Following a succession of major surgeries and treatment Nick went into remission; unfortunately the cancer returned to the lungs in 2011 and has spread to the spine therefore giving him a terminal diagnosis.

Given the circumstances Nick has decided to donate all his proceeds from the sale of his first 1,000 copies of the novel to the Roy Castle Lung Foundation.

Nick started this project back in 2007 and the main body of the story only took five months to write. The publication of the story got derailed due to illness and other matters but now it is ready to share, hope you enjoy the read.

'Off Plan' is a fast-paced, gripping adult thriller set in the tough urban playground of Liverpool. It tells the tale of a ruthless family of property developers who also control the city's drug business.

Future projects include further adult thrillers and a love story.

CHAPTER ONE

The sirens wailed; the engine roared as the ambulance weaved in and out of the rush hour traffic with the precision of a slalom skier, attempting to make its way across town. It was heading to the Accident & Emergency department of The Royal Hospital that lay on the outskirts of Liverpool. Two paramedics, assisted by a bearded doctor, busily attended to their precious on-board cargo, as they fought to keep James Robertson alive.

Up front, the female driver and her young male attendant tried to navigate through the maze of traffic that lay before them.

"Stand back!" one of the paramedics shouted as he charged the built-in defibrillator.

"Clear!" replied his assistant, as the doctor continued to monitor all the vitals that were displayed before him on a large colour screen, periodically stroking his beard as he processed the information.

The pungent smell of singed hair filled the ambulance as the defibrillator's pads discharged their current. The charts remained unchanged as the doctor recited the latest readings whilst encouraging the driver to go faster through the intercom.

"For fuck's sake, we're losing him! Women drivers...."

Another shot of adrenaline was administered by the medical crew, who were desperately trying to bring their ailing patient back to life. As the contents of the syringe began to run around the veins of the dying man, the sirens became noticeably louder, piercing the dulling skies above. In a last-ditch attempt to save their desperate patient, the ambulance had been joined by a couple of motorbike cops.

Whilst the dials in the back of the ambulance remained stable, the speedometer in the front began to increase with some intensity. The outriders started to move the cars and buses, pushing them to the side of the road, creating a passage through which the ambulance could safely pass.

The blue flashing lights reflected in the rear-view mirror of the Mercedes SL 500. The sirens drowned out the local radio station that was playing, as they combined to arouse the driver from his semi-comatose state. He had been sitting in the rush hour traffic attempting to return home to his penthouse on the waterfront for over half an hour now, and was not in the best of moods.

As the first two outriders passed his car, the ambulance mounted the kerb to undertake him, clipping the passenger side mirror of his beloved motor.

"Ah, for fuck's sake...." he exclaimed. "Is there really any need for that, knobhead?" Tony Barlow was having yet another bad day.

Needless to say, the procession continued on with haste in an attempt to reach its destination, bidding to save the life of its cargo, another self-destructive junkie. This druggie was a multi-millionaire – not just a regular user or low-life dealer, but also the son of "Mr Big", Liverpool's biggest distributor.

Tony Barlow was left to inspect the damage to his vehicle. As he moved around to the passenger side he could see the glass from the shattered inbuilt indicator lens on the road. The wing mirror was hanging off and bore the scars of dull white paint from the ambulance.

"Fucking great, I won't get any change out of four hundred rips for that!" Barlow shouted in annoyance as the storm clouds began to build in his troubled mind.

"Hey mate, move your fucking motor – haven't you got a home to go to?" the driver of the old white Transit van that was directly behind the Mercedes shouted, accompanied by the continuous sound of car horns. The traffic had finally begun to move as Tony continued to inspect the damage.

"Alright, keep your hair on!" he shouted at the driver of the battered van.

Another day in paradise, he thought to himself – things always happen in threes. The day had not got off to the greatest of starts when he was awoken at three a.m. by a cheap-looking tart banging on his front door looking for the punter who had just called for her services. It turned out she was a junkie prostitute looking for the occupant of apartment 401 and not 403, where he lived. It was not long before the third thing happened.

He switched on Bloomberg to find out that the NASDAQ had crashed, down over 300 points on the day. His shares in HERITAS, a high-tech company, had been trashed in the process, closing at thirty-two dollars and change, having started the trading session at a shade over forty-eight bucks. A quick calculation soon gave him by far the worst news of his latest bad day: he had lost, on paper, over a hundred and twenty thousand pounds.

As the demons flooded into his troubled mind, his mobile vibrated and distracted him. It was a text from some fit blonde chick that he had met in town on Friday night. His spirit lifted and his pulse quickened. It read, "Shud b with you by 8 at the latest, really lookin 4wd 2 c in u x x G."

Since returning from his apartment in London to his birthplace, two years ago, all had not gone according to plan. He had divorced his wife of over twenty-three years, losing his beautiful five-bedroom detached family home that backed onto the golf course in the process. His relationship with his kids, Sara, 21, and his son Sam, 19, was in meltdown because he had started seeing one of his ex-wife's best friends, amongst a string of other women. Tony had a big sex drive. He used high-class escorts on a regular basis and had enjoyed attending a few swinging parties in London.

Over recent times he had been, not through choice, subjected to living with drug addicts and low lifes at what were supposedly some of Liverpool's finest new addresses, as bent property developers sold their souls; in the main to Irish and out of town investors who bought masses of apartments "off plan", looking to make a quick buck, only to rent a high proportion of them on completion to any Tom, Dick or Harry, as long as they had enough money to cover the rent.

Millions of pounds of dirty money got laundered through a system that had more holes than a sieve. Drug dealers, so called property developers, city planners, councillors, council officials, and politicians all conspired to make their fortunes on the back of a chance of a lifetime – the regeneration of Liverpool. None of them gave a shit about who got hurt along the way – who they ripped off, whose lives they destroyed with their deceit. All they cared about was their greedy selves and how much money they could all make.

Palms were greased, brown envelopes exchanged with the regularity of a heartbeat. The destruction of decent, honest, law-abiding people had begun and was gathering pace on the streets of Liverpool.

The intercom buzzed, and the TV screen immediately changed to the security channel on his Bang & Olufsen. The vision that filled the huge plasma screen was sex on legs. Blondie had arrived bang on time and looked a picture. He released the lock and within a minute she was at his front door.

Dressed in a tiny figure-hugging black miniskirt that resembled more a belt than a skirt, a pair of black patent leather stilettos and a stylish black and white zebra print jacket, Blondie thrust a chilled bottle of Chablis into Tony's mitt and gave him a big kiss on the lips and a welcoming hug.

She smelled great and was far more attractive and toned than Tony remembered. Barely inside the apartment, she slipped her coat off to reveal a tiny black top. Her nipples stood to attention. Tony simply could not resist as he felt his blood race and his cock stiffen. She sank to her knees and quickly unbuttoned his jeans and pulled his throbbing dick towards her. She looked up at Tony and smiled before taking him deep into her mouth. His dreadful day was starting to get a whole lot better! She licked the head of his cock, dragging her tongue across his helmet. He saw her manicured hand moving up and down his penis as the other hand moved towards his arse. She began to stroke his arse before slipping her index finger into it.

Tony tried to think of all things ugly just to distract him – he was so turned on and wanted to explore her body, but knew he was about to come. He managed to get on the cold wooden floor beside her, his cock still firmly inserted in her mouth. He moved towards her pussy, first his hand, then his mouth. God, she was wet. He slipped two fingers inside her and began to lick and nibble her shaven pussy. She groaned and moaned as Tony set to work. She tasted so good, so sweet.

"Bite it, bite it," she demanded. "Finger my arse." Tony duly obliged and as the intensity arose, she screamed, "Oh my God, that is so good – harder, harder, harder!" she shrieked as she came in his mouth.

"I want you to come over my face. Would you like that?" she said. Tony was so turned on and so erect that his cock hurt and his head banged, he just had to release. She sucked and pulled and licked and fingered until he felt the sudden hot rush and came at first in her mouth and then over her beautiful face. His hot white sperm ran down her bronzed skin and over her red lip-gloss.

The Chablis rolled on the floor besides them as they composed themselves. Tony struggled to his feet; still feeling dazed by the unexpected experience, and moved towards the bathroom to get some toilet paper and wipes. He gazed at himself in the bathroom mirror admiringly. Not bad, son, not bad at all. He did not even know her name – she was just Blondie. He cleaned himself up before returning to the empty hall. He quickly checked the kitchen, followed by the lounge. There was no sign of life.

"Blondie, Blondie," Tony called. But his calls were met with stony silence.

The bottle of Chablis lay alone. Blondie had upped and gone.

As Tony began to try and rationalise what had just happened, his mobile vibrated on the hall table.

The text read, "That was so good … Hope to c u around town thanx G xxx."

Tony Barlow was a high-powered executive. For the past five years, he had run a business called Storage Solutions. He was a man who only wanted the best for his family and himself. In pursuit of his goals of buying the next big family home, privately educating his children and paying for the biannual exotic summer vacations, he had been subjected to an ever-increasing amount of stress and time away from home.

His current employers had forced him to buy a flat down south five years previously, apparently in an effort to demonstrate his commitment to the post. Politics dictated that he had to be based down south, within a 25-mile radius of Storage Solutions' head office in Maidenhead, even though he spent very little time there.

Whilst the money had rolled in, his relationship with his wife became intolerable, mainly as a result of too many nights away. Sure, Barlow was a bit of a lad. However there was no other woman in his life – just many one night stands that he had used or paid for to satisfy his sexual desires.

He had simply grown apart from his cold wife, who resembled more of a motherly figure than a partner. Tony had paid the price of his ambition and infatuation with money and had picked the wrong girl.

The divorce cleaned him out. He did not want his kids to suffer as a result of the marital breakdown, so he was far more generous than he needed to be, with the asset sharing as well as the maintenance payments that he committed himself to.

He was forced to radically change his lifestyle. He had been living the high life, and now had to adjust. He really didn't like the prospect of this. Following a couple of cheap flat rentals, he progressed to a two-bedroom penthouse on the marina in West Ferry Quay.

The modest penthouse was bought off plan from Formby Homes for a hundred and sixty-five thousand pounds. At a little over eight hundred square feet, it was functional but certainly not grand – the kitchen wasn't big enough to swing a cat in.

The apartment was very tastefully decorated, like everything about Barlow's lifestyle – he paid meticulous attention to detail. It sat proudly on the top floor of a four-storey block on the water's edge, constructed of yellow brick, and featuring distinctive black PVC frames that wrapped around large glass panels.

Tony had a taste for the nice things in life: designer clothes, fast cars, good food and great company, but only on his terms. He had become a materialistic obsessive compulsive, coming from a broken home – his father had upped and gone whilst he was stuck in his mother's womb. Tony was unsure that he had ever really loved anything, really loved … sure, he thought that he loved his wife; he loved his kids, but this word *love* he struggled with.

In his opinion people used it far to freely. He had no recollection of being loved as a child; no cuddles from his mum, who worked around the clock to give him the private education that put him in good stead for the rest of his days. No father, or indeed, father figure had been present during his formative years when he needed a man in his life to guide and encourage him.

Barlow was a bit of a loner, a very private individual who did not let people pass his inbuilt barriers without detailed scrutiny. Tony had grown to enjoy his own company during years of hopping on and off transatlantic flights and endless nights alone spent in drab hotel rooms.

Nowadays, it was ordering the next sports car or buying a luxury watch or the next toy that gave him a buzz. This feeling of warmth and egotistical self-satisfaction – some people might call it "Love".

Once the builders had fixed the creaking roof, sealed the leaking bedroom windows and cleared the site, Barlow began to settle into his new home, venturing out most weekends with his pals to enjoy the nightlife that was on offer on his doorstep.

* * *

Over the water on the Wirral peninsula, Fraser Robertson drew long and hard on his finest Cuban cigar relaxing in the drawing room of his Caldy mansion, periodically sipping Louis X1V brandy from Stewart crystal. His third wife had already retired for the night to one of their eight bedrooms. They slept apart.

Robertson was in his late fifties, a portly man, with very pale, almost transparent skin. He stood no more than five foot six, but his thick grey hair gave him the appearance of being a distinguished looking man. Nothing could have been further from the truth. Robertson was from the gutter, a real lowlife. Whilst he had been privately educated, he had quickly become embroiled with Liverpool's mafia in an attempt to make his fortune.

To the naïve public, he came across as a well spoken local businessman, raised by his Amish parents within their community until the age of twelve, when they broke with Amish tradition by placing Fraser into one of the top schools in the Midwest, his place had been paid for by a rich uncle.

The Amish stress simplicity and humility. They avoid anything associated with self-exaltation, pride of position or enjoyment of power.

Amish believe that the community is at the heart of their life and faith, and that the way to salvation is to live as a loving community apart from the world. Individualism is avoided.

Amish values include:

- Putting God and community ahead of the individual
- A life of 'goodness', rather than a life of intellect
- Wisdom, rather than technical knowledge
- Community welfare, rather than competition
- Separation from, rather than integration with, modern worldly society

Fraser Robertson and his sons had absolutely no respect for these values. In the main, they represented everything that would have been abhorred by their forefathers.

Fraser's firstborn, Simon, was heir to his lavish empire, had been conceived by Maria, a hairdresser, who was Fraser's first wife. Simon was in his early thirties, married with a son aged six who had recently begun his education at Liverpool College, one of Merseyside's finest educational establishments. Simon's wife, Gina did not work – there was no need for her to work. Her days were filled with regular visits in her new Porsche 911 to Toni & Guy, shopping for the latest designer labels in Manchester at Harvey Nichols and Selfridges, eating at the finest tables that the North West had to offer and a regular glass or two of vintage Champagne.

Manicures, pedicures and general pampering were weekly treats for Gina. She had Botox every three months at a luxury spa in the heart of Cheshire. A personal trainer twice a week kept her figure as she wanted it. Gina Robertson only really cared about herself and her equally phony friends.

Simon Robertson was nothing like his half-brother James. Simon was a very private lad. He loved his wife and he loved his son. He dreamt of him growing up and going on to play for his beloved Liverpool Football Club. Whilst it was believed that he was ashamed of his father's business dealings and all that he represented, he loved the power his dad had and he thought that maybe when the time was right, Fraser would pull a few strings for his son.

Simon enjoyed a drink at home. He had no real pals – he had let them all go during his courtship with the beautiful Gina. He devoted all his social energy to her. She, however, had not given up any of her friends. He even looked after his boy Mark every Friday and the occasional Saturday whilst she went out.

Gina had been fucking the father of one of her son's friends for about six months, having met him at the college whilst they cheered their boys on during a mini soccer game. She had also recently pleasured her personal trainer in the toilets at the gym.

James, Fraser's second son, lay in an induced coma in a private suite at The Royal Hospital, having been rushed across town by ambulance. He had taken a couple of tabs prior to injecting himself with pure crack; grade 'A' stuff from Afghanistan, all from his father's stockpile. Luckily he was with a local escort in his penthouse at the time and she had raised the alarm.

At this stage, the doctors did not know if this time he would have severe brain damage as a result of his latest drugs fest. They had managed to save his life again, but it was too early to assess what further damage he had inflicted on himself.

James was a bad junkie who enjoyed the entire product range of his father's business – crack cocaine, heroin, ecstasy, poppers, and white lightning. He was also a manic-depressive who for the past eight years had been in and out of rehab with the regularity of a fiddler's elbow.

James had been totally neglected and beaten by his dad during his adolescence; he was a nuisance, he just got in the way.

James Robertson was an absolute embarrassment, not to mention liability to his father. Like his half-brother he was a director of Robertson Holdings, the property development company that his father presided over. In the ten years that he had worked for his dad, he had been off sick for at least fifty per cent of the time. Even the days that he had managed to turn up for work, he had hardly contributed, other than by snorting or injecting some of the profits.

James also had a love for prostitutes. He had to pay for sex; being devoid of personality, he was sick. There was no way that he could entice a normal girl. It was rumoured around the city that James was the father of at least three kids born to three different call girls; he did not pay maintenance for any of them. If the bastard's mothers got too vocal with their demands, then the heavies were sent round to give them a good hiding.

Fraser Robertson was as dangerous as an epidemic of a killer virus breaking out on the streets of Liverpool.

CHAPTER TWO

The Reds had just beaten Ipswich Town 5-4 on penalties after a dull 1-1 score line following extra time, to scrape through to the fifth round of The League Cup. Barlow had been a season ticket holder at Anfield for twenty-five years. He had watched his beloved Liverpool win many major honours and play some fabulous, attractive, effective football.

In recent times under Gerard Houllier and Roy Evans, the football that was being played resembled watching paint dry or grass-grow. The Reds no longer played entertaining football; Barlow was considering giving his seats up as a protest that no one would listen to. It was supposed to be enjoyable, but the football that was on display just added to his depression. For now, he decided against it.

He headed home in the driving rain, the windscreen wipers struggling to clear the torrents of water that battered the windshield. It was quite ironic, he thought to himself as he arrived home, that in just six hours he would be up and heading down to Ipswich for a number of meetings with BT. He could have got on the Ipswich team bus, not that there would have been much of an atmosphere on it.

By 11:30 p.m., after checking that the bedroom windows had managed to withstand the heavy rain, he was tucked up in his king size bed. The alarm had been set for 5:04 a.m., not 5 a.m. but 5:04. Barlow was peculiar about time: always punctual but never compliant. He soon sank into a deep sleep.

Bang, bang, bang – this was not the sound of the alarm; he glanced at the bedside clock. It was 2:28 a.m. The banging continued. The noise was coming from directly below his apartment. Some weird looking guy had moved in at the weekend.

"Police, open up, we know you're in there, Victor," the officer screamed.

All of a sudden the front door lost all resistance to the constant pounding of the police battering ram. Several armed officers ran into Victor's apartment, led by the superintendent carrying the warrant. "MSDS – Merseyside Special Drugs Squad," shouted an officer who had already pulled a gun out of his holster. Two more officers with Alsatians, who were frothing from the mouth, just baying for some action, entered the hallway.

Tony Barlow lay motionless, pulling the duvet and fluffy pillows over his face in an attempt to drown out the reality of what was occurring directly beneath him. His pulse quickened.

"Put the knife down and let the girl go!"

"No fucking way, I will kill her if you don't all fucking do one right now," Victor yelled.

"Please, please … do as he says," cried the semi-naked girl with the bread knife at her throat, "he'll kill me, please…." Tears streamed down her cheeks, and her body shook uncontrollably. She felt the bile in her gut start to ascend into her throat.

Victor stood directly behind her, using her slim body as a human shield; his eyes were wild from the coke he had snorted earlier. His right hand, holding the serrated blade, shook violently; a used syringe lay next to a rubber tourniquet on the small, cheap-looking coffee table. By now, there were six armed officers and two Alsatian dogs, plus a couple of paramedics in a parked ambulance waiting outside for the signal to spring into action.

"Come on, Victor, put the knife down – don't make things even worse than they are," one of the officers tried to reason with him.

"Get out, fucking get out, I won't tell you again," Victor raged.

"You know we can't do that, Victor".

Whilst the dialogue continued, Victor now had no less than four laser-sighted guns locked on various parts of his anatomy.

As a shot rang out, the girl fell to the floor; blood gushing from the artery in her neck that Victor had just severed. The vomit that had been stuck in her throat released explosively. He fell beside her, dropping the knife, clutching his left shoulder that had been hit by the lone bullet. She shook uncontrollably; blood filled her mouth and nasal passages as it ran down her naked breasts and began to congeal with her vomit.

The medics were up the stairs and in the flat in no time tending to the wounded. This is not what the MSDS had in mind. It was supposed to be a drug raid, acting on a tip off from a paid informant.

Victor Knight was no small-time dealer. He was a trader, a broker, and a user who was employed by a local building firm as a labourer – cash in hand, no cards in. He was also involved in some unemployment benefit rackets.

Sure, Victor had a record. It didn't begin to reflect the real crimes that he had committed over the years on the streets of the city. Time after time, no matter what evidence the cops had on him, the message would come down from on high to release him without charge. Victor was more important to "Mr Big" out there trading his wares than banged up behind bars.

This time, even by Victor's low standards, he had been sloppy.

The cops were quick to restrain him whilst caring for the girl.

"Bag up all the evidence and search this place from top to bottom, leave no stone unturned." The syringe and tourniquet were bagged; the dogs and their handlers went to work.

The girl was a local prostitute. She was in her mid twenties – quite a pretty looking thing. She was tough – had to be to do what she did. During the day, she tended to her little girl, Samantha, who had just enjoyed her third birthday despite having no daddy. At night, she earned her corn.

Samantha's mum lay fighting for her life in a pool of blood and stenching vomit next to her assailant. He was quickly removed from the crime scene and she was hurriedly transferred to A & E in a bid to save her life.

* * *

Tony Barlow was wide awake, prowling around his apartment in an attempt to find out what the hell had happened just a few feet below him. From his apartment window, he saw two bodies being bundled into separate ambulances before they sped away, sirens blaring. He also spotted the Alsatian dogs and their handlers joining a handful of police officers as they filed into the back of the police van.

He knew something pretty serious had occurred at 303 West Ferry Quay – he had heard a gunshot and had been subjected to most of the proceedings, listening to the dialogue that was exchanged between the cops and the other parties through the paper-thin walls of his new abode.

"Jesus", Tony thought, "my dream home that I have bought with the remnants of my divorce is on top of a criminal playground. How on Earth can someone who is involved in an early morning shootout with the police possibly be living below my penthouse?

"What a disaster. This will be all over the papers, nobody will want to live here." His brain raced and he began to panic. Barlow could not believe what was happening to his life; he was not good at dealing with problems or any kind of negativity. Little did he know that it was going to get a whole lot worse.

The joiners were boarding up the front door of 303 as Barlow prepared to leave, albeit an hour earlier than planned. He stopped to ask what the hell had gone on, only to be told by the workmen that they had no idea, they were just doing their job. Bloodstains interspersed with wet muddy boot prints were ingrained in the recently fitted pale grey carpet on the stairs. A pungent smell hung in the stale air. Tony was in some way relieved that he would be away for a few days.

As he drove towards Ipswich, there was only one thought that was occupying his mind. He needed answers, and he needed them fast. He dialled directory enquiries from his car phone.

"How can I help?" the operator enquired.

"Merseyside Police, please,"

"I have a general number for the headquarters in Queen Street."

"That's fine."

"Should I put you through?" the operator said.

"Yes, please," replied Tony.

"Connecting you to 0151-707-4427 at forty-two pence a minute through your mobile operator."

"Merseyside Police, Detective Sergeant Roper, how can I direct your call?"

"Oh hi, I live in the new marina development in West Ferry Quay...." Before Tony could continue, the sergeant interrupted him. "Lucky you", he said, with his poor attempt at humour. This was definitely not a time for humour.

"Not so lucky me – there was a major incident in the apartment below me, number 303, a few hours ago. I heard gunshots being fired, two people were taken away in ambulances and the place is now boarded up. I need to know what has gone on."

"I am aware of the incident, Sir; it is being dealt with by MSDS. Unfortunately, I cannot divulge any information as it breaches data protection rights."

Barlow could feel his pulse quickening. "Data protection rights? You must be joking! Now listen to me, sergeant, I have just spent a lot of money on a penthouse suite at this development, it is not every night that there is a police raid where you live, especially directly below you.

I need some answers, sergeant. I have a right to know what I am living on top of."

"I am really sorry, Sir. I can take your contact details and pass them onto the investigation team explaining your obvious distress. I'll ask them to call you, but I'm fairly confident that they will only tell you what I have already told you. Would you like me to do that?" queried the desk sergeant.

"Absolutely. I need to speak with them urgently, please get them to call me as soon as possible." Barlow gave his mobile number out and finished the call, his hand still shaking with rage as he replaced the handset. He felt the inner rage surge inside him. He hated this all too familiar sensation.

What have I done he thought to himself? During the past few years, he had lived in the relative calm of Windsor, a stone's throw from the castle. He ran most mornings in the beautiful surroundings of The Great Park. Tony had been as free as the deer that ran alongside him. Apart from his marital difficulties and the demands of his job, the rest of his life was relatively peaceful and predictable – he felt that he was in control, as long as his life was not full of too many issues and challenges.

Following his meetings at BT, Tony checked into his hotel and immediately ran a hot bath to soak away the stress of the past sixteen hours. As the bath began to fill, he switched his mobile on – it had been off all day whilst he had been in his meetings. It rang straight away.

"You have five new messages," the pre-recorded voice said. He switched off the taps so that he could listen to them.

The first two messages were to do with work; the third was from his daughter Sara. Barlow immediately recognised the sheer panic and concern in her voice – the drug raid and shooting were all over the local evening paper and news channels, and she was worried about him. The fourth was from his son, Sam, who was equally concerned. The final message was from Detective Inspector Finch of MSDS returning his call, leaving a number if Barlow wanted to get in touch with him.

After calling his kids and reassuring them that he was fine, he called Detective Inspector Finch. Finch played his cards very close to his chest; offering platitudes as opposed to facts and solutions. Barlow explained his grave concern not just for his safety, but also for his investment. During the conversation with Finch, he learned that the guy who had been arrested was a known local criminal.

The police had acted on a tip-off from an informant. The girl was a prostitute she was also known to MSDS for some minor offences; she was recovering in hospital and was expected to be released within the next 48 hours. Victor Knight had already been discharged, as his shoulder injury was only superficial.

Despite Tony's best efforts, he could not get any more information from Inspector Finch, who advised him that things should calm down and that he should get on with his life.

That evening, Tony's phone was hot with calls from his Scouse mates who had read about the incident in *The Liverpool Echo* or heard about it on *Radio City* and the regional TV news. His so-called friends were not offering their sympathy but taking the piss out of him for buying an apartment in a drug den. "What's it like living in the Bronx?" one of them said. "Welcome to Scouse Harlem," another one jibed. Bastards! Fucking bastards!

Tony was gutted but put on a brave face, joining in with the laughter of his so-called friends who were seizing the moment to inflict a few more mental scars on his already battered brain.

On Friday evening, he returned to the relative calm of West Ferry Quay. The journalists and reporters were long gone, and a peaceful quiet had descended on the area, although the stench of vomit still hung in the seaside air. Tony was looking forward to going out into town for a few beers with his pals. He knew well in advance what the main topic of conversation would be.

As he entered his apartment, a rancid smell filled his nostrils. He had only been away for a few days. "What the hell is that?" he cried to himself, quickly opening all the windows and spraying air freshener in every room like it was going out of fashion.

The smell resembled Indian food mixed with rubbish that had gone off – it was disgusting. He quickly checked to ensure that he had not left any stale food in the kitchen, although he knew that he had not – it would be impossible even with the distraction of the police raid. Barlow was an obsessive compulsive; he would never do such a thing. He was, of course, right. The smell was coming into his penthouse from Victor Knight's flat below.

Without a second thought, Barlow went down the stairs to number 303. The door was still boarded up and double locked with two huge black bolts, one at the top and one at the bottom, each of which was further secured by industrial strength padlocks. Merseyside Police tape was stuck to the doorframe in a cross pattern. There was no sign of life. The air was filled with the pungent smell that had taken up residence in Barlow's apartment.

Victor Knight was not at home; he had been discharged from hospital and released from police custody to a safe house upon instructions from on high. Knight was to lie low for a while until things settled down. He would get a beating from his paymasters for his behaviour, not to mention the fact that they had been forced to call in a very expensive favour to protect one of their assets in their multi-million pound Business.

The prostitute, Mercedez, was resting at home in Toxteth, counting the crisp twenty pound notes – the contents of a large brown envelope that had just been delivered by a mobster, along with a stark warning about keeping her mouth shut. She was instructed to stick to the storyline that she had provoked Victor by telling him that she was fucking all his mates, that he only had a little dick, a crap body and was a lousy lay. She called him a total loser, a waste of skin. It had not taken long for Victor to completely lose it in his drug-induced state.

Mercedez had slipped onto the knife trying to escape from his clutches; of course, no drugs had been found at 303. The syringe had been misplaced; all the loose ends were being tidied up. "Ten grand," the mobster said. "If you don't want to hear from me again and you wish to see your little girl grow up, you keep your mouth shut, understand?" Mercedez nodded as she clung to her daughter, closing the door on the messenger.

If she hadn't been the mother of James Robertson's daughter, she would probably be at the bottom of the River Mersey now.

Victor Knight had also been saved because of his association with Fraser Robertson and his boys.

CHAPTER THREE

James was continuing to make progress. He had managed to escape brain damage, and the doctors expected him to make a complete recovery. Fraser had alerted The Priory Clinic to his imminent arrival in yet another bid to rid him of his evils.

Simon Robertson was babysitting his son, much to his father's disgust. He had been told to go out, to get a life, to socialise. Little did Robertson know of his daughter-in-law's regular activities, but it was only a matter of time before he found out. Gina, sporting a tight-fitting black dress and a pair of killer heels, bid her farewell to Simon and her son Mark. She was having a meal in town with her friends – well, that was the story that she had spun. She was actually meeting with Brian, her personal trainer, who had booked a suite in the best hotel in town.

Brian had already checked in. He had texted her with the room number where he she was going to get a good seeing to. Gina was playing with fire. All in all, it was a typical Friday night in Liverpool.

Simon had an early night with his son; he didn't hear Gina return a little after 2 a.m., he was in a deep sleep. She slipped off her little black number, took her makeup off, cleaned her teeth and carefully climbed into their king-sized bed that had not seen much action recently. Gina was exhausted after her night of passion with the super-fit Brian: he had thrown her all round the hotel bedroom and they had fucked each other stupid. Her trainer was extremely well endowed; Gina had experienced multiple orgasms and so had he.

As a contented smile broke out on her beautiful face, little did she know that she had been spotted leaving the hotel shortly after one-thirty. She had not spotted her father-in-law enjoying a nightcap with a couple of council officials in the hotel reception area. He had been treating them to a slap-up meal in La Brasserie, notably one of the best restaurants in town. Unfortunately for Gina, Fraser had seen her as she hurried through reception and into the back of the taxi that she had booked through the concierge.

A few moments later, Fraser had successfully incentivised the concierge with a fifty-pound note to disclose that she had been in the hotel all evening. Another fifty got him the information that he craved – confirmation that she was not alone. Gina had spent the entire evening in one of the hotel's suites, room number 505, with Mr Brian Wright. His home address and mobile number were also provided as part of the deal.

Whilst Gina slept at home with her family, Fraser Robertson was putting the wheels in motion. Nobody, absolutely no one interfered with his family. Family was sacred and above all else.

Brian Wright lived in a modest townhouse that overlooked the marina with his wife and son. Brian was thirty-six – a good-looking, muscular specimen. He was obsessed with his body: he worked out every day except Sundays, when he would devote some time to his missus and his lad, Daniel, who was nine. He really enjoyed taking him to the local park and kicking a ball with him. Brian had recently opened his own gym on the outskirts of town; the bank had given him a two hundred and fifty thousand pound loan, taking his house as security.

Despite the exertions of the previous night, he arose at 7.a.m., showered, grabbed a quick breakfast and headed off to his gym. He switched on his mobile, and – bleep, bleep – two text messages quickly filed into his inbox.

The first message was from a client cancelling a session later in the day.

He did not recognise the number for the second text. He opened it. The second message read – "Hi Brian, hope you had a good night in room 505 last night. If you value your health then stay away from her."

He read it again and again. His heart sank, his pulse raced. What the…? Who on Earth…? How the hell…? All of a sudden from feeling on top of the world, Brian Wright was not feeling so good.

I'll call the mobile that the text was sent from, he thought, I'll bloody well show whoever it is that I am not going to be intimidated. Maybe not such a good idea, as I would be acknowledging receipt of it and then by implication confirming my mobile number, he decided against this. This was a shot across his bows; an early warning, but from whom?

What about Gina, should I tell her? If I do, that will be the end of our relationship, and we are only at the very start of a steamy liaison. His mind flashed back to the amazing sex that they had shared together just a few hours ago. No, I can't tell Gina, not yet, anyway.

What about Kelly, his wife? What if whoever had sent this anonymous text was going to tell her. Should he confess? Say it was just a one-off and it will never ever happen again; beg forgiveness in an attempt to save his twelve-year marriage? No, no, stay calm – don't do anything at this stage. Let's see what develops. Try and carry on as normal, he decided.

Brian Wright was a decent man, a good husband, and a loving father. Apart from a one-night stand at a Christmas party three years ago with a female personal trainer, he had not strayed. Gina Robertson was hot; she was a sex bomb who from the moment she had stepped into his gym wanted to get her claws into him. She had an agenda and Brian was it. He simply could not resist her advances and now he wanted more. He could not let go – well, at least, not just yet.

* * *

The sound of the roof creaking combined with the shrill of the gulls circling above his penthouse was enough to break Tony Barlow's deep sleep. The bedside clock read 8:15 a.m. After taking a long shower and consuming a bowl of cereal, Tony headed into town. Saturday was always a good day to get things done, like ironing, cleaning, and shopping.

The regeneration of the city centre was gathering pace; all the approach roads into town were being dug up, sadly all at the same time. New developments were being built; old buildings demolished to make way for fancy new ones. Everywhere that you surveyed the landscape, there was a crane.

Four thousand new flats spread across twenty-five developments had already been granted planning permission. Some of these were just breaking ground; others were near completion. Everton FC had applied to build a world class fifty-five thousand-seater stadium on the waterfront, and a number of respected retailers who had always shied away from Liverpool had announced their intentions to "come and join the party" by committing to open brand new retail outlets in what were soon to be revitalised, fashionable areas of the city.

Liverpool City Council had entered the race to become "European Capital of Culture 2008". Plenty of taxpayers' money was being spent on supporting the bid with fancy marketing presentations and expensive public relations exercises. Large brown envelopes and party donations were being made, in the main by bent property developers and dishonest council officials, in return for favours down the road.

The bid was driving newfound optimism through the city and backhanders had never been so rife.

Liverpool was up against some pretty stiff competition: Newcastle, which was expected to win, Cardiff, and Bristol, to name but a few. Even though 2008 was five years off, the government were due to announce the winner next year.

It was fifty years too late, but at least this was a chance for Liverpool to put itself back on the world map. For far too long, tens of millions of pounds of money had poured out of Liverpool and into the coffers of retailers, restaurateurs, publicans, hoteliers and concert promoters' pockets in nearby arch-rival Manchester.

The Scousers had helped Manchester rise from the ashes by spending their hard-earned cash down the East Lancs Road simply because Liverpool had very little quality anything to offer. Potential investors had been scared off by the poor history of this great city and decided to spend their money in favour of backing its near neighbour.

Tony Barlow had an awful opinion of the way that his beloved city had been misrepresented, abused and raped over the past fifty years by militant, corrupt politicians, bent council officials and general lowlifes. He felt embarrassed every time he switched the television on or picked up a national newspaper to read or hear about another national or international organisation that was pulling out of Liverpool because of incessant strikes that were damaging their business or racketeering that had scared them away in the first place.

Apart from The Beatles, The Cathedrals and Liverpool Football Club, there was little to shout about.

He had absolutely no faith in what he had seen or read about since his return. There was no one, from what he could tell thus far, who was in a position of power that possessed any charisma or commercial acumen; they were all just looking to feather their own nests. Despite his concerns, he did feel that it was going to be an exciting time to be living in the city, even though things had not got off to the greatest of starts.

He passed by Albert Dock en route to his first port of call – the Mercedes dealer at Mann Island had his car booked in to have the passenger wing mirror replaced having been damaged by the ambulance. After dropping the car off, Tony decided to walk along the waterfront past two of the three graces towards Princess Dock, where a lot of residential development was happening. He thought he would have a nose.

What looked like a multi-storey car park was being erected, and a couple of hundred yards away, the foundations had been laid for what the developers' sales board described as a stunning ten-storey development of one, two and three-bedroom apartments, some with river view, with completion due in the spring of 2004.

On the opposite side of Pall Mall, work was well underway on completing what was to be Liverpool's tallest residential development – a forty-storey skyscraper that from street level looked like it touched the roof of the sky.

'Robertson Heights' was situated on what was the old St Paul's Eye Hospital site. St Paul's had been a long-standing establishment, caring for the community for over seventy years. Barlow had been there with his mum some years ago – she needed to have cataracts removed. Wow, he thought, the views must be awesome, especially from the city-facing units that would benefit from both river and city views.

The sales board boasted Liverpool's finest address, a luxurious development of 220 one- and two-bedroom apartments, complemented by seven exclusive penthouses, secure parking, 24-hour concierge service, and landscaped Japanese gardens. The development was attached to Liverpool's first five-star hotel, the SAS Radisson, with 24-hour room service for the penthouses. Barlow was smitten; he had never seen anything like this outside New York, where he regularly travelled on business.

A bright yellow banner across the developer's board announced, "Units released for sale, grand launch at The Platinum Lounge, Thursday, February 23rd. Prices from £140,000,00 to £1.5 million."

"My God, that's this Thursday," Barlow said to himself.

He made a note of the phone number for sales enquiries, stuffed it into his jacket pocket and proceeded into town for a much-needed shot or two of caffeine. As he drank his coffee, he read the local newspaper. There was nothing of any real note. Everton's plans to build their new stadium dominated the front page. They had received backing and support from Vision 90, some dodgy consortium that represented the city council, the developer and the political party that presided over the local ward. More than a few brown envelopes being exchanged there, Barlow thought. The stadium was going to cost over two hundred and fifty million pounds. Certain unscrupulous individuals in positions of power will be looking to top up their pension funds on the back of this development, at the expense of the working- man.

The inside front pages featured an interview with Fraser Robertson, the property developer behind *Robertson Heights*. He was boasting about his organisation's ground-breaking new development setting new standards in Liverpool. He told the reporter that he had no doubt that all the units would sell very quickly off plan, with most of them expected to be snapped up at Thursday's launch in The Platinum Room, a nightclub and bar that he also owned. For effect, he talked about the social mix of the apartments, with the majority being one-bedroom units aimed at offering a real opportunity for first-time buyers to get on the property ladder.

The more that Tony Barlow read about *Robertson Heights*, the more his passion's stirred. He could visualise himself sitting in a penthouse in the sky, surveying all below him, as he waited for the concierge to bring him a filet minion accompanied by fresh vegetables and béarnaise sauce, all washed down with a nice bottle of Fleurie. He had already decided that he was going to get himself on the guest list for the launch; he was now working out the financial implications of buying a penthouse.

After dropping off his cleaning and ironing, Tony decided to walk back the same way as he had come into town, so he could catch another glimpse of what in a few months' time could well become his new home. He spent a good fifteen minutes inspecting the development from every angle, trying to visualise the finished structure, prior to collecting his car that was sitting on the cobblestone forecourt waiting for him.

CHAPTER FOUR

Simon Robertson was up early on Saturday with his son, Mark. He left the lovely Gina in bed, fast asleep. She looked a picture. Mark had soccer practice at the nearby park in Woolton. Simon had enrolled him in Woolton juniors from the start of this season. The club took boys from the age of five up to sixteen.

Woolton FC had a proud history. It had spawned a couple of kids who later went on to play for Liverpool, and the coaching set-up was impressive. Simon wanted to give his son all that the world had to offer. He did not want him to grow up like he had, in a split family, never seeing his father, being subjected to constant rowing. Simon loved his boy; he wanted the best for Mark, his only child.

"Good morning ... Simon, isn't it?" enquired Peter Swann as he ushered his son onto the field of play.

"Good morning," Simon replied as he turned to face the stranger.

"Peter Swann. My son, Gavin, goes to the College with Mark. I've seen you a couple of times dropping him off, but have never had the opportunity to introduce myself."

"Well, pleased to meet you, Peter," replied Simon, as the two men shook hands.

Peter Swann was in his late thirties: a relatively tall, slim man with an athletic build. He had a tanned complexion, deep blue piercing eyes and short, neat fair hair. Peter was recognised as one of the top divorce lawyers in the North West. He ran his own practice in the city centre. There was plenty to keep his practice very busy in this sordid town.

Little did Simon know that Peter Swann had already introduced himself and worked his charm on his beautiful wife Gina. He had been shagging her for six months now. The couple met either in a hotel or at his swanky apartment in town most Wednesday afternoons, when Mark was picked up by his Nan and taken for tea.

As Gina awoke, her hangover kicked in straight away. Her head throbbed whilst her stomach ached from the excesses of the night before. She felt lousy. Gina searched around the bathroom cabinet for some Alka Seltzers to ease her plight. She found them on the back shelf next to some old condoms of Simon's that had gathered dust.

They had not made love for over three months. She could not bear him near her. Her attention turned to the events of last night. She searched for her mobile so she could text Brian as she drank the fizzy concoction.

"Morning big bad boy, can't wait to have you on Tuesday Love G" the text read.

Brian's mobile beeped as Gina's text message was received. The noise of the inbound text startled him. Could this be another sinister message? Brian opened it and was relieved to see that it was from Gina. He read it and smiled.

Brian texted back, "See you Tuesday Sexy Love B x". He had already decided that this dangerous liaison was going to continue no matter what. She read it and deleted it.

Gina washed, dressed and readied herself for the day ahead. She enjoyed Saturdays, not as much as Tuesdays when she saw Brian or indeed Wednesdays when she saw Peter, but nonetheless Saturdays were a chance to meet up with the girls. They would catch up on the gossip as well as get their hair done alongside some general pampering and a bit of shopping. Gina thought she would treat herself to some really sexy new lingerie as a treat for one of her co-conspirators – maybe a Hollywood wax, too.

As Gina pulled off the driveway making her way down the leafy lane to join the main carriageway into Liverpool, she failed to spot the guy in the black BMW 5 series pull out from the lay-by and tail her into town.

The private detective kept a safe distance as he followed Gina from the car park to the department store, where she bought a black silk basque and some fishnet stockings to match. Gina proceeded to Starbucks where she met her friends Jenny and Jane, both of whom were married; both of whom were having affairs. She stayed in the coffee house for about forty-five minutes, during which time she shared the sordid details of her steamy night with the personal trainer with her trusted pals. Jane told the girls how she had given some guy called Dave – whom she had met at Spiders, a local nightclub – a blowjob in the toilets after doing a line of charlie with him.

Jenny also took drugs – she was a raver – but on this occasion had nothing to report as she had stayed in nursing a migraine. Jenny was seeing a Jewish estate agent named Miles. It was great because they shagged in a different property every week. Miles spoilt her rotten. He was besotted with her Italian looks. Dark, sultry, and sexy, she was a beautiful looking woman. Miles was after a threesome with her and Jane, and by the sounds of it, the girls were up for it, too; they just needed to negotiate the correct fee.

Gina said her goodbyes and walked back into town to do the grocery shopping before stopping off at the beauty spa for her Hollywood and a manicure. She arrived back home shortly after four p.m. The groceries were unloaded whilst her silky purchases were left out of harm's way in the front boot of her Porsche 911.

"I'm home," she cried.

"We're in the lounge," Simon replied.

As she unpacked the groceries, Simon walked into the kitchen to give her a hand.

"How did Mark do at football?" Gina enquired.

"He did really well, the next David Beckham...." said the proud father. Mark, who began to search through the shopping bags for some sweets, joined them.

"Hey, I met a really nice guy at the football, Peter Swann, do you know him?" Simon enquired.

Gina could feel her cheeks begin to colour and burn.

"Peter Swann.... Err, yes, I think I have spoken to him a couple of times, err, Gavin's father."

"Mummy, you know him, you're always talking with him at the school, giggling and joking – you seem to really like him," said an innocent Mark.

Gina could feel her face flush with guilt and embarrassment. Thankfully, Simon had been distracted with a score flash on the large plasma television that hung on the kitchen wall – Liverpool had just taken the lead against Arsenal at Highbury.

"Oh yes, Peter, I was getting him mixed up with someone else."

"We should have him and his wife over for dinner sometime, what do you think? They could bring Gavin with them too, it would be company for Mark."

Before Gina could reply or even collect her thoughts, an overexcited Mark was jumping up and down in front of her. "Oh please, mummy, please, that would be so good, please...."

"Well, let's see...." Gina hastily responded.

"No, come on love, it would be good to entertain, Gavin seems a nice boy too. Peter gave me his business card, divorce lawyer, you know. I shall call him and invite them. How about a week on Saturday?"

The house phone rang, much to Gina's relief. She picked it up. "424-6996," she said.

"Oh hi Gina, it's Fraser, is Simon about?"

"Yes, of course ... Simon, it's your dad."

Gina passed the receiver to her husband.

"Hi dad, what's up?"

"I need a favour, son."

"Of course, dad, you name it."

"As you know James is out of the business again for some time. I have a large shipment – ten kilos – coming into Brunswick Docks first thing Monday morning on The Soviet Star. Victor Knight was supposed to meet Alexi over the weekend to pay for the shipment, but he's in a safe house following a major police incident.

"I'm entertaining some of our council buddies in London, so I need you to go to the office, take two million out of the main safe and arrange to meet with Alexi either later tonight or sometime tomorrow to complete the transaction."

"No problem, dad."

"I'll text you Alexi's number. The shipment is coming in as reinforced PVC window panels for *The Heights*, specially manufactured in St Petersburg. A cherry pick complete with crew has been arranged. The crew will load the windows onto one of our flat backs, which will take the cargo to our supplies depot in Bootle. Martin Derbyshire is taking care of the operation but you need to be involved with this, Simon – this is our biggest shipment to date and has a street value of over five million pounds."

"I understand, no worries, text me Alexi's number. I'll speak with Martin."

"Good boy. How's my grandson doing?"

"He's great, I'll put him on." Mark spoke with his grandad, telling him all about his football coaching and his friend Gavin before handing the phone back to his dad. "Take care, see you and Gina at the launch on Thursday," said Fraser, the secure line went dead.

"What was all that about?" Gina enquired.

"Dad needs me to do some work tomorrow prior to the big launch on Thursday, so I'm going to have to go into the office. Is that OK, honey?" Simon asked.

"Of course it is – you don't have to ask me," she replied.

Simon's mobile beeped. It was Alexi's mobile number.

As Fraser replaced the receiver in his suite at The Dorchester Hotel, his mobile rang. He recognised the number straight away. It came up as "Joe Deech PI" on his cell's display.

"Not a lot to report, Mr Robertson," the voice said. "She met with a couple of girlfriends in Starbucks, did the grocery shopping, treated herself to some sexy new underwear before pampering herself at the spa and returning home shortly before four. Not a man in sight", the private detective continued.

"Excellent," said Fraser, "Keep me posted."

The detective hung up. Fraser thought about the sexy new underwear – they were not for his beloved son. He felt the blood surge in his veins. He was onto his daughter-in-law. She was not going to get away with her little escapades. Gina was going to pay.

The timely interruption of Fraser's call had proved to be a distraction to her husband. It appeared at least for now that the invitation of one of her lovers to dinner had been averted.

CHAPTER FIVE

Fraser Robertson checked himself in the ornate mirror, adjusting his black bow tie and giving his freshly laundered dinner suit a final inspection.

He was hosting a table of senior Liverpool council officials, politicians and dignitaries at a grand gala dinner in aid of the shortlisted candidates for European Capital of Culture.

Fraser was a confident, arrogant, man who had established himself as a property developer some twenty-five years ago following a scam that involved Daniel Rosenberg, a Jewish property magnate, Alan Grimshaw, who was head of inner city planning and development for Liverpool and himself.

The scam was clever, to say the least. Rosenberg owned a street of dilapidated terraced houses in Grimley Street, just off Scotland Road. Grimshaw, an associate of Rosenberg's, issued a demolition order on Rosenberg's property company. It was going to cost the council three million pounds to carry out the work and make good the area for redevelopment, not to mention the redevelopment costs. Robertson, who was running a small property development company at the time, mainly offering refurbishments of existing houses, joined forces with Rosenberg and Grimshaw to defraud the city council out of one and a half million pounds.

The plan was delightfully simple. Instead of the city council spending in the region of five million pounds on a redevelopment project that fell under Grimshaw's total authority, they would spend one and half million, by way of a development grant made to Robertson's company, to refurbish all the houses on Grimley Street. The proposal went into Grimshaw, he duly authorised the expenditure, and a budget of ten thousand pounds per house was allocated which came out of the three-way split. The cowboys moved in and cleaned up in the process.

Robertson's company, with a little help from some local trusted cronies, supplied fake invoices to cover the allocated budget. Grimshaw signed off on the work, and the triumvirate got rich quick, all walking away with a little under four hundred thousand pounds apiece. The working class, decent people of this once great city were thrown out on the street without so much as a second thought.

Grimshaw had gone on to be knighted for services that he had provided to the local community. It was an absolute disgrace, as people in the know knew he was totally corrupt. He could not give a shit about the local community or the people of Liverpool. All he cared about was himself. Grimshaw had pulled strings on the land sale for *Robertson Heights* that had been earmarked for a special needs school. He was on Fraser's table with his wife, Lady Eileen, who was also active in Liverpool City Council. She was presiding over the city's planning committee

Paul Gibson, Head of Planning, Jim Russell, leader of the city council, Chief Constable Julian Wilberforce, and Arthur Moores, Head of City Infrastructure, along with their partners, joined their host and paymaster, Fraser, at the table of Robertson Holdings for this glittering occasion. Fraser was unaccompanied; he had recently married wife number three following the breakdown of his marriage to his second wife, Nicole. She was a beauty consultant who had fallen for the public schoolboy image that masked a real monster. She had lasted just under two years. She could not tolerate his lies and deceit, and she hated all that he stood for.

Fraser mingled with the assembled masses dressed in a mixture of penguin suits, expensive evening dresses and ball gowns in The Grand Ballroom of The Dorchester Hotel. He rubbed shoulders with the culture secretary, who would announce the winner early next year, and he shared a drink with the deputy prime minister before returning with a couple of wine waiters to his table, armed with half a dozen bottles of Dom Perignon vintage Champagne.

He was in a good mood. Apart from Gina, who could well become a problem in the not too distant future, he felt optimistic. Business was doing well, especially his illicit drugs trade. This was being fuelled by the feel-good factor that had taken over Liverpool. His largest shipment of drugs was on its way from St Petersburg, carefully stashed away in PVC window and doorframes, from prying customs officials, most of who were not on his payroll yet.

Fraser Robertson was doing what he was really good at – portraying himself as something that he was not: an upstanding, charming citizen who cared for his fellow men and women. However, if you pulled back the veneer, you would see that the real Fraser Robertson was in fact a cheating, revolting, disgusting individual who was depriving Liverpool of its future generation by destroying them with his wares.

After the top table had been clapped in, the customary toasts would be followed by a sumptuous six-course banquet. The formal proceedings and speeches would bring the gala dinner to a close. The MC rose, banging his gavel. "Order, order," he said, "please be upstanding for the Right Honourable Janette Walters". The Culture Secretary rose from her seat whilst granting permission for her audience to return to theirs by waving her outstretched arms in a downward motion.

She started by saying how honoured she felt that one of Britain's finest cities was going to be crowned "European Capital of Culture" in just a few months' time. She congratulated the assembled council officials and politicians on their bids: "They are simply outstanding and the competition is much too close to call," she declared. "I have never seen such compelling proposals; you have all done an incredible job." Fraser sat and listened, occasionally taking a slow controlled drag from his finest Cuban cigar. Her speech drew to a close with,

"In my eyes, you are all winners – good luck." Rapturous applause broke out as she lowered herself back into her seat.

Robertson knew that if Liverpool was successful in its bid, then he stood to make tens of millions of pounds. He would make an absolute killing with his drug trade, as more and more visitors flocked to the city. Fraser was aware that he would have to expand his dealer network; he also knew he was all set to make a fortune from his property business by acquiring land from his bent council contacts at ridiculous, knock-down, unopposed prices that bore absolutely no resemblance to their true market value. The future looked bright on all fronts for him.

Sheila Gibson, the wife of Paul, who was head of Liverpool's city planning department, was a playmate of Fraser's. In return for him providing her with a regular supply of cocaine, she would have sex with him. Sheila was a lot younger than her husband Paul. She had fallen for the charm of the aspiring council official six years ago when she met him at one of the local nightspots. She still looked considerably younger than her forty years. Sheila looked after herself by attending regular aerobics and spinning classes. Fraser had introduced her to coke at a wild swingers' party he hosted some four years ago. Sheila had gone with Paul in an attempt to spice up their lagging sex life but to no avail as Paul had quickly disappeared with some brunette.

Robertson had wasted no time moving in on his prey. He had fancied the pants off Sheila since he had been introduced to her at a council do that he had attended. After consuming a bottle of Cristal between them, he enticed her to his bedroom, which was kept under lock and key. He laid out a couple of lines of coke on the glass-topped dressing table, rolled up a fifty pound note and passed it to Sheila. He swept up the remaining line before entering into wild sex with her. She was hooked and had been in Fraser Robertson's pocket ever since.

The chief constable and his wife said their thank yous and bid good night. Mr and Mrs Moores, Sir and Lady Grimshaw and the Russell's quickly followed them. Robertson slipped his suite number, 1001, to Sheila. He knew that it would be difficult as she was with her husband. However she had that glint in her eye – she needed a fix and so did he.

"Great night Fraser, the meal was superb," said Paul Gibson.

"My pleasure, I'm really glad that you enjoyed it. If you would both excuse me, there are a couple of people that I need to see. Then I'm going to take advantage of a reasonably early night, I have a massive week coming up," he continued. "Feel free to put any drinks on my tab".

"Sure, sleep well, Fraser,"

"Good night, Fraser," Sheila added as she gave him a kiss on the cheek.

Within ten minutes, Fraser Robertson had cut and laid out two perfect white lines of very pure cocaine, awaiting the arrival of Mrs Gibson. He poured himself a cold beer from the well stocked mini bar and a glass of Champagne for her.

The bell went on his hotel suite door. He looked through the spy hole to see the lovely Sheila. She looked so sexy in a sleeveless black sparkling mini dress that showed off her toned legs to their best. He knew she would come, but he also knew they would not have much time.

As Fraser opened the door, she quickly entered the room, making her way over to the huge king size bed.

"God, you look hot," Fraser said.

"Where's my fix?"

"On the table," he replied.

She quickly snorted it up like a vacuum removing some offending dust from the pristine table. As Fraser inhaled his line, she took a gulp of Champagne.

"I told him I was feeling unwell, that my tummy was off," said Sheila. "I left him talking to some bloke from Gateshead that he knows. With a bit of luck, he'll occupy him for a while".

"Now for your payment...." Sheila unzipped Fraser's trousers and started rubbing his cock. He was already aroused from the anticipation of what was happening. Unfortunately, he was not well endowed. She sank to her knees, pulling his erect penis out of his pants and went down on him, sucking and biting his cock. As she sucked, she started wanking him, furiously stroking his balls with her other hand. He came quickly, just like she had hoped.

"God, that was so good, baby," Fraser cried.

"Good, I always aim to please. Now I must go before Paul finds me missing." Sheila picked up her bag and left Fraser to clean himself up.

Thankfully for Sheila, she had not been missed. She returned to find their hotel room empty. He must still be at the bar, she thought. She had a quick shower, took her makeup off and climbed into bed alone.

That night, she had broken sleep interspersed with violent dreams that were probably brought on by the line of coke. She awoke to find her husband fast asleep beside her. Sheila felt relieved, yet agitated.

CHAPTER SIX

Back in Liverpool, Brian Wright woke up with his wife in his arms, thinking of Gina. He had received no more text messages, although he remained nervous about switching his phone on. Maybe he would leave it off today. Gina lay with her husband thinking of Brian and the fact that it was only a couple of days before she would see him again. She felt horny as she recalled the events of Friday evening.

Simon cuddled his wife. He was in need of warmth, support, and reassurance. His mind was racing thinking about what lay ahead today, meeting Alexi and handing over two million pounds. His heart pounded. He despised this lucrative side of the family business, but what choice did he have? His father controlled him like every other person that entered Fraser Robertson's life – there was simply no escape.

Gina closed her eyes and kissed her husband, at first softly then with more vigour. He caressed her, fondling her gorgeous breasts. Her nipples quickly hardened, and so did his penis. Within minutes, his cock was inside her. Her mind flashed between images of her personal trainer and the divorce lawyer. Simon penetrated deep inside, thrusting his penis in and out of her shaven pussy.

He wasn't as big as either of her "bits on the side". She forced him onto his back and mounted him like a jump jockey in an attempt to compensate for his size and her desire; her eyes remained tight shut throughout the whole proceedings, which did not last very long.

Simon began to groan and shout, "Oh my God, oh my God". She soon felt his hot sperm release inside her. As soon as he came, she felt empty and full of remorse. Gina had visualised shagging her partners and not her husband – she had not climaxed. Simon, however, was ecstatic.

"Wow, that was so good. I know it's been a while, but oh boy, that was good, I love you so much," he said as Gina made her way to the shower, not uttering a word. She spent the day at home, cooking a traditional Sunday roast that Simon and her son enjoyed with her. Simon met with Alexi as planned and completed the transaction without a hitch.

Fraser Robertson, the councillors, local politicians and the chief constable made their way back to the city to prepare themselves for another week following the excesses of the previous evening. Brian Wright enjoyed a day off with his wife and son. They went for a stroll in the local park. He did not switch his phone on all day. The Soviet Star made headway towards its final destination, cargo intact. Victor Knight, James Robertson and the hooker all rested, as their bodies continued to heal prior to normal service being resumed.

* * *

Tony Barlow awoke to find that his female companion from the night before had already upped and gone. He spent most of Sunday at his local gymnasium working his body back into shape. Ever since he was a boy, he had played sport – there was something about pushing his body to its limits and constantly challenging himself, striving for new heights. He was fiercely competitive, always had been – he hated losing. Nowadays he played squash at county level. He was also a very capable golfer, playing off a handicap of four.

Tony planned to start playing competitive squash for his local club again now that he had returned home. He was also going to apply for membership to a decent private golf club, but today he needed to burn off some calories, dump some stress and tone his muscles. He loved beating himself up.

Monday was a big day in more ways than one, After Tony had cleared all his e-mails, he took the piece of paper from his trouser pocket – "*Robertson Heights* 0151-722-0414, Anne or Emma". He dialled the number. After a couple of rings, his call was picked up.

"Good morning, Robertson Holdings, Beryl speaking, how may I assist you?" said a shrill female voice, trying to be professional but sounding very much like a local girl.

"Ah, good morning. I need to speak with one of your sales ladies, either Anne or Emma, regarding *Robertson Heights*, please."

"Oh yes, there has been a lot of interest in this development. I don't think Anne is in yet, probably sleeping off the excesses of the weekend ... ha ha ... but Emma is in, I'll put you through. Who should I say is calling?" Her cheap attempt at humour not only failed, but also confirmed Tony's initial thoughts – definitely a local girl.

"My name is Tony Barlow, thank you."

The line went silent for a few seconds before it was picked up.

"Hiya, Emma speaking", she sang in a Scouse accent.

"Oh hi, Emma, my name is Tony Barlow. I'm interested in finding out more about your development *Robertson Heights*. I would also like to attend the launch event this Thursday," Barlow said enthusiastically.

"There has been a lot of interest in the development, but we do still have a few units, plus I believe a couple of penthouses left, but I would need to check with Annie and she is not in at the moment."

This was not the response that he was looking for. It knocked him back a bit, temporarily disengaging his normally razor-sharp senses.

"Hello, hello…." she repeated.

"I'm still here. When you say you have a few units left, I understood that the development was not being released for sale until this Thursday."

"Well, Mr Robertson, his associates, employees and friends have all bought off plan. I've bought a couple myself," she said proudly. "Would you like me to get Annie to call you? Should I send you an invitation?" Emma continued.

"There's really no need to get her to call me. However, I would appreciate it if you would send me an invitation." Tony gave her his home address and hung up.

He now wanted an apartment in *Robertson Heights* even more. Like all things in life that have a rarity value or simply are out of reach, they always increase the desire for ownership. There again, she could just be spinning a sales pitch, he thought. Tony Barlow was a top salesman. He was at the pinnacle of his profession. For the past twelve years, he had been selling and managing in the IT industry. He could spot a bullshitter at forty paces.

The Warrington office was beginning to fill up, with employees logging on to catch up on what had happened over the weekend, preparing themselves for weekly sales forecast calls with their managers. Tony grabbed a piece of paper and began writing down some figures with his Mont Blanc pen, trying to assess what he could afford to spend or borrow in order to secure an apartment at *Robertson Heights*.

Despite being cleaned out by his divorce, Tony earned a lot of money – the IT industry paid well, and he had amassed a bit of cash over the last two years. This financial year, he was looking at potentially stellar earnings, somewhere in the region of half a million pounds. It all depended on him closing two big contracts with BT, but things were looking good. His borrowing power was also impressive, as he had consistently earned in excess of a quarter of a million pounds a year for the past ten years.

Tony quickly worked out that he could spend up to a million pounds if he needed to. He would need to borrow heavily and sell his current penthouse. He had at least a year to do that and Liverpool was at long last on the up. Let's hope they have some decent units and it is as good as it sounds, he thought to himself.

Barlow spent the rest of the day in and out of internal meetings; he called his contacts at BT just to ensure that the contracts were on track and that they had all they needed at this stage. All seemed positive.

Meanwhile at Brunswick Docks, the Soviet Star had docked, and the cargo was secured and successfully unloaded onto the flat back trucks prior to being transported across town to Robertson Holdings' depot in Bootle. The depot looked like any other builder's yard from the outside, with wooden pallets scattered around the broken cobblestone perimeter.

The inside of the run-down building told a completely different story. Hidden behind huge steel doors that were protected by state of the art laser-controlled alarms and a couple of lookouts that changed shift every eight hours around the clock, seven days a week, was "the powder factory". There was nothing cosmetic about the place – this is where the contents of the specially manufactured

PVC window and doorframes were emptied, cut and bagged. This was the heart of Fraser Robertson's drugs operation.

Only trusted family members and long-term friends were employed in the powder factory. Fraser adopted a Sicilian approach and methodology to running his business: trust was absolutely everything, and nothing else really mattered.

He recognised that it would only take one employee to turn bandit on him, and that would be the end of that. A few words in the wrong ears; information deposited with the authorities – it would not take much to bring him and his empire crashing down. As a consequence, all of his employees were extremely well looked after and paid significantly over the odds for their services and loyalty.

Despite the fact that nobody had stolen so much as a gram from him since a trader mysteriously vanished some five years ago, mainly because they feared for their life, each and every employee that entered the factory was searched on the way out – Fraser left nothing to chance.

Simon returned to the office to let his dad know that the snow had arrived in Bootle as forecast.

CHAPTER SEVEN

Gina Robertson threw her gym bag onto the front seat, engaged reverse gear and backed off her pathway. As she continued on down the cul-de-sac to join the main road, her body tingled with anticipation. She was like a schoolgirl going on her first date. Her makeup looked more like she was going on a night out rather than a workout at the gym with her personal trainer.

She had not heard from Brian since Friday – nothing unusual in that, although she did expect maybe a text following their memorable night of passion. Still, at last the day had arrived. She was feeling so turned on, her pussy tingled as her 911 powered its way through the morning traffic, carrying her ever closer to fulfilling her sexual desire. The SugarBabes billowed out of her Bose sound system, drowning out the road noise. She was in her zone and nothing was going to distract her from her mission.

The Porsche circled the car park looking for a space. She had plenty of time, so there was no need to panic. A white Transit van beeped its horn to attract her attention – the driver had seen that she was looking for a space.

"I'm going, love," he shouted. Gina nodded and raised her hand to thank the workman as he vacated the place next to a black BMW 5 series. She was blissfully unaware of the man sitting behind the wheel of the Beemer wearing an earpiece as she locked her car and headed for the gym.

Brian was finishing his previous session with a rather overweight-looking bald man as she entered the aerobic area. The man's face was bright red. It looked like it he was about to suffer a heart attack. Sweat was pumping out of his every pore as he clearly struggled to finish the session. Brian looked fit in his torso-clinging sleeveless T-shirt and skin-tight shorts. His kit left very little to the imagination, revealing almost every muscle in his body. She caught his gaze as he stretched the big guy off; he smiled and mouthed to her, "I won't be long now – get warmed up on the treadmill."

She followed his instruction and began her warm up routine. Her heart rate was already up as the running machine belt whirred into action.

"Good morning, Mrs Robertson," Brian said in a formal voice as he joined his lover and client by the side of the treadmill.

"Good morning, Mr Wright, and how are you today?"

The gym was reasonably quiet, with only a handful of people working through their morning routines, whilst elsewhere in the city; people went about their daily routines.

"You look gorgeous, babe," he whispered.

"You don't look too bad yourself," she responded giving him a cheeky wink into the bargain.

"Was everything OK on Friday ... no problems?" Brian enquired.

"Yes, Simon was asleep when I got back, out for the count – he didn't say a word."

"How about you?" she asked as Brian increased the speed on the treadmill to nine kilometres per hour, forcing Gina to break into a jog.

"Err ... fine, why do you ask?" he said, unconvincingly.

"Because I care about you."

"So what have you been up to, babe?"

"Not much, really, I met with the girls on Saturday for a coffee and catch up, did the shopping, bought something for you and then went to the beauticians for a little pampering. Sunday was spent at home with Simon and my little boy; I didn't go over the door. How about you?"

"You bought me something, hey? Have you told the girls about us?"

"No, of course not." "We both have way too much to lose – I wouldn't tell anyone". As for your present ... Well, you will have to wait and see."

"Good girl. God, you're beautiful, Gina."

She smiled. Somehow they managed to complete her forty-five minute session without expending too much energy and without laying a hand on each other. She could see he was aroused through the bulge in his shorts. Her expensive makeup and composure had remained intact.

Brian had another client due in twenty minutes. They headed for the ladies' changing room. He took a couple of towels and a large bag of ice with them. Gina was the only woman in the gym and he could lock the changing room door from the inside. The plan was that, if they were unexpectedly interrupted, that she had twisted her ankle during the session and Brian was attending to it. He was unsure as to what he would do with his erection but maybe that's where one of the towels would come in handy.

As he locked the door, Gina stripped out of her kit and showered, rubbing perfumed suds over her magnificent body. She had a near-perfect hourglass figure, size 8, with silicon enhanced 32 E's, having put the recent operation on one of the credit cards that was paid by her loyal husband. Her body was superbly toned, with a cute peach-shaped firm bum. She had baby blue eyes that sparkled like the purest cut diamonds. Her toenails were painted ruby red, her fingernails beautifully manicured, and blond short cropped hair further enhanced her appearance.

Brian sat on one of the benches. He, too, had stripped off. He played with his stiff black cock as he watched

Gina's index finger slip into her pussy. Her other hand stroked her erect nipples. She fixed her gaze on his tool as his hand moved up and down its thick shaft; she inserted another finger into her vagina and started massaging her clitoris.

Brian reached into his gym bag for his phone and started videoing her. She didn't object. In fact, it seemed to stir her to greater heights of passion. Gina played to the camera as it recorded away.

"Christ, I am so turned on," she screamed, "come here, I want to suck your cock."

She knelt in the shower and took him deep into her mouth. He continued to capture the event. My God, she was gorgeous, he thought. His cock looked so good in her pretty mouth he wanted to come there and then, but resisted. She tossed him off as she sucked and licked his dick.

"Fuck me, fuck me hard…." she instructed as she picked herself up and bent down with her back to him, pushing her cute little arse out, spreading her legs whilst putting her hands on the shower tiles to balance her. Gina was so wet, she had already made herself come, but needed to come again, and she knew it wouldn't take long. She felt his throbbing cock enter her vagina as he pulled her towards him and then away again, controlling the movement of her waist and pubic bone with his strong forearms, hands clasped firmly round her sides.

"Give it to me. Oh my God, you are so big, I want to come," she wailed. Brian was hurting her as he thrust forward. He held her slight body up, and then released it again. Gina began to burn inside she felt her juices rushing towards a huge climax. He increased the pace and ferocity of his cock moving in and out of her shaven pussy. His hands moved from her waist. He grabbed her hair and pinched her nipple hard as they both exploded together.

Gina stood upright, her body quivering. She was panting. Brian embraced her and held her tight, still clasping the phone in his right hand.

As the temperature had risen, the bags of ice had begun to melt. They composed themselves. Brian picked up a towel and the bags of icy water. Depositing the phone in his bag, he left Gina to get changed.

"God, that was amazing. I'll text you, babe," he said as he unlocked the changing room door on his way to meeting his next client.

"You better had", an exhausted-looking Mrs Robertson replied.

She left the gym feeling on top of the world. Brian was so fit, he was a great lover; Gina had never experienced such physical and emotional pleasure. She knew she was playing with fire, especially when Peter Swann was thrown into the mix as she had feelings for him, too – he was more of a gentleman, showering her with expensive gifts, he treated her like a lady. Brian was more from the street; sex was different with both of them. As she arrived back at the car park and unlocked her Porsche, she remained oblivious to the man with the earpiece in the black BMW parked next to her having a conversation with someone on his car phone.

"She's just returned, Boss ... No, she's alone."

"Anything unusual to report?" Fraser Robertson asked the man with the earpiece.

"Not really, other than she wore full make up to go for a session with her trainer. She looked hot!"

"Don't speak like that about my daughter-in-law."

"Sorry, Boss, I was trying to paint a picture for you."

"I've got the picture, send him another text from one of the other chipped mobiles. Say, "Hi Brian, Gina looked a little more made up than we would expect for her session with you today. We really do hope you are behaving yourself, the consequences of not being a good boy are unthinkable."

The line went dead. The message was duly despatched.

Gina pampered herself with a leg wax and relaxing massage before meeting up with Peter Swann at The Holiday Inn. She wore tight fitting washed out denim jeans and a cropped white short-sleeved T-shirt. Leopard skin high heels and a matching shoulder bag completed her casual but extremely sexy look. Her eyes were shielded from the sun behind a large pair of designer sunglasses.

As she walked through the marbled reception area on her way up to Room 706, heads turned to both admire and acknowledge her natural beauty.

The private detective sat outside in the hotel car park, awaiting the arrival of her personal trainer. As the car clock continued to advance, there was still no sign of Brian Wright. Half an hour passed. Maybe he's been held up, he thought. He couldn't have been already in the hotel because the concierge had already checked the guest register and there was no Mr Wright. Even if he had used a pseudonym, it didn't matter as he had a photograph of the personal trainer, who was nowhere to be seen. Maybe she was in the lobby having a coffee … no, she was dressed to kill. Where was she and more importantly, who was she with?

An hour later, following another afternoon of unbridled passion, Gina Robertson was spotted coming out of the elevator, stupidly arm in arm with another man, Peter Swann.

"What the…?" exclaimed the private detective as he snapped away silently on his two megapixel mobile phone camera. The images were good, crisp and sharp.

The private detective knew that he had to work quickly on this. How am I going to break this to Fraser? He thought, knowing full well the rage that would follow. She bid farewell to the tall, rather elegant looking gentleman by kissing him on the cheek, leaving the hotel whilst he moved over to the reception area to settle the bill.

"Bingo! Gotcha...." cried the detective to himself.

"Room 706, check out, please."

"Sure, was everything OK for you, Mr Swann?" asked the hotel receptionist.

"Excellent, thank you."

Swann paid the bill and left, the detective shadowing him. He hailed one of the waiting black cabs, blissfully unaware that he was under surveillance. The private dick jumped in the next cab in line.

"Follow that cab," he instructed the driver.

They soon reached Castle Street and the offices of Peter Swann & Partners, specialists in divorce law. As Swann disembarked and entered the plush-looking suite of offices, the detective's head began to spin. Divorce lawyers, she couldn't possibly be thinking of divorcing Fraser's son, could she? Surely not, I mean for the personal trainer guy? If she was, then why did she not meet him at his offices? Why meet in a hotel room?

Wait a minute – she was having an affair with this guy too! He needed to unscramble all the information that had hit his brain over the past couple of hours. He needed to focus.

The private detective told the black cab driver to take him back to The Holiday Inn. He had to check a few facts before passing judgement. After all, it would not be an easy call that he had to make to Fraser Robertson and there was absolutely no margin for error. The consequences of getting this wrong did not bear thought.

Peter Swann's desk phone rang. He pressed the speakerphone button and connected the call. It was his PA.

"I've got Simon Robertson on line one for you."

"Simon Robertson," he said nervously.

"Yes, he said it's a private matter." He paused to collect his thoughts. Surely Simon had not found out about his affair with Gina. My God, it didn't bear thinking about. Swann, like other local people knew of the reputation of his family, in particular his father.

"Put him through," he instructed his secretary.

"Peter, it's Simon, I hope you don't mind me calling you at work?"

He sensed by the tone of his voice that he was not aggressive or upset. Simon Robertson was not displaying any of the characteristics of a man who had found out that his wife was having an affair.

"Not at all, what can I do for you?"

"Gina and I would like to invite you and your wife over for dinner a week on Saturday if you don't have any plans. Bring Gavin too, he will be company for Mark."

"Dinner, a week on Saturday – that would be great. As far as I know we don't have any plans. I will check with Fiona but thank you, we will look forward to that."

"Shall we say seven o'clock unless I hear to the contrary?"

"Yes, seven will be fine."

"Good, I will get my PA to send you our address, it's easy to find."

"Thank you, Simon."

As Swann hung up he mopped the sweat from his brow with the back of his hand. He took a couple of deep breaths in an attempt to relieve the stress. His secret was safe, well – at least for now.

"Can you confirm this guy is Mr Peter Swann?" the private eye asked the receptionist at The Holiday Inn.

"Why do you ask?" enquired the receptionist.

"Because I think that he may be having an affair with my boss's son's wife." He showed him a photograph of the lovely Gina, slipping two crisp fifty pound notes under the picture. "I need to know."

"She is gorgeous," he acknowledged.

"That's him, alright," he confirmed, tucking the two crisp new fifty pound notes into his waistcoat pocket.

"He has become a bit of a regular over recent months, has our Mr Swann."

"How regular?"

"It will cost you," the receptionist said confidently.

"How much?"

"Well, by the sound of it, this it is pretty important and if I got caught, I would lose my job. So for five grand cash, then it's worth the risk, anything less then I am not really interested."

"Five grand, you are having a laugh," interjected the detective. "Listen, fuck face, you don't know who you're dealing with". He stepped forward, opening his jacket so the receptionist could see his shoulder holster. The information is worth a grand tops or the equivalent in charlie."

"I'm not a user, thanks". "A grand it is, then."

The private eye took a small brown envelope out of his jacket pocket and placed it on the counter. The receptionist beckoned him to the office at the back. He asked another cute-looking young assistant to cover for him.

He began to scroll through the hotel's guest registry database and conducted a search on Peter Swann. The PC began to spew out information as a host of dates became visible on the screen. Further inspection showed that the dates and times spanned a period over the past six months.

They showed a pattern of deceit. Every Wednesday afternoon, Swann checked in around one thirty, checking out between three and four p.m., with only a couple of exceptions. The bills covered accommodation, lots of Champagne and nibbles. The receptionist printed the data out at the request of the detective.

"Now back to the photograph. How many times have you seen her in his company? Let's face, it he's not drinking all that Krug alone."

"To be honest, I would be pretty sure that I would remember such a stunner, although if she arrives and leaves via the express lift it's unlikely that I would see her – I'm typically bound to the front desk. Now I know, I'll keep an eye out."

The detective stuffed the print outs into his jacket pocket, passing the brown envelope over to the receptionist, removing five hundred pounds. He gave him his business card. It read Joe Deech, Deech Enterprises. His mobile and office number stood out in a ruby red embossed print.

"I will give you the balance and who knows, maybe a little bonus when I get the rest of the information," he said. He left as the bemused receptionist deleted the printer queue records.

* * *

Simon Robertson could not wait to get home and tell Gina that he had invited Peter Swann and his family over for dinner a week on Saturday; he knew it would be a nice surprise for both her and his son Mark, who he had just collected from school.

As he pressed the home link device in his silver Aston Martin DB 9 to open the impressive electronic nine feet tall black and gold leaf wrought iron gates onto the private select development, he spotted Gina's Porsche 911 on the driveway.

"Honey, we're home," he yelled as he kicked his shoes off, placing his Mulberry leather briefcase in the imposing entrance hall. Mark left his muddy tarnished school shoes in the porch before dumping his school bag by his dad's case.

"You'll never guess who I spoke to today," he said as she came down the stairs and into his field of vision. She was still wearing the tight-fitting jeans and white cropped T-shirt. Mrs Robertson looked an absolute picture.

"No idea."

"Your friend Peter Swann."

She stopped in her tracks as she heard his name. What on Earth had her husband been doing calling one of her lovers?

"Peter Swann," she repeated.

"Yeah, I called him at his office. I've invited him over with his wife and kid a week on Saturday, thought we could cook a nice dinner and share a bottle of wine or two with them."

Before she could say anything, Mark probably saved the day by doing a jig in the hall whilst shouting, "Yippee! Yippee, oh thank you, daddy. Gavin and I can play in my room."

"Anyway, he has accepted, subject to checking with his missus."

* * *

Brian Wright finished a long day at the gym. His mobile had been dormant since he finished making the movie of delectable Gina and him enjoying each other's bodies in passion-fuelled sexual acts. He couldn't wait to watch that back. As his mobile flashed into life, his incoming messages tone bleeped four times.

The first message was from his wife saying that she was taking their boy around to her sister's for tea. She had left his meal in the fridge, it just needed microwaving.

The second was from one of his mates, Dave, asking if he fancied going out on Friday for a couple of beers.

The third was from Gina saying how much she loved his cock exploding inside her – she was still sore.

The final text had been sent from an unknown number. His heart skipped a beat as he quickly cross-referenced it against the number of the sinister text that he had received on Friday. Fearing the worst, he was temporarily relieved to find that it was not the same number.

He opened the text. It read, "Hi Brian, Gina looked a little more made up than we would expect for her session with you today. We really do hope you are behaving yourself, the consequences of not being a good boy are unthinkable."

Brian felt palpitations in his chest. He felt lightheaded as his blood pressure surged, and he could feel the colour drain away from his face as his hands began to shake. Brian began to ask himself a host of questions. He had convinced himself, rather naively, that the text he received on Friday was a one off – that whoever had sent it would just go away. Why the change in number, he thought to himself? Brian was in a blind panic, and for the moment, totally out of control.

He could barely eat the meal that his wife had left him. He pushed the food around the plate, taking the occasional mouthful. Who is it? He asked himself time and time again. Is it someone I know? It must be someone from the gym, of course they would have seen us together today, but how does that fit with Friday?

He racked his brain and continued to torture himself searching for answers; explanations, but none came. Once again, Brian decided not to share this with Gina.

Surely if she was getting similar texts, she would say something to him.

Brian could not let her go – she was gorgeous, and he was smitten. Still, he decided to call off Friday night's intended rendezvous. He would make an excuse nearer the time that he wasn't feeling well and cool it for a few days.

CHAPTER EIGHT

Liverpool's finest gathered at The Platinum Lounge for the launch of *Robertson Heights*. The sun shone on the decked patio area, where gangsters, drug dealers, and council officials mingled with a handful of honest, decent local people who were genuinely interested in this ground-breaking development, as opposed to the money, the pay offs; the numerous brown envelopes that had already been deposited in exchange for favours during the acquisition of land, planning and construction phase so far.

Apart from the bling and the audacious designer handbags that accompanied the WAGS, it was hard to differentiate the good folk from the bad guys.

Tony Barlow handed in his gold-embossed invitation to one of the two hostesses who greeted him with a chilled glass of Champagne. She introduced herself as Kylie. Her accent gave her away as a local girl. She put a marker pen through the name of Mr. T. Barlow.

"Welcome, please help yourself to some food. The presentation will start in thirty minutes."

Tony wandered through the dark lounge onto the bright patio, passing an impressive-looking architectural scale model of *Robertson Heights*. He made his way over to the buffet. A couple of chefs were barbecuing chicken, prime beef and sausages. It smelled delicious. He grabbed a plateful and found a table in the corner so he could enjoy the hospitality that was on offer.

From his good vantage point, he began to survey the assembled guests. Barlow recognised a few bad men that he knew from around town. They were talking with a respectable-looking gent with silver-grey hair that had been cut short and combed back from his forehead. He was dressed in a smart charcoal grey single-breasted suit, white shirt and red polka dot silk tie with matching pocket-handkerchief. Black Oxford brogues completed the outfit of the man, who looked like he was in his late fifties, possibly sixty.

A couple of blondes who were a lot younger than their partners chewed gum, periodically tossing their heads, swirling their long locks from side to side for effect. As the Champagne glasses removed their lip-gloss, they regularly reapplied it.

Silicone combined with both Botox and gleaming white veneers were widely visible throughout the impressive venue. Barlow did a quick scan of the room. He reckoned that there were over two hundred people here.

A smart, young-looking man in a navy jacket accompanied by a stunning-looking blonde lady joined the older gent in the charcoal suit. He greeted the man warmly whilst merely acknowledging the presence of his beautiful partner.

Barlow could not stop staring at the sexy blonde. She looked so familiar. At first he could not place her and then, bingo! It was Blondie. Wow, she looked hot. He could not take his eyes off her. She wore a cream mini skirt that just about covered her bits and a tan figure-hugging blouse that was unbuttoned, revealing her cleavage. A killer pair of tan shoes with four-inch heels showed off her athletic tanned legs to their absolute best. His cock bulged as he recollected the night of pure passion they had enjoyed together in the hallway of his apartment. She had not spotted him yet. Tony wasn't the only guy in the room who was captivated by Gina Robertson's natural beauty.

An auburn-haired lady stepped up to the lectern and formally welcomed everyone on behalf of Robertson Developments to what she described as the official launch of Liverpool's premier address.

"Please put your hands together for Fraser Robertson, Chairman and CEO of Robertson Holdings," she said.

The elderly man in the charcoal suit and red polka dot tie greeted polite applause.

"Thank you, Rita, and may I add my sincerest of welcomes to each and every one of you. I am somewhat overwhelmed by the turnout this evening – maybe we need to build another one," he joked in a public schoolboy accent.

A few nervous laughs were heard from the more remote corners of the patio.

"We are truly proud to have developed *Robertson Heights*; it has brought new standards to both design and affordable luxury city dwelling. *Robertson Heights* stands proud on the banks of the River Mersey and benefits from magnificent sweeping views of our great city and majestic waterfront.

"It will be the tallest building in the city and comprises two hundred and twenty, one and two-bed apartments plus seven executive penthouses. The development is physically attached to Liverpool's first five-star hotel and all owners will enjoy one year's free membership to the hotel's state of the art health club. Penthouse owners will also be able to order twenty-four-hour room service from the hotel at the touch of a button.

"All apartments will be finished to the very highest standards with top of the range German custom-built kitchens, granite work tops, and Bosch appliances. Bathrooms will be fitted with Villeroy & Boch classic white sanitary ware. Mahogany planked floors will be laid in the entrance halls and living areas."

As Fraser continued to deliver his pitch, Tony's mobile vibrated silently in his trouser pocket. "Meet me in the end cubicle of the ladies now! X." His pulse raced as he quickly followed Blondie's instructions.

"Now let me turn to security. *Robertson Heights* will have an around the clock concierge service available to provide you with a range of personal services including receiving mail for you and dealing with any dry cleaning or ironing that you may need to be collected. They will provide valet parking for your guests – in fact, just about anything within reason that you can think of.

"Quite simply, we want your living experience to be blissful and without stress. The penthouses will enjoy two secure underground parking spaces with access code protected security via a couple of express lifts up to your apartments. Video entry phones and on screen displays will be fitted as standard to all apartments".

"I don't know how many of you have been down to see the site, but for those of you who have not let me tell you that construction is well underway and ahead of schedule – we expect completion within the next six to nine months.

"Apartments are very reasonably priced from £145,000 up to over £1 million for some of the penthouses. So whether you are looking for a fabulous new home or maybe you are looking at Investment, then this ground-breaking development is for you.

"We are taking reservations tonight. Fifteen hundred pounds will secure your apartment with exchange at 10% of the full value within thirty days. We take cheques, credit cards or good old cash," Robertson joked with his audience. Those on his payroll laughed.

"Before I close, I would like to introduce you to some of my helpers tonight who will only be too happy to assist you with any queries that you may have – first of all my son and Managing Director of Robertson Developments, Simon Robertson". The guy in the navy blue jacket stepped forward and raised his hand, turning around to acknowledge the people behind him. As he did, Tony ejaculated his hot white sperm into Blondie's mouth. She swallowed hard before licking the last drops of cum off his helmet. She looked up at Tony and placed her index finger to her smudged lips and beckoned him to go. Neither of them had noticed the tiny recessed camera in the ceiling void.

As Tony composed himself to leave the ladies' toilets, he could hear the next bloke being introduced. It was the architect of *Robertson Heights*. As he re-entered the main lounge area, he bumped into a tall, rugged-looking man with an earpiece. Tony thought nothing of it as he watched the architect, James Thirsk, like Simon before him acknowledge the crowd. He was a gaunt-looking, pale man in a scruffy cheap suit.

Fraser continued with his introductions in his posh voice as Gina swept by the man with the earpiece.

"Annie Evans, head of sales, Emma Sefton, sales negotiator, Beryl Purvis, sales assistant and of course, there is me. So please don't be shy, mingle, ask us any questions you want, drink, eat and be merry – the bar is open till 11:30. Thank you for your support and attention."

Applause broke out and people started to move away from what had become their base for the past twenty minutes or so, rushing forwards towards the scale model where the directors and employees of Robertson Developments were gathered.

Tony Barlow joined the throng with a view to seeking some further information. A waitress offered him a fresh glass of Champagne and he duly obliged, savouring each sip as he studied the model of the Heights and reflecting on the act that Blondie had just carried out on him.

The model resembled a very large cigar tube. The first thirty-seven floors had six apartments on each floor, apart from the fifteenth floor that only had four larger flats. This was to strengthen the infrastructure, and it also housed the air conditioning units.

The next two floors had three penthouses. Each of the ones situated on the Western side of the development benefited from downtown city views, whilst the Eastern end looked down the mouth of the river towards Seaforth Docks. The Top floor housed a spectacular executive penthouse of over 3,500 square feet.

Barlow had decided that West was best. One of the sales ladies approached.

"Can I help you? My name is Annie, I am head of sales for Robertson Developments." Annie had taken advantage of the garlic bread that was on offer. Tony took a step back.

"Yes, I am interested to find out more about the larger apartments on the western side of the tower from say the 35th floor upwards. I would also like to understand the price and availability of the penthouses."

"I only have 3901 left, which is a 2,350 sq foot penthouse, on at £900,000."

"I thought that this was supposed to be a launch event," Barlow sarcastically replied. "How can you only have one penthouse left at a launch event?" Barlow also thought that it was strange not to see any of the great unwashed at the event. After all Fraser Robertson had been banging the moral drum for weeks now in the media that the development was mainly about giving Liverpool's 'working class' the opportunity to get on the property ladder and enjoy the delights of living at Liverpool's finest address. Was this just a sham to get the press on board? Was Fraser hiding something?

Annie became uncomfortable "The development has been really popular, I have worked for the company for fifteen years and have never known anything quite like it," she bullshitted. "Mr Robertson and a lot of his business associates, family and friends have all bought off plan."

She had clearly missed the point, but Barlow thought better of pursuing it.

"Tell me about 3901, the penthouse."

Annie explained that it was a three bed, two bathroom unit; in addition to the host of features that her boss had relayed moments earlier, it benefited from under floor heating in the bathroom and en-suite, a choice of kitchens with a budget of £45,000,00 and had air conditioning throughout.

Barlow did not like the layout – it looked cluttered. He wanted to open it out so he asked if it would be possible to change the layout and customise it.

She looked round to find Fraser Robertson. He was busy, so she grabbed his son, Simon.

"Simon Robertson, how can I help you?"

I wouldn't mind spending the weekend with your wife, Barlow thought to himself.

"Tony Barlow."

"Pleased to meet you."

"I'm interested in buying one of the penthouses, 3901; however, I don't particularly like the layout. I would want to change it to a large two-bedroom unit with a dressing area. Some of these internal walls need to go, so the apartment is more airy and bright. Finally, I would like to customise it with some special fixtures and fittings and negotiate the price – it's too expensive."

"Let me grab the floor plans and the architect, James Thirsk, we can see what's possible."

Tony was ushered to a private table in a raised area that had been roped off. Simon soon returned with the architect, who had the plans rolled up under his arm. A hostess brought a fresh bottle of Bollinger and a freestanding ice bucket and poured the fizz into clean chilled flutes. Simon's wife joined the party and cast

Tony a cheeky smile. He felt his cock twitch. He wanted to fuck her brains out.

Following the introductions, they got down to business, although Gina's presence and her natural beauty did prove to be a bit of a distraction, especially considering that only a few minutes earlier, she had sucked him off.

After a couple of glasses of Champagne and much debate, it was agreed in principle that 3901 could be redesigned and customised to meet Tony's requirements at an all-inclusive price of £875,000 with a five per cent deposit on exchange of contracts within the next 60 days. Barlow was a shrewd cookie. He gave Robertson a post-dated cheque for five working days in advance for fifteen hundred pounds to cover the reservation fee along with his business card. He had not been so shrewd with his liaison in the ladies. The man with the earpiece was speaking with Fraser and pointing to Tony as he continued his negotiations.

"I have post-dated the cheque so you have a reasonable amount of time to process the amended floor plans and confirm to me in writing everything that we have agreed including all the extras. If you could e-mail me and then send a signed hard copy to my home address then that would be great. If for some reason I don't receive all the information, then I will instruct my bank not to honour the cheque.

"Gentlemen, Mrs Robertson, it was a pleasure meeting you all and I look forward to wrapping everything up over the next couple of days."

Handshakes and further platitudes were exchanged amongst the group.

As Tony prepared to leave, he thought he noticed a familiar face engaged in conversation with Fraser Robertson. The unshaven, dark haired, scruffy looking individual seemed agitated. Robertson looked like he was trying to move away from him. As Barlow drew nearer he could not believe his eyes: Victor Knight was back on the scene, but what on earth was he doing talking with Fraser Robertson?

CHAPTER NINE

Victor Knight did not return home that night, which at least was some consolation for the fact that he had reappeared. The front door of 303 West Ferry Quay remained boarded up. Tony did not sleep well and rose early. He had to attend a sales meeting in Warrington. He was hopeless when he had things on his mind that challenged his fragile mental state. He also could not get Gina Robertson out of his mind. He wanted her so bad. In spite of her connections, he had to have her.

Gina Robertson was also up and about with her son Mark. It was her turn to do the school run on this bright warm summer's morning. Simon had headed into the office an hour earlier nursing a bit of a hangover. She was still coming to terms with the fact that her unsuspecting husband had invited Peter Swann for dinner. He should have invited Brian and had done with it, she thought.

After dropping her son off at the college, Gina was heading into town. She had a hair appointment booked with Peter at Toni & Guy for nine thirty, followed by a manicure and pedicure at twelve thirty. Gina wanted to ensure that she looked at her best for another night of passion with her personal trainer.

Joe Deech was getting used to following Mrs Robertson into and around town. He kept a healthy distance from his prey, parking up in the multi-storey car park a floor above her Porsche. After confirming that she was going to be in the hairdressers for a good hour or two, he decided to grab a coffee and catch up with the morning's news. His mobile rang.

"Joe Deech," he said assertively.

"Oh hi Mr Deech, it's Colin Dennis, head receptionist at The Holiday Inn, just to let you know that Mr Swann has just confirmed a reservation for Wednesday."

"Excellent, Colin, thanks for letting me know, see you Wednesday."

A short but highly informative call came to an end. She just can't get enough of it. Joe amused himself with the thought. Silly girl, it will all end in floods of tears.

Gina and Joe's next port of call was The Spa for her manicure and pedicure. She received a text just as she was checking in. It was from Brian. Probably some dirty foreplay ahead of tonight, she thought. As she began to read it, her immediate disappointment must have been obvious.

"Are you alright, Mrs Robertson?" the receptionist enquired.

"Yes, I'm fine, thanks, just a bit of unexpected news, that's all."

The text read, "Really sorry babe I am not going to make it tonight. I have gone home ill with some sort of stomach bug, hope it's only a forty eight hour thing – look forward to our session on Tuesday, so, so sorry Love Brian xxx."

Ah well, it looks like a night in with an expensive hairdo and lovely nails. Gina texted him back. "So sorry to hear that you are not well. I was looking forward to seeing my baby tonight, guess I will have to wait until Tuesday, look after yourself xxx."

Joe put in a call to Fraser Robertson. "Tonight's the night, boss. She spent two hours in the hairdressers and an hour and half in the beauticians. I am going to grab a couple of hours' shut eye, I could be in for a long night."

"Call me later Joe. I want you to be all over this little slut like a rash. I have to protect my son and put paid to her misgivings – you do understand, don't you?" Fraser Robertson replied chillingly.

"Fully understand, Boss, I will speak with you later." the private detective hung up and headed home. Following a couple of hours' kip and a quick shower, Joe was back on duty. He waited patiently in the layby at the end of the road where Gina and Simon Robertson lived. He felt excited as he listened to Steely Dan belt out "Here at the Western World". Joe picked up the beat and began to play the drums with his hands on the top of the dashboard. The car's clock showed 20:30 and there was still no sign of the lovely Gina.

Steely Dan belted out several more songs. Gina still hadn't shown. Joe glanced at his wristwatch. 21:15. He began to question himself. She could not have passed without him seeing her; there was only one way in and one way out of the exclusive development. She couldn't have used Simon's car, because he would have spotted it. No taxis or private hires had gone past him. He decided to wait for another half hour. Then he would head into town and check with the friendly head receptionist if she had somehow escaped his surveillance and was sharing a night of passion with her personal trainer.

It was time to go, as 21:46 on the BMW's clock confirmed. Joe headed into town. He began to feel a little anxious. After all he had boasted to his boss like a proud fisherman that tonight he was going to land his big catch.

Joe arrived at the hotel a little after ten fifteen. There was no sign of the friendly receptionist, Gina or her personal trainer. Like a good detective, he checked with a young receptionist if a Mr Wright had checked in. He drew a blank. Maybe he had used a different name. He checked again, this time showing a photograph of Brian Wright that he had downloaded from his gym's website. The picture was greeted with an obligatory shake of the head.

Deech thought he would do a quick scout around the other city centre hotels armed with photographs of both Gina and Brian and his customary wad of cash. He began his last ditch attempt to track them down. By one o'clock, he was done. He had drawn a blank and needed to check in with Fraser Robertson, whom he knew would not be too happy with the news.

"Joe, what's happening?"

"Nothing, boss, she didn't show."

"What do you mean, she didn't show?" Fraser said irately.

"She didn't meet up with him, as far as I can tell." The private detective then relayed the events of the evening, giving chapter and verse to Mr Big. Joe even suggested that maybe the text messages had scared the personal trainer off.

"It's time for you to get fit, Joe," his boss said. "I want you to join Brian Wright's gymnasium and book a couple of one to one sessions with our Mr Wright. We have to work on the inside. He's not going to give her up that easily."

* * *

"Snow Drift" was doing a roaring trade on the streets of Liverpool. Shifts at Robertson's powder factory had been extended to cope with the increased demand. Initial reports suggested that this was the best gear so far. Plucked from the 165,000 hectares of poppy fields in Afghanistan's Helmand Province, it had a 7.0 purity rating. Normally regular users and dealers would expect anywhere between 0.5 as a low and 5.0 as a high. 7.0 was off the scale.

Fraser Robertson's growing army of dealers worked tirelessly on the streets and in the pubs and clubs. To encourage new users, they had launched a trial pack of "Snow Drift", a sampler that would give an instant high and claim the welfare of a bunch of new clients. This was proving to be an instant hit in the city, especially with the clubbers.

The street price was also dropping like a stone as distribution increased. Needless to say, Robertson's profits were also on the increase as he began to control more and more of Liverpool's drug trade. It was estimated that as much as one-fifth of Liverpool's economy revolved around drugs. The streets were starting to get out of control.

James Robertson, a victim of his father's trade, was strong enough now to be transferred back to The Priory. His father had made arrangements for him to be chauffeur-driven from his private hospital to the clinic in southwest London. A nurse and a doctor but no family members accompanied him. Fraser was far more concerned about his own wellbeing than that of James. He had proved to be a total embarrassment to his father. His mother had not contacted him since divorcing his father some fifteen years ago.

James was a desperately weak boy who had turned to a life of hard drugs and alcohol in search of happiness. Despite being a director on a salary of one hundred and fifty thousand pounds a year plus a lucrative profit share scheme from the property development business, he shirked all his duties and responsibilities. In recent times, he had become virtually incapable of fulfilling even the most basic of tasks.

Over the past few years, James Robertson had become a manic-depressive. He had made what can only be described as two pretty poor attempts at taking his life and ending his misery. Like most aspects of his existence, he had failed miserably. It was more a cry for help: attention-seeking, rather than genuine attempts to end it all. James had been on and off anti-depressants, supplemented by sporadic attendance at cognitive behavioural therapy sessions for twelve years now.

He had no real friends. His associates or the "hangers on", as his father referred to them, were only after his money and notoriety. During the ever-decreasing times of casting off the shackles of his almost hermit existence, when he did go out in public and party, then the "hangers on" would flock to him to gain access to VIP areas and admittance to the top night spots in town, enabling them to mingle and rub shoulders with the cream of the city's ladies, footballers, celebrities and gangsters.

He had no love in his life, no warmth, no wife, no girlfriend and no partner. He paid for female company. James had spent tens of thousands of pounds on prostitutes over the years. Robertson junior had allegedly fathered three children to different local working girls. His father, unbeknownst to him, looked after their welfare. This time one of them had saved his life, but how long would it be until the next time? At twenty-nine years of age, James Robertson was out of control, in need of friendship, love and direction in his life.

James had been a junkie since he was fifteen. Like most druggies, he started smoking weed, but soon progressed onto the hard stuff when he found some tablets amongst the condoms in his dad's bedside drawer. He could not resist taking one of them with his last real friend, Sam. The white lightning did not take long to take effect – he was hooked. The only thing that kept him going was the hatred of his father, that raged like an inferno inside him.

This was to be his tenth visit to The Priory. In some respects, it was not only a waste of money, but also a complete waste of everyone's time that was associated with this latest attempt to rehabilitate him.

CHAPTER TEN

Victor Knight, who was also in need of rehab, started his daily rounds along with three other trusted traders. They divided the city up into four quarters. Victor looked after the Eastern sector.

It had been a busy Friday, with lots of out of towners partying ahead of the big concert on Saturday. The traders were expecting a huge Saturday, as "Creamfields" was being staged out at Speke; forty thousand revellers would converge on the disused airfield in South Liverpool, each paying fifty pounds for the privilege of getting off their heads to their favourite music. Amongst the acts that had been confirmed were Groove Armada and Faithless, with The Chemical Brothers topping the bill.

Fraser Robertson had come up with an ingenious idea. He had taken a stall at the festival site where they would sell "Snow Drift" as mere confectionery. A tiny amount of sugar had been added to the potent white powder and bagged. Branded as a "sherbet dip", it was going to be sold complete with lollipop and plastic spoon for £4.35 as a taster.

They were hoping to sell 15,000 units and hook some new punters. Robertson had hired some trusted users to man the stall and mingle in the crowd offering their wares from trays that were strapped around their necks, resembling those that ice cream vendors that had been selling refreshments in cinemas for years.

The stall had been secured under a bogus company through Jim Russell, head of the city council, and authorised by Grimshaw, his old mucker. They would trade under the name of "Fizzy Dips". The real money, of course, would be made by the dozens of dealers, posing as revellers throughout the proceedings. They ensured that appetites both old and new were duly satisfied.

Robertson expected to clear at least sixty-five grand on the day. After he had paid his traders and given the high-ranking council officials their backhanders, he would clear fifty gees – not bad for a day's work. Of course, he had a fall back plan just in case it went pear-shaped. The company was not traceable. The council's authorisation had all been by word of mouth and e-mail. The villains would of course disappear into cyberspace.

As the concertgoers sampled their first taste of "Snow Drift", James Robertson was administered his initial dose of methadone.

* * *

The smell of Indian food interspersed with Frankie goes to Hollywood penetrating into Tony Barlow's penthouse signified the return of Victor Knight, much to Tony's disappointment.

"Unbelievable! The lunatic is back in residence," he screamed.

"How the fuck can he one minute be the victim of a police shootout, not to mention drugs raid and conducting a knife attack on a local prostitute, then the next minute he is back making my life a fucking misery again"?

"The man is a fucking gangster, what was he doing talking with Fraser Robertson?" "Surely to God he can't be following me to *Robertson Heights*, can he? I mean, how can he possibly afford to live here, let alone Liverpool's premier new address?" Tony's mind was all over the place as he continued to search for some answers.

He convinced himself that Victor Knight had to be a big cog in the machinery that drove Fraser Robertson's Industry and that was definitely not property developing.

"Relax, don't do it when you want to move through it. Relax, don't do it when you wanna come, when you wanna come."

Tony stamped on the floor to register his annoyance with the sound level of the music. He could not use any appropriate signal to table his disgust with the smells that were entering his apartment. He wanted to go and bang on Victor's front door and give him a piece of his mind; however, he managed to restrain his basic instincts and curb the rage that raced around his brain.

* * *

The guy with the earpiece entered the downtown gymnasium, duly completed a membership form and relevant paperwork, paid his joining fee and booked his first "one to one" session with Brian Wright for Tuesday, an hour's slot just before Gina Robertson. He did not use the name Joe Deech – he used a pseudonym, Alan Wild.

Fraser Robertson's generals had called him on the safe line to confirm that the takings for "Snow Drift" had surpassed even their wildest expectations, £78,425, with nothing else to report other than a lot of sweat from the adoring public as they danced throughout the concert ... no arrests, no disturbances – just thousands of enlarged pupils and young people off their heads.

Initial reports from The Priory were that James Robertson had settled in and the early signs were that he was responding well to treatment.

Monday morning Tony was up bright and early. He decided to go for an early morning run along the waterfront. The sky was a magnificent shade of pale blue and the sun shone, warming him as he set off. There was not a cloud in the sky.

Tony felt energised so he thought he would attempt 10 km and aim to do it in less than fifty minutes. His best time was forty-one minutes and twenty-two seconds, but that was a few years ago now. As he got into his stride, the seagulls circled above and accompanied him, their shrill cries in unison with his rising heartbeat. He checked his wristwatch and heart monitor – he was making good time. His heart rate was up to a hundred and seventy, and the sweat began to flow freely.

He passed a number of runners en route, each one with a different personal goal and various degrees of drive and commitment. Tony Barlow pushed himself to the limit in everything he did, regularly beating himself up, whether that was on the squash court – where he could let off some real steam and had broken numerous racquets by smashing them into the sidewalls – or the golf club, where he expected to conquer the course every time he teed off.

In business, where he needed to be the best, he was his own worst enemy. Tony Barlow set himself exceptionally high standards in all walks of his life. He expected everyone else to measure up to his metrics, too.

Barlow finished his run with time to spare – forty-eight minutes and eighteen seconds. He felt a sense of achievement as he warmed down and stretched on the embankment outside his apartment.

There was no sign of life from number 303, Victor Knight's place. The cheap-looking, crumpled mesh curtains had been drawn in a fashion, but all appeared calm. Junkies tend to sleep during the day and then party or have their fix at night.

Formby Homes' after-sales service were due out today to have a look at the roof again and also investigate the smells that were coming from 303 into Tony's apartment. As he finished his stretching, the workmen arrived. That will be the end of your lie-in. Victor, he thought. The workmen had already told Barlow that they would have to gain access to 303 to find out exactly where the pungent smells were coming from.

"Morning, Guvnor," one of the labourers shouted, "is it alright to go up?"

"Good morning, yes, of course."

They made their way up to his apartment whilst he completed his warm down and stretching routine. Tony showered whilst the workmen first attended to the roof. He could hear their footsteps above him as he relaxed under the hot water, letting it rain down on him from his power shower.

By eleven o'clock, the roof had been fixed – they had found a problem with one of the supporting joists that needed attention. They had also determined that the horrendous smells that were entering Tony's penthouse were coming in through the bathroom waste pipe work. Large gaping holes were quickly filled with industrial foam. Five bin bags of stale rubbish were also removed from Victor Knight's apartment.

It was much needed job well done. Tony gave the labourers twenty pounds for their troubles to buy a drink or two.

"You shouldn't have any problems now, boss, those pipes should have been sealed; the roof's metal torsion wires may need a further slight adjustment, but for now everything is looking good.

"We can't vouch for the geezer downstairs to put his rubbish out though. He seems a bit of a weirdo if you ask me and the place is a real mess, it smells like a fucking karzy."

As Tony said goodbye to the labourers, his mobile rang. It was Robertson Developments.

"Good morning, Mr Barlow, Annie Evans from Robertson Developments. Is there any chance that you could call into our offices over the next couple of days to review the plans for your penthouse? We have received the amended plans back from James Thirsk and want to run over them with you."

"I can get in tomorrow, say around 12 noon?"

"12 noon it is. We will look forward to seeing you tomorrow."

"OK, can you confirm that we will be able to agree on the asking price and the extras that I require?" Tony asked.

"Let me just check on Simon Robertson's diary as he will need to give the final authority ... It looks like he is in the office and has a slot free between 12 and 1 so yes, we should be able to resolve everything tomorrow."

"Great, see you tomorrow".

Apart from texting Blondie, the rest of the day was pretty uneventful. It was the calm before the storm.

Chapter Eleven

Alan Wild rose early and made his way to Brian Wright's downtown gymnasium for his first and maybe only session, depending on what information he could glean about the relationship that was going on between the lovely Gina and the personal trainer.

Gina Robertson was also up and about preparing herself for her session, or should we say sessions, with Brian. She was so looking forward to seeing her man and hoped that he had made a complete recovery following his stomach upset. Gina chose a real figure-hugging black Lycra top with matching shorts that showed her body off to its absolute best. She set off for her destination, but the man with the earpiece, did not follow this time. Little did she know he was already training with her lover.

"So what do you want to achieve, Alan?" asked Brian Wright.

"Basic fitness and body tone. I used to work out on a regular basis but have let it go over the past year or so."

The private detective did not want to give too much information away for obvious reasons.

"OK, so what I suggest we do today is put together a basic programme and get you set up on the machines."

"Sounds good to me."

Brian's phone beeped as an inbound text arrived.

"Excuse me," Brian said as he opened the message and read it.

"God I am feeling so horny maybe we should skip the session and just lock ourselves in the ladies changing rooms for an hour, Love Gina xxx"

"Sorry about that, it's from my next client."

Brian switched the mobile off and slipped it into his tracksuit jacket pocket.

Joe nodded his head. Boy, I would like to read that, he thought, not to mention what other stuff could be on that phone. I need to get the phone. That was his mission.

As Joe's first session neared an end, his body began to ache, but his mind remained alert. Brian had taken his tracksuit jacket off and hung it on the end of the running machine as he demonstrated various muscle group exercises to his client.

A vision entered the gym. Of course, it was the lovely Gina, looking hot to trot, with not a hair out of place, full make up and the skimpiest of gym kits. A hint of perfume filled the air. Not your typical gym look, thought Joe.

Brian left Joe to warm down with some brisk walking on the running machine whilst he went over to Mrs Robertson, giving her a warm embrace. As he was distracted, Joe pounced to capture his prize. Within ten seconds, the mobile was stuffed into the pocket of his shorts. The private detective left hurriedly not even bothering to shower. He could not wait to see the contents of the phone.

As he sat in his BMW, he first of all looked at the mobile's text inbox. It did not take him long to find the first message from Gina Robertson. It read:

"Morning big bad boy, can't wait to have you on Tuesday Love G".

He confirmed that the mobile number was that of Gina Robertson. It was.

The next text was sent from Brian to Gina in response to hers. It read:

"See you Tuesday Sexy, Love B x"

The third text was from Gina. It was dated last Tuesday. He had to read it a couple of times for it to sink in.

"I love your big cock exploding inside of me, I am so sore Love G x"

The next one was sent from the personal trainer to his lovely client.

The text read "really sorry babe I am not going to make it tonight I have gone home ill with some sort of stomach bug, hope it's only a forty eight hour thing – look forward to our session on Tuesday, so, so sorry Love Brian xxx"

Joe paused for a second. That must have been after the text I sent him – scared him off a bit....

The response from Gina was relatively short and to the point:

"Really sorry to hear that you are not well. I was so looking forward to seeing my baby tonight, guess I will have to wait until Tuesday, look after yourself xxx".

So that's why she didn't show on Friday night, Joe mused to himself.

This was really powerful stuff. He then turned his attention to the photo gallery section of the phone. There was nothing much to reveal under the "my photos" tab other than pictures of a woman and a boy, who he presumed to be Brian's wife and son.

He moved his attention to "my video clips". He pressed select and scrolled down the menu. There were a couple of videos of the woman and the boy and Brian and the boy playing football in the park. The final clip was dated last Tuesday at 11:08. He pressed the play button to reveal the contents of the footage.

The clip opened with the sight of Gina naked under a hot running shower, playing with herself.

"Christ, I am so turned on!" she screamed. "Come here, I want to suck your big black cock."

She knelt in the shower and took Brian's stiff cock deep into her mouth. She tossed him off as she sucked and licked his dick and nibbled at his balls.

"I want you to fuck me, fuck me hard," she instructed as she picked herself up and bent down with her back to him. Pushing her cute little arse out, she spread her legs and put her hands on the shower tiles to balance her. His throbbing dick entered her vagina as he pulled her towards him and then away again, controlling the movement of her waist and pubic bone with his forearms; his hands clasped firmly round her sides.

"Give it to me, oh my God, you are so big, I want to come," she wailed. He held her slight body up against his then released it again. The personal trainer increased the pace and ferocity of his cock moving in and out of her shaven pussy. His hands moved from her waist. He grabbed her hair and pinched her nipple hard, as they both appeared to come together.

The recording stopped...

Joe knew the consequences for both of them, but in particular Brian Wright. His boss Fraser Robertson would have him seen to. One of his henchmen would be assigned and he would be in for a big bonus once Fraser

Robertson had calmed down – and that may take some time, he thought. Not only was his precious son's wife playing away with not one but two blokes, she had been caught red-handed with her black trainer. Fraser Robertson was a bad man, a very bad man and amongst it all he was a racist – he hated blacks.

Whilst Joe Deech was indeed proud of his swift, masterful piece of detective work, he was concerned as to how he would break the news to Fraser. There was no easy way – he could not dress it up. He would just have to come out with it and then wait for the explosion.

Fraser Robertson sat quietly sipping a double espresso in the corner of Starbucks, waiting for Joe Deech to arrive. He was reading an article on "*The Big Dig*" in Liverpool as he was interrupted by a mobile phone being thrown on the coffee table before him.

"It's all in there, boss – but before you look, I have to warn you, it is very explicit, and maybe it's not a good idea for you to see everything," the private detective said nervously.

"What the fuck do you mean? What is this? What the fuck is going on, Joe?" Fraser screamed angrily, attracting the attention of some nearby customers.

"Well, Boss, this is Brian Wright's phone. There are texts that confirm the affair between your daughter-in-law and the personal trainer. There is also a very explicit sexual act that looks like it was taken in a shower at his gym."

Fraser Robertson's face began to glow red, then purple. His eyes showed the inner rage that he was feeling as the awful truth began to dawn on him. He slammed his clenched fist into the table, making the remaining contents of his coffee cup spill over onto the newspaper.

"Show me, Joe. Show me everything. I need to see it."

"Are you absolutely sure, boss? As I said...."

"Show me!" Fraser screamed at the top of his voice, making heads turn from every corner of the coffee lounge.

"OK Boss, as you wish".

First of all, Joe Deech showed him the exchange of texts. The veins on Fraser's forehead and in his neck started to bulge. Next was the video clip. As it began to play, Fraser Robertson caught his first sight of the black personal trainer. He only watched a few seconds of the footage. That was all he could stomach.

"Switch it off, switch it off!" he yelled before storming out of the coffee shop into the main street to catch his breath and collect his thoughts.

Joe followed him out onto the street. "I'm really sorry, Boss."

"Hey Joe, as always, you have done a great job and there will be a handsome bonus in this for you."

"What are you going to do, Boss, not that it's any of my business?"

"Mr Wright will be dealt with, fucking dirty black bastard. You keep tabs on my slag of a daughter-in-law, because she is still seeing our Mr Swann and God knows who else, fucking whore."

"OK, will do."

"Do whatever it takes, Joe. I need hard evidence like this of them both together, the more sordid the better. Dealing with her is going to be more challenging – after all, she is the mother of my grandson."

"I need to make a couple of calls, Joe, will you please excuse me?" Fraser moved on up the street, punching some numbers into his mobile as he walked.

Whilst the number rang, Brian and Gina were engaged in another sexual act, this time in the ladies' toilet of his gym. Little did either of them know as they fondled, sucked and enjoyed each other's bodies that this would be the last time they would be seeing each other.

"Hi Boss, what can I do for you?" the gangster asked.

"I need you and a couple of the boys to conduct a contract torture for me. The target has well overstepped the mark with a member of my family, causing great dishonour. He needs to pay. I will send you all the details later over the secure network from The Factory. Put your most evil bastards on this one, I want him to suffer, I want him to feel pain like he has never experienced, I want him to shit his pants, piss himself, choke on his fucking spew and scream with sheer fright...."

"I've got the picture boss, consider it done. Whatever you desire, we will deliver – just make sure it's in the instructions with all the details."

"You will have everything you need within the next twenty-four hours." Fraser hung up.

Around 12 p.m. the next day, Tony Barlow arrived at the plush offices of Robertson Holdings to hopefully finalise a deal on *3901 Robertson Heights*. Annie Evans, Head of Sales for Robertson Developments, and James Thirsk, the architect who had designed Robertson Heights greeted him.

Barlow was ushered into a plush-looking office that was adorned with black high back leather chairs and a mahogany boat-shaped table. Prints of Liverpool's four graces hung at various points around the boardroom.

A pot of coffee arrived as the three of them sat down to work out what was possible in terms of a redesign and thrash out the details of a final deal. After forty minutes of deliberations, it was agreed that the plans would be amended to Tony's requirements, which included a custom-built kitchen, dressing room with the master bedroom and a feature bathroom that incorporated a wet room. They agreed on a final price of £875,000. Tony Barlow had got himself exactly the deal that he wanted. He felt very satisfied and excited at the prospect of becoming the proud owner of one of the swankiest penthouses in town.

CHAPTER TWELVE

James Robertson's blood tests had come back from pathology at The Priory. There were clear instructions on his file to only communicate the results with his father.

Fraser was finalising the confirmation for his heavies to see to Mr Wright when his secretary alerted him to the fact that Doctor Clegg from The Priory was holding for him on line one.

"Put him through," Fraser instructed his secretary.

"Mr Robertson, its Doctor Clegg from The Priory, is this a convenient time to talk?"

"Yes, what is it?" Fraser replied abruptly.

"It's about James, we have had the results back today from his first batch of bloods and there is a complication to his condition that I need to make you aware of. Can you get to the clinic in the next 24 hours? It's extremely important."

"What is it, Doctor? I'm very busy right now and wasn't planning on visiting James for at least another ten days, so please tell me."

"With respect, Mr Robertson, it is unethical to discuss any patient's condition over the phone; we do really need to have a face to face meeting."

"Listen, Doctor Clegg, I understand and appreciate your ethical policies, but I'm too busy right now to drop everything and come down to meet you – so whatever it is you feel there is a need to make me aware of, then you have my permission to tell me now, otherwise it will have to wait for my next visit".

"Your call, Doc".

"Very well, Mr Robertson, have it your way – it will have to keep until your next visit." The doctor hung up.

What the bloody hell was that all about? Fraser muttered to himself. He was paying them a king's ransom to look after his embarrassment of a son. Let's face it, how much worse could it get? James was already an alcoholic, drug addict, and manic-depressive, so whatever they had found could surely not be that bloody serious.

Across town in one of Robertson Developments' safe houses, a couple of his heavies were preparing for the arrival of Brian Wright. They were making sure that they had everything that they were going to need in order to carry out Fraser Robertson's instructions to the letter. The men were in their early thirties – ex-marines built like brick shithouses. They were killing machines that had executed a dozen men between them. They had no feelings or fear.

They connected Brian's mobile to a large plasma screen that was attached by two metal chains that hung from the ceiling, dangling down in front of an old dentist's chair that had been modified with the addition of both foot and hand straps. On the opposite side, a video camera perched on top of a tripod was ready to record the proceedings for their boss's pleasure.

The chair was positioned to give its occupier the perfect view of what was being transmitted to the screen. The basement room was bare and cold with no floor covering. It was dimly lit and smelled of stale piss and shit from previous visitors. A variety of tools, including some large scalpels, were laid out in a big oval steel plate that rested on an old walnut table next to the dentist's chair. A couple of tailor's steam irons hung in brackets on the wall, but there was no sign of an ironing board or indeed any tailors.

Tonight's movie would be Brian and Gina, filmed, directed and produced by Mr Brian Wright.

The two ex-marines were satisfied that their preparations were now complete and set off in a black Transit van, destination Brian Wright's gymnasium. Within ten minutes, they arrived and found a parking place on the street at the back of the gym. They moved the bollards that Fraser's council chums had placed around the suspended parking bay awaiting their arrival.

They knew that Brian always entered and left his place of work by the back door. It was perfect as it backed onto a very quiet cobblestone street that very few people used away from the main thoroughfare. The plan was to restrain him and throw him into the back of the van, then move Brian to the safe house, a move they had perfected – it took no more than fifteen seconds.

One of the marines phoned Fraser Robertson on a secure line, as was protocol, just to confirm that nothing had changed and their mission was still "Active."

"Confirmed, please proceed," Robertson told the heavy.

"Green light," he told his buddy, "Now all we have to do is sit and wait for the cheating nigger."

CHAPTER THIRTEEN

It did not take long for Brian Wright to emerge from the rear door of his gym alone.

One of the heavies checked the identity of the personal trainer against the man in the photograph that lay on the dashboard whilst the other checked that all was quiet on the street. The taller of the two ex-marines approached Brian from the front whilst the stocky one moved around towards the back of him.

"Hey mate, have you got any change for the pay and display, I've only got a fiver," said the taller of the two thugs to an unsuspecting Mr Wright.

Brian dropped his gym bag knelt down and reached into one of the zipper pockets where he kept his change. Within a couple of seconds he was unconscious and bundled into the back of the van with blood pouring from the open wound. He had no warning as the baseball bat powered down into the base of his skull.

The stocky marine went in the back of the van with their victim. He tied Brian's hands and ankles with ship rope, gagged his mouth with packing tape, and a black cotton bag was tied over his head. For now he lay in a crumpled heap, dead to the world and blissfully unaware of his plight.

As the Transit van approached the safe house, Brian was starting to regain consciousness. He moaned and groaned as he felt the pain surging through his head and the back of his neck. He tried to focus; to understand where he was, and whom he was with, in an attempt to gain some sort of perspective on what had happened to him. As he continued to come around, he could feel that his feet and hands were bound. He could taste sticky glue on his tongue and lips from the packing tape. As he opened his eyes, all he saw was darkness. Brian knew he was in trouble – big, big trouble.

"He's coming around."

"We're nearly there. If he gives you any shit, hit him with the baseball bat again, but this time even harder."

What the fuck is going on, who are these people, why have they attacked and kidnapped me? Brian's brain tried to compute. It tried to find some answers so he could make some sense of it all, then all of a sudden it began to dawn on him: the text messages, Gina ... oh, my God.

"Move again, arse wipe and I will break your fucking leg!"

Brian knew that it made sense not to make a struggle, so he lay motionless on the floor of the van until it came to a halt. He was bundled out of the Transit and taken a short distance into some kind of building and taken down some steps, presumably into a room. The cold, stale air hit him. It was rancid. He could almost taste the stench of a cocktail of piss, shit and vomit. It made him heave.

Brian was dumped in a chair that had seen better days. The seat was manually adjusted so his body was in an almost upright position. He could hear the men flicking switches. They removed the bindings from his ankles and wrists, only for them to be replaced by four taut metal restrainers, one on each ankle and one holding each arm with the palms of his hands uppermost. The bag remained tied around his head. The gagging also stayed in place.

"Who's been a very naughty boy, then?" one of Robertson's thugs piped up.

"Who's been a really stupid boy?" the other one added.

"Why didn't you heed the warnings, Brian? You were given a couple of chances to repent on your sins, but no, Brian thought he could carry on fucking the brains out of the lovely Gina and get away with it."

Whilst the men teased him with their conversation, they removed his training shoes and socks.

The black cotton bag was next to go. Brian rapidly flicked his eyes several times, trying to adjust from the pitch black of the last ten minutes to the dimly lit room. His eyes began to water as the chill of the air hit his eyeballs. The gagging was the next to go. His mouth felt dry, his lips slightly chapped and rough. As he began to see his environment, he sensed the absolute desperation of his position.

Brian saw two muscular men both protecting their identities behind black balaclavas. He was strapped into what appeared to be an old dentist's chair. A huge plasma screen hung down directly in front of his gaze. He could see a video camera that looked like it was recording the events as they were unfolding.

The tall marine piped up, "And now Brian Wright Productions in association with Robertson Holdings proudly present tonight's feature movie, *Mrs Robertson Goes Training*, and I have to say, boys and girls, it's quite a workout!"

"Maestro, please," he beckoned his assistant.

As the movie started, the irons began to reach the desired temperature.

"Listen guys, I can explain. I know I should have taken your warning. I'm a happily married man, I have a beautiful son, and I've been stupid, for Christ's sake."

The movie continued to roll.

"It's a bit late for saying sorry and regrets now, Brian, you had your chance, not one warning but two, and you have messed with the wrong girl from the wrong family. Mr Robertson does not tolerate fools, and you are a fucking fool, boy."

"Mr Robertson, you mean Gina's husband?" Brian asked.

"No, Mr Robertson as in Mr Big, Gina's husband's father."

Brian knew this was it; they had revealed the identity of their boss, so there was no way that he was getting out of this alive.

"Mr Robertson likes us to do things nice and slow, especially for people who disrespect his family. He has requested extra special treatment for you, Brian."

The first iron was carefully removed from the bracket. The marine spat on the sole plate, and it hissed back at him. The second iron was removed from its holding, billowing steam; the test repeated. It too hissed back to confirm it was up to the required temperature.

The taller man stood over Brian, who had already pissed his pants in anticipation of what was about to happen. The red-hot sole plate was wafted over his face. He could feel the searing heat, as it hovered no more than a couple of inches above his cheek. The man's accomplice stood at the bottom of the chair, clutching his steaming hot iron with a clenched fist.

As the movie ended, the iron was driven into the bare flesh of Brian's right sole and heel. He screamed as the unbelievable pain hit his brain and central nervous system. Flesh hung off the sole plate as it was pushed into the base of his other foot.

Brian vomited, he yelled like a dog; he just about managed to plead. He was now begging for his life, as the video camera continued to capture the horrific events. It was now the turn of the taller thug to dish out his torture as he plunged his iron into the palm of the personal trainer's right hand and ran it up and down it a couple of times.

"Please, please, I am begging you I will give you anything you want, please...."

Brian did not speak again; he lost consciousness as they finished the task by ironing his other palm before sealing his fleshy lips together.

If Brian thought that this was the end of his troubles, little did he realise what was yet to come as he was bundled into the back of the black Transit van.

Whilst the ex-marines drove into the night sky, Fraser Robertson was putting the finishing touches to his appearance. He left nothing to chance when he was entertaining the ladies. He moisturised his freshly shaved skin, plucked a couple of rogue eyebrows and then trimmed both his nasal and ear hairs before splashing on some of her favourite aftershave. He looked dapper but far from cool in his navy pants and pale blue shirt.

The Cristal was chilling nicely by the sofa in the lounge area of his hotel suite, and freshly cut lines of "Snow Drift" were laid out side by side on the glass-topped dressing table awaiting the arrival of Sheila Gibson. Fraser had taken a 100mg of Viagra about twenty minutes earlier – these days he needed all the help he could get.

As the ex-marines and their freshly pressed cargo neared their destination, Sheila arrived at Fraser's suite. Unlike the tortured personal trainer, she knew exactly what was going to happen to her over the next couple of hours.

The Transit approached the deserted public car park that once served the festival gardens site. The driver dimmed the van's lights as he parked as close as he could to the entrance to the overgrown, deserted vast expanse of land that ran along the riverfront. His assistant went around the back of the van to collect its tortured passenger for the next abusive phase of treatment that had been specifically ordered by Fraser Robertson.

The marine looped a coil of rope around his right shoulder and picked up a couple of searchlights, a canvas ice bag and a tool box before throwing Brian Wright over his left shoulder into a fireman's lift position.

The military men knew that the next part of their journey was going to be the most physically as well as mentally demanding as they began the two mile journey on foot across dense, dark wasteland that was only illuminated by their flashlights. They were taking the personal trainer to the remotest spot on the site. He was just about conscious, breathing through his nose. His body resembled a rag doll, as it lay lifeless and limp, occasionally gravitating up and down as the land climbed and then fell away again.

"Have you got his mobile?" enquired the stockier of the two henchmen.

"Yeah, I was just about to switch it on...."

"Got the Viagra?"

"Yeah, I have a pocketful of little blues."

"Good, let's keep going, I will take over in a couple of minutes, give you a blow."

"Sound, mate."

Brian's mobile burst into life with the arrival of several texts and a couple of voicemails from his wife enquiring as to his whereabouts. The first message was left at 19:06 and the second at 21:02. The thug laughed as he listened to the panic in Mrs Wright's voice. "Brian, I am so worried, where are you? I was expecting you at 6 o'clock – this is so not like you. We are all worried. Please call as soon as you pick this message up. I have also texted you."

"It's your missus, mate, she's worried about you – your dinner is in the bin!" Laughter erupted and echoed in the deserted wasteland.

"You've got a couple of texts from your lover ... She is asking what she should wear for her session with you tomorrow and is there anything that you would like her to do to you?"

"Let's have a bit of fun with the lovely Mrs Robertson," said the thug.

Brian was sufficiently conscious to understand precisely what was going on. Despite the acute pain that he was experiencing, he tried to keep some sort of focus in the hope that against all the odds he may somehow get out of his horrendous ordeal and survive.

Brian's captors texted back to Mrs Robertson.

"Hey babe, I want to eat your pussy and come all over your face x."

The ex-marines chuckled as they sent the text. Brian mustered all his strength in an attempt to show his assailants his disgust with them.

Brian's phone flashed as a text came into his inbox.

"That was quick."

"What does it say?" enquired the shorter of the two thugs.

"Sounds great honey, I am playing with myself just thinking about you eating my pussy night, night x."

"Come on, let's get back to business."

Before the stockier heavy took over the task of taking Brian Wright to his final destination, he forced a Viagra into the corner of Brian's narrow mouth, pinched his nostrils together and poured some water down the small gap in his lips to make sure he swallowed the tablet.

As they made their way, Fraser Robertson was snorting another line of "Snow Drift" from the city planner's wife's navel before he moved down to give her wet pussy some attention. She duly obliged by returning the compliment. It did not take long for Fraser to ejaculate.

Finally, the ex-marines arrived at the clearing miles from civilisation. This was to be Brian's final place of execution. First of all, he was stripped naked. His ankles and wrists were then bound with the rope. They dumped him down at the base of a tree. He was trembling with fear and began to wail through his sealed lips.

The taller marine knelt down alongside him and began to play the movie of Brian and the lovely Gina. The Viagra started to have the desired effect as his cock stood to attention.

"Enjoy your last erection, big boy," the stockier marine uttered.

As the movie advanced, the personal trainer's erection became harder, the stockier marine pulled a butchers knife with a nine-inch blade from the toolbox. Brian became distracted from the movie at the sight of the gleaming silver blade. He began to howl. His mind raced in competition with his pulse as his thoughts began to run away with him.

The razor sharp blade was placed at the base of Brian's black penis. His face contorted; his eyes bulged. He tried to scream and beg, but all to no avail as the blade cut through his cock. Blood spurted like water from a garden hose, covering the marine's white paper suit and gloves.

Brian's last howl reached its pitch and then died away to silence as he lost consciousness. His penis was placed in the ice bag. The marine removed the blood-soaked paper suit and gloves and burnt them. As the fire began to die, they made their way back to the car park, leaving Brian Wright to bleed to a most indignant death. He had paid more than he could ever have imagined for his affair with Fraser Robertson's daughter-in-law.

Within fifteen minutes, the heavies were back in the Transit van with their trophy that their boss had specifically instructed them to take.

Fraser Robertson's mobile phone rang on the bedside as he lay on the king-sized bed with Sheila cradled in his arms. He recognised the number as he answered.

"Mission accomplished, Boss."

"Thanks for letting me know." He hung up.

"Cause for celebration," he said to Sheila as he poured a couple more glasses of Cristal.

CHAPTER FOURTEEN

"He left the gym around five-thirty." the gym assistant informed the extremely distressed Kelly Wright. "I do apologise for calling you at this late hour."

"Did he say he was going anywhere?" she asked.

"No, he just said that he would see me in the morning."

"I am so worried, I have texted him and been calling his mobile all evening, but he won't pick up. This is so out of character for him, I'm really concerned."

"No problem, I am so sorry that I can't help, Mrs Wright. I am sure he will turn up."

It was now approaching midnight and still no sign of Brian. His wife had called all his friends and associates but to no avail. It was time to call the police.

The desk sergeant was not much help. He offered little assistance and sounded like he was reading robotically from a script.

"When was the last time you heard from him?"

"Who was the last person to see him?"

"What time was that?"

The questions came thick and fast.

"Was he in any trouble?

"I will make a note of our conversation and give you a provisional crime reference number. If he has not returned home by, say nine in the morning then call back and quote the number; we will then open an official case."

She noted the number and name of the desk sergeant before hanging up.

Gina Robertson had slept well, as did her father-in-law. Brian's wife had not sleep a wink, she just stared at the clock waiting for it to show nine o' clock so she could phone the police station again. She just knew that something was very wrong.

Bang on nine, with no sign of her husband Kelly dialled the local police station, quoting the provisional crime reference number. After about twenty minutes, the preliminaries were completed. A policeman was going to be assigned to the case that they were treating initially as a "missing persons", with no obvious motive, grudge or reason.

Police Constable Roberts would call at both Brian's place of work and visit the family home during the course of the morning to begin with official enquiries, as right now this case did not appear to add up.

Following a briefing at the station, the assigned officer headed off to Brian Wright's gymnasium to question staff.

Gina Robertson arrived at the gym for her session with her lover looking ravishing as ever. As she passed through reception she caught the police officer with her gym bag.

"Sorry officer."

"No problem," he replied.

She was stopped in her tracks by one of Brian's assistants, Leroy. He took her to one side to explain that her lover had been reported missing by his wife late last night. No one had seen him since he left work yesterday around 5:30.

"That's impossible, he texted me last night around 11:30 to confirm our session this morning."

The policeman overheard the conversation and intervened.

"Please allow me to introduce myself, I am PC Roberts. I have been assigned to investigate what we are treating as a missing persons case the disappearance of Mr Brian Wright. You are...?"

"Gina ... Gina Robertson."

"What is your association with Mr Wright?"

"He is my personal trainer; I'm here for my weekly session with him."

"You said you received a text from him late last night to confirm this morning's training?"

"Yes, I did."

"What time was that?" enquired the police officer.

"Around 11:30 p.m.," Gina replied.

"11:30 ... that's kind of late for your trainer to text a client to confirm a training session, isn't it?"

"Not really," replied Gina, who by now was starting to be deeply concerned at Brian's sudden disappearance. She managed to contain her emotions.

"Do you have your phone with you, Mrs Robertson?" the policeman enquired.

"No, I left it at home charging ... why do you ask?"

"We will need to take a look at it. Not only may it help us with our enquiries, but it could also well be used in evidence. I'll need to take your name and home address – I'll collect it later."

Gina felt her body quiver; she absolutely did not want the police visiting her at the family home. Where was Brian? What had happened to him? Multiple thoughts whizzed in and out of her brain at an alarming rate.

"I won't have the text, officer – I delete my texts once I have read them."

"Don't worry, we will be able to pick up all the phone records, both calls and texts, from the phone company."

Oh shit, Gina thought, that would almost certainly throw the cat amongst the pigeons. Surely it would not be long before their affair was revealed. What a mess, what a bloody mess.

"If you really need my phone, I would prefer to bring it to the station," she said.

"I am sorry, that won't be possible. I will have to accompany you back to your house now, Mrs Robertson, as right now you are classed as a source of information to assist the police with our enquiries."

"OK." Gina had little option. However, she thought that at least Simon was at work and her son at school, so with a bit of luck there should not be a problem – well, at least for now.

As they left the gym to return to Gina's home, her mind raced as to what was on her mobile and how she could possibly erase the evidence prior to handing it over to the police.

Thankfully for Gina, nobody was at home as she entered her family home with PC Roberts– all was quiet.

"Can I offer you a drink?" she asked.

"No, thank you, I am already running late I have to visit Mrs Wright, have you ever met her?" he enquired.

"No, I will go and get my phone and you can be on your way."

The mobile was charging in the study. Gina could not remember if she had erased all the texts that Brian had sent her. She was pretty sure that she had; however, the phone company records would probably blow the relationship wide open, not to mention the affair that she was having with Peter Swann.

She had no time to check her phone and thought that it would be a pretty worthless exercise, anyway. As she removed it from its cradle, she noticed that she had received another text from Tony. She quickly deleted it.

Gina walked back into the kitchen and handed the phone to the officer. She felt sick to the pit of her stomach; she could not believe that her near-perfect life was about to be wrecked, especially if something had happened to Brian.

PC Roberts switched on the phone and asked Gina for the PIN number to activate the handset. Within a matter of seconds the phone lit up and he went straight to her text Inbox. Much to Gina's relief, the last saved message had been from her friend Jenny asking if she fancied meeting up for a coffee.

There were no texts in the sent box as she had it set to not retain any sent messages.

After satisfying himself that there was nothing incriminating either in her text messages or in her voicemail, he made a note of her mobile number and, much to Gina's surprise, handed the handset back to her.

"Thank you for your co-operation, I will be in touch when we have some news." He left and made his way to Kelly Wright's house.

Gina was still shaking as she bid the policeman farewell, although she felt deep inside that it was only a matter of time before she would be hearing from PC Roberts again.

Kelly Wright had still not heard from her husband as the front doorbell rang and she let the police officer into her home. She had told her son that his dad had left for work early. During the next forty minutes or so, PC Roberts filled out all the official documentation and asked a lot of questions. Kelly Wright sobbed through most of the conversation, as she knew that her husband was in some sort of trouble – it was totally out of character for Brian to behave in such a manner. She passed on some recent photographs of her husband to the officer.

"We will notify all the other local forces and publish Mr Wright's photograph across the locality if he does not get in touch with you in the next 24 hours. One final question: did your husband ever mention a lady client of his, Gina Robertson?"

"No, I have never heard of her, why do you ask?"

"No real reason, I bumped into her at his gym."

They bid farewell to each other. Kelly shut the door wandering whom Mrs Robertson was and if she had anything to do with Brian's disappearance.

* * *

A tall, thin, gaunt-looking young man entered the crowded public area at Paddington Station. He made his way hastily to the locker area behind the ticket office, bumping into several commuters en route.

He arrived at his destination and pulled a piece of crumpled paper from his jeans pocket – 7297, it read. He fiddled with the silver dials on the padlock until it released the lock. The grey locker door swung open to reveal a large brown holdall that looked like it had seen better days. The sight of the holdall brought a smile to the ill-looking man's face.

"Come to Daddy," he said to the brown leather bag that had a large zip pocket secured by a small gold padlock. He closed the locker door and headed for Costa Coffee on the other side of the complex. The coffee shop was heaving, as he had hoped. After ordering an espresso, he found a table in the corner where he could enjoy his drink and inspect the contents of his bag

He inserted a small gold key into the padlock on the holdall. The lock sprang open and was duly removed. He looked up and surveyed the scene before unzipping the bag to reveal its contents.

His pulse raced as his eyes bulged, focusing on the contents of the bag. All present and correct, just as he had left it a couple of years ago for a "rainy day".

CHAPTER FIFTEEN

"Good morning, Robertson Holdings," the receptionist recited almost in military fashion as she answered the incoming call.

"Fraser Robertson, please, I need to speak with him urgently."

"Who should I say is calling?"

"Doctor Clegg."

Fraser Robertson was mulling over the daily papers that his secretary had brought in earlier, along with the morning's mail and his regular pot of piping hot coffee. His inner peace was about to be disturbed.

"I have Doctor Clegg on line three," his secretary informed him.

"Put him through," Robertson retorted abruptly.

"Doctor Clegg, I am sorry that I have not been in touch, I have been tied up with the business, I am planning on visiting James at the weekend, I am aware that we need to discuss the results of his blood tests."

"Mr Robertson, by the sounds of it, you have not heard from your son; I was rather hoping that he had at least contacted you. Unfortunately, he has gone missing."

A deathly silence descended across the phone line. Fraser Robertson could feel his blood pressure rise as the inner rage built inside him.

"Gone missing? What the fucking hell are you running there, Doctor, some kind of open house where troubled people in need of serious around the clock attention can just stroll about and wander in and out at their will?" "My son is a very sick boy. I am paying you a fucking fortune in an attempt to get him better, to give him some stability and lessen his dependencies on hard drugs and alcohol so that he can at least live some sort of normal life and you tell me he has escaped!" screamed Robertson. "You fucking moron!"

"Calm down, Mr Robertson."

"Don't you dare to tell me to calm down! Your organisation is a disgrace, Doctor Clegg."

"There really is no need for this language – it is not going to help us find James. I fully understand that you are deeply upset and extremely angry, and I can only apologise, Mr Robertson. We really should put all our energies into finding your son."

Doctor Clegg took advantage of the pause that followed by continuing.

"We know that he has been missing for up to three hours. We can determine this because the last time his room was checked at 7:30 a.m., and he was asleep in his bed. Does he have any friends in the London area, is there anywhere that he would go, a safe haven, perhaps?"

"Listen, Doctor, James did not have any friends. He lived in a dark world where the stable diet consisted of a few lines of coke and a couple of shots of heroine, complemented by a bottle or two of vodka and fifty cigarettes. That is why he has been in and out of your establishment on a regular basis over the past ten years or so."

Robertson drew breath before continuing. "I will be with you sometime this afternoon, in the interim period, notify the police and alert the local media. I will put up a reward of £200,000 for his safe return. You should have an up to date photograph of him on file that you can distribute."

"We have and are already in the process of making the necessary contacts; I will see you later today. Once again, please accept our sincere apologies for this indiscretion."

Fraser Robertson hung up and banged his clenched fist on his desk a couple of times in an attempt to let of some steam. He called his assistant through the intercom.

"Get me a car to take me immediately to The Priory and cancel all my engagements for the next couple of days."

"Certainly, Mr Robertson."

Within an hour, Fraser Robertson had cleared his desk and was heading to The Priory in search of his son. Fraser made good use of the travel time sitting in the back of his chauffeur-driven Bentley surrounded by all the toys that money could buy. He called into the powder factory to check on the weekend's takings, and he spoke with a couple of his bent council official cronies about tying up a deal on some land that was about to become available, offering them rich incentives if they could ensure that the sale bypassed the required formal tendering process and was offered to his company for silly money.

He checked in with his ex-marines who had done such an admirable job the previous evening to congratulate them and give them specific instructions for the final heinous act.

❖ ❖ ❖

His daughter-in-law, the lovely Gina, was in a flap. Where the hell was Brian? Why had he not returned home – was he in danger? Nothing made sense to her. Her stomach churned as she thought of her encounter with PC Roberts and the prospect of the phone company's records exposing not only her torrid affair with the now missing Brian but also Peter Swann.

Gina knew that she had to cancel her rendezvous with Peter and somehow see if she could persuade Simon to call off the weekend's dinner party, albeit much to her beloved son Mark's extreme disappointment. After much deliberation, she decided to call Peter at work, not from her mobile but from the landline.

Her luck was in. The call went straight through to Peter. She told him that she was feeling unwell and was not up to meeting up tomorrow. She was relieved when he became sympathetic rather than confrontational. She also slipped into the conversation that they may well need to reschedule the dinner party. Once again, Peter was charming and said that he completely understood.

She felt at least some temporary relief, unlike Kelly Wright, who was quickly heading towards a breakdown as the police failed to deliver any positive news over the next couple of days. Kelly had broken the news to her son that his dad had gone missing. After an initial outburst where the boy blamed his mother for driving his dad away, he had calmed down and began to show maturity beyond his tender age, tending to housework, taking messages from the police and trying to comfort his distressed Mum.

Simon Robertson had noticed the change in his wife. She was edgy, short-tempered and agitated. Despite not hearing anything from PC Roberts, she had developed an annoying habit of looking at her mobile phone every few minutes, checking if any communication had landed in her inbox. Gina had not left the house for two days, apart from dropping Mark off at school. She had forgotten how many times she had called Brian's mobile from the house phone, but all in vain – he would not pick up. Like his wife Kelly, Gina knew that Brian was in some serious trouble.

In an attempt to cheer herself up, she decided that a visit to the hairdresser's and a new set of nails was in order, even though she did not feel up to venturing out and entering into cheap, meaningless dialogue with hairdressers and young beauticians.

As Gina drove back up the driveway of the family home some four hours later, looking and feeling a little better, armed with a new set of white nails and a designer haircut, she noticed a brown cardboard box that had been left on the doormat. She parked the car and collected the parcel, taking it with her into the kitchen. The package had a large white address label that was marked in black felt tip pen:

Strictly Private & Confidential

For The Attention of Mrs Gina Robertson

Hillbark

4 Cedar Close

Calderstones

Liverpool

Merseyside

L18 3SX

Only to be opened by Mrs Robertson

There were no other distinctive markings on the parcel other than the TNT sticker. The box was no bigger than a case of wine but a lot lighter.

Gina was not expecting a delivery. She had no idea what it could be. She reached into the cutlery drawer for a knife to cut through the light brown sticking tape and open the package. The butcher's knife made light work of the sticking tape; she pulled back the flaps and peered inside the box to find another smaller package beautifully wrapped in very expensive high gloss black gift-wrapping. A magnificent silver ribbon tied in a bow accompanied by a matching gift tag completed the package. Gina felt excited: a present, maybe from Peter? No – surely he would not risk sending something to the house. Maybe it was from her husband Simon?

The gift tag did not help. It simply said, "Hope it fits x."

Ever since she was a little girl Gina loved opening presents, she ripped through the expensive gift wrapping splitting one of her new nails in the process; "Shit! This better be good."

As she peeled back the paper she saw a tasteful red leather Cartier jewellery case embossed in gold leaf with an antique clasp. She pushed the clasp in, lifting the catch at the same time to open it. An unpleasant smell filled her nostrils as the lid opened. Her eyes locked onto the contents. As she focused, Gina could feel the bile in her stomach begin to ascend into her throat. She threw the box across the kitchen floor. Her body shook uncontrollably as she vomited in the kitchen sink.

All of a sudden, everything went black as Mrs Robertson passed out, collapsing on the kitchen floor.

Less than two minutes later, Gina regained consciousness. She was sweating profusely. Her brain began to recollect the events that had lead to her attack, the unknown parcel, the beautiful gift wrapping, the Cartier jewellery box and what must be confirmation that her lover was dead – Brian Wright's castrated black penis lay on the ceramic floor tiles.

Her head was spinning. She could not comprehend what had happened. As she picked herself up, she felt the nausea return, vomiting again.

"Oh my God, oh my God...." she repeated.

Who on Earth could have conducted such a barbaric act? Whoever has done this? How do they know about me? Has Brian lost his life because of our affair?

She caught her breath as she gulped water from the kitchen tap; she cupped her hands and soaked her face with the cold water in an attempt to regain some composure.

Gina tried to collect her thoughts – what should she do next? If she told the police, then it would implicate her, not to mention the possibility of her becoming embroiled in a murder investigation, as well as the distinct prospect of a divorce, culminating in the end of her lavish and exciting lifestyle.

If she didn't tell anyone about it, then whoever had sent the package had her where they wanted her – or had they committed their final act and life would go back to relative normality?

After much deliberation and soul-searching, Gina decided to clean up and shut up. She felt trapped not knowing the identity of her persecutor.

She donned a pair of rubber gloves and began a clean-up operation. She tentatively picked up Brian's penis with a pair of tongs and placed it in a garden refuse sack, along with all the packaging and jewellery case. She mopped the floor thoroughly and restored the kitchen to its pristine best. She sprayed the room and opened the large window in an attempt to get rid of the smell of sick.

Gina put the bag in the boot of the car and headed for the council tip. Her luck was in: the gates of the council site were open and the security hut unmanned. She hurriedly took the bag out of the boot and threw it into one of the green skips before beating her retreat back to the relative safety of her family home.

Thankfully, the smell in the kitchen had started to subside. Gina poured herself a large brandy, slugging it back to calm her shattered nerves.

For the next thirty minutes, Gina Robertson sobbed as she reflected on her affair with her personal trainer.

Chapter Sixteen

"And the winner of European Capital of Culture for 2008 is ... Liverpool!" the culture secretary announced to the gathered masses of reporters, TV crews and banks of photographers who had assembled for the press conference.

Over the next few hours, the news quickly spread of this unbelievable and unexpected news. Newcastle was expected to land the prize. The Geordie city's odds had fallen considerably in the run up to the announcement, and they were clear favourites to win.

Tony Barlow was at a sales conference in London when he heard via text message that his home city had been crowned. The cynic in him immediately turned his thoughts to huge brown envelopes being exchanged between politicians, councillors and dignitaries in exchange for this massive favour. He was obviously delighted as he reflected on his £850,000 investment, probably growing by at least ten per cent on the back of the news.

Fraser Robertson stood to make significantly more from the news: millions of pounds, if not tens of millions, from his drug business as hordes of thrill-seeking foreigners descended into the European Capital of Culture to see what all the fuss was about, not to mention a few bob from his so-called legitimate business, Robertson Developments, that was about as straight as a curve.

He continued to buy up prime real estate from his council and political contacts for a fraction of its real market value. His visit to meet Doctor Clegg had proved to be less than fruitful. He had stormed out of The Priory threatening to sue them for gross negligence, describing the security arrangements as a joke.

Gina Robertson had been lying low. She had not received any more parcels or texts, her visits to the gymnasium had ceased and she had started to put on some weight. At first she thought that this was probably down to the fact that she had stopped exercising, but she had also missed a couple of her periods.

The police, having initially stepped up their search efforts for Brian Wright had now scaled back, almost resigning themselves to the fact that he had disappeared without trace or motive. The records from the phone company had confirmed that he was sexually involved with Gina Robertson; however, they had not connected the relationship to his disappearance.

"*The Big Dig*" continued unabated, bringing misery and chaos to thousands of city-bound commuters and dwellers. Backhanders that had been part of Liverpool's economic culture for over fifty years were on the increase and looked like going into overdrive on the back of the announcement as cowboy property developers looked for special favours and concessions from bent political allies and council officials who were in search of early retirement.

Robertson Heights continued to progress towards completion.

The indicator on the home pregnancy tester turned blue, indicating that Mrs Gina Robertson was pregnant. She did not want a baby at this stage of her life; it would be an inconvenience that interfered with her lifestyle. Furthermore, she had no idea who the father was; it could be one of three – Brian Wright, Peter Swann or her husband Simon.

The worst-case scenario would be Brian, quickly followed by Peter and the best of the three outcomes would of course be Simon. Their sex life had not been entirely active of late – one quick bonk in the past six months, some ten weeks ago now. Their firstborn, Mark, had taken a couple of years of regular intercourse and a crash course of fertility treatment to conceive, so how convinced would Simon be? She had to tell him – she had no choice.

In just a matter of a couple of months, Gina Robertson's near-perfect life had fallen apart. She had been forced to bottle everything up. She had nobody to confide in that she could really trust.

Simon Robertson had been embroiled in his father's businesses of late. He had supervised another shipment of "Snow Drift" hidden in the latest batch of PVC window and doorframes for *Robertson Heights*. Simon had also been supervising the initial phase fitting of the nearly completed tower.

He was concerned about the disappearance of his brother, even though they did not see eye to eye. Simon was acutely aware of his fragile condition. His wife's unusual behaviour was also concerning him deeply.

As he headed back to the office to sign some contracts for *Robertson Heights*, he received a text from his wife asking what time he would be home as she had some special news for him. He texted back that he could be home by 5:30 p.m. and could not wait to hear her news.

Perfect she thought as his text came in, I will cook us a nice meal and I can break the news this evening. We can then tell Mark that he is going to have a little brother or sister and from there it will spread like wildfire to family and friends.

Gina made a quick trip to the local butchers to pick up a couple of fillet steaks, Simon's favourite. She would make some béarnaise sauce; cook some fresh spinach and sauté potatoes. A bottle or two of Pinot Noir would be the perfect accompaniment. She knew that she was going to have to produce a truly convincing display.

Simon arrived home early, eager to hear Gina's news.

"So come on, honey, what's the news?" he enquired as he entered the house.

"You'll have to wait a little while longer, why don't you jump in the shower then dinner will be ready and all will be revealed."

"Sounds exciting; can't wait. What's for dinner?"

"Your favourite."

"Great, you are spoiling me... where's Mark?"

"He's round at Gavin's, his mum said that she would bring him back around 8."

As Simon showered, she lit the candles, poured two large glasses of Pinot and prepared to serve dinner and break the news. The steaks fizzed and crackled in the pan as Simon entered the kitchen and took his usual place at the head of the table.

"So come on, honey share it with me and put me out of my suspense."

Gina passed her husband a small gift-wrapped package.

"Open it," she instructed staying close to his gaze.

"What is it?" he enquired as he unwrapped his unexpected present to reveal a white plastic predictor where the indicator had turned blue. An uncomfortable pause followed as Simon computed what was in front of him. It was broken with a howl of delight. "You're pregnant, you're pregnant!" he repeated enthusiastically.

"You're going to be a daddy again," Gina responded.

Simon threw his arms around his wife, giving her a big hug, tears streaming down his face.

"Oh babe, that is fantastic news, are you sure? How many weeks pregnant are you?" The questions came thick and fast.

"About seven weeks," Gina replied.

"This really does call for a celebration, let's break out the Champagne. I can't wait to tell Mark and my dad".

As Simon popped open the Champagne, his euphoria was tamed as he thought about the fact that he and his wife had hardly made love over the past few months, other than the quickie they had shared a couple of months ago. Maybe that was it? It certainly fitted in terms of timeframe, or maybe it was not his. He decided not to spoil the moment, as deep down, he wanted the baby to be his. He loved his wife and had always wished for a large family.

The happy couple toasted the news with a glass of chilled Krug each as well as polishing off a bottle of Pinot Noir and devouring the succulent steaks.

Mark was dropped off by Gavin's mum around 8:30pm Simon and Gina were clearing away the dishes when he enthusiastically bounced into the kitchen to announce his arrival home.

"Mum, Dad, I had a great time with Gavin, he wants me to stay over at the weekend, can I, please, please?"

"We'll have to wait and see, if you are a good boy, then maybe". "Anyway, we have some exciting news that we want to share with you," Gina said.

"Oh wow, what is it? Tell me, tell me mummy".

"Well, how would you like a little brother or sister?" his Dad asked enthusiastically.

"Oh yes, please, can I have a little brother? I could play football with him."

"Mummy is expecting – we are going to have a new baby".

Mark was very excited. He thought that it would be great to have a younger brother. He did not really fancy a little sister though – he was at an age where baby girls were not on his agenda. The family embraced to celebrate the news. For the time being, Gina was as safe as she could expect to be, given the circumstances.

CHAPTER SEVENTEEN

He climbed up the old stone steps and pressed the highly polished brass bell that had been a fixture of the Harley Street practice for over a hundred years. A pretty blonde lady in her late thirties opened the large entrance door and welcomed the tall, gaunt-looking man carrying a brown leather holdall.

"Good morning, Mr Harris."

"Good morning," he replied.

"We need to complete a few formalities and get you admitted; your surgery has been booked for 12 noon. Dr Aziz and Dr Saleh, who are performing the procedure, will be in to see you to discuss any concerns that you may have prior to taking you down for surgery."

"That's fine," he acknowledged.

The pretty receptionist completed the paperwork and the formalities before taking Mr Harris to his private suite.

"How will you paying the balance for the surgery?" she enquired.

"Good old-fashioned cash. What's the balance?"

"Thirty-thousand pounds, please."

He reached into his holdall and took out a pile of fifty-pound notes and handed them to the receptionist. She nervously accepted the bundle, putting it into her desk drawer. A tall brunette nurse arrived to take the patient to his private room, where she would check his blood pressure and perform the preliminaries.

"Mr Harris, I am Sister Goodall, can I help you with your bag?" she enquired.

"No thanks, I have got it."

The private suite resembled a quality five-star hotel executive room. There was virtually nothing that related it to a clinical establishment other than the drip that stood at the head of the double bed and the clipboard that was hung over the decorative metal railing at the foot of bedstead.

Contrasting blackberry-coloured velvet drapes and matching bed cover complemented a lush mushroom-coloured carpet. A huge flat screen plasma TV hung on the wall above an ornate marble fireplace. A display of fresh flowers sat on the mantelpiece. White fluffy slippers were placed on top of a towelling robe that had the clinic's logo embossed onto the breast pocket.

"I think you will find everything to your liking, Mr Harris," said the nurse as she turned down the bedspread. "I will leave you to settle for a while. Is there anything that I can get you – a newspaper, maybe?"

"No thank you, I will be fine."

The sister left the room. He locked the door behind her before emptying the contents of the brown holdall onto his bed, amongst the countless bundles of fifty-pound notes were a few clear plastic bags containing white powder.

A Colt 45 handgun came to rest on one of the bundles of cash next to a large A5 brown envelope. He grabbed the envelope, opening the flap and removed some detailed photographs of a man's face taken from various angles. The pictures focused on the features of the face, nose, cheekbones, lips, eyebrows, and teeth. The British passport that accompanied them was brand new and in the name of Mr Robert Harris. The passport photograph was a perfect match to the photos. The date of birth was three years and three months after the actual date when James Robertson entered the world. He had now decided to live the rest of his natural life as Robert David Harris.

The contents of the bag were quickly replaced in the holdall that was duly locked and put in the in-room safe. The surgeons, who were reputed to be amongst the finest in the western world, discussed in great depth the desired outcome of the facial transformation. Attention to detail was absolutely critical in any identity change operation.

Following eight hours of surgery, which was a complete success, master craftsmen had created Robert David Harris... James Robertson was no more.

* * *

A sale price of two hundred and fifty thousand pounds was agreed with the Greek chip shop owner for 403 West Ferry Quay. Tony Barlow was delighted to be moving on from the relative nightmare that he had been subjected to over the past nine months, living above a drug dealer and all the delights that had condemned him to.

Barlow was particularly excited about moving into his super swanky new penthouse. For once in his life, things were looking good. Matters had been progressing nicely. Professionally, he was doing well, having recently closed a couple of large transactions with BT. The West Ferry Quay chapter in his life was about to close and a promising new one begin.

The removal men arrived at West Ferry Quay on the dot at eight a.m., armed with numerous cardboard boxes and large rolls of bubble pack plastic wrap, plus a couple of large rolls of brown packing tape. Two of them began wrapping valuable items in the bubble wrap. Portable wardrobes, of which there were eighteen, began to stream into number 403. Tony loved his designer clothes and had insisted on portable wardrobes so he could hang his more treasured items of clothing. He was paranoid about how his Prada suits and business shirts would look following the relative short journey down the road to *Robertson Heights*.

Tony had decided to go on ahead to his new penthouse, his new home in the sky.

When he arrived at *Robertson Heights*, he parked in one of his allocated spaces before proceeding through the car park on level -2 to the express lifts. One of the first things to hit him was the fact that none of the common area walls or doors that he had advanced through had been painted. The bare concrete and wood-panelled security door looked far from welcoming. He dismissed this as work to be completed.

The lift door opened. It resembled a small wooden crate with chipboard panels stretching floor to ceiling on all three walls. He pressed floor 39 and inserted a small card into the recess on the keypad. The penthouse floors had a special security code that was built into the card to gain access. Barlow soon arrived at Level 39, where he was greeted by the smell of paint. The door to his apartment was open, and he was rather surprised to see a posse of workmen in his new penthouse.

"What's happening guys?" Tony enquired.

"We're experiencing some technical problems with your air conditioning and heating system."

"What kind of problems?" asked Tony.

"The system keeps shutting itself down for some reason. Don't worry, we're working on it," replied a chubby looking bearded man.

"I'm moving in today, so it's important that you resolve this."

"We may have to take the ceiling down in your master bedroom en-suite".

"You are joking, of course ... is this a wind up?" Barlow, raising his voice, continued, "I have paid eight hundred and fifty thousand pounds for this place and you are telling me before I move in that a ceiling may have to come down".

"We will do all we can – it's just that the main controller unit is situated in your bathroom ceiling". "For some reason best known to the architect, the controller unit is at the furthest end from the access hatch, so it's impossible to work on. We have to take part of the ceiling down to get to it."

Tony proceeded through the upstairs living area. He felt agitated with the news. Negative thoughts began to occupy his mind as he wondered what was going to happen next. It would not be long before he found out. As Barlow moved swiftly into the master bedroom, he immediately noticed the feature glass panel wall that separated the bedroom area from a dressing room, complete with walk-in wardrobes, had been glazed with transparent glass, as opposed to opaque glass as instructed and agreed.

"Shit, this is unbelievable!" he exclaimed. Tony knew that the wall and the wardrobe doors would have to be replaced or at least taken away to be treated or sandblasted to remove the transparency. Each panel was three metres high by a metre wide and there were nine of them – no, make that 12, as he confirmed that the guest bedroom had the same problem.

Tony could feel the blood begin to boil in his veins. He reached for his mobile phone to call Fraser Robertson and give him a piece of his mind. He could not get a signal so moved into the hallway to make the call.

"Good morning, Robertson Holdings, Sara speaking, how may I direct your call?"

"Fraser Robertson," Barlow responded sternly.

"Can I ask who's calling?"

"It's Tony Barlow."

Barlow did not get through to Fraser Robertson, who had just come off the phone from his son, Simon, telling him about his wife's pregnancy, news that both concerned and angered him. He spoke with his personal assistant instead.

"I am sorry, Mr Robertson is not available, can I ask what your call is in connection with?" his PA enquired.

"You certainly can. I have just paid Mr Robertson eight hundred and fifty thousand pounds for a penthouse in *Robertson Heights* where the heating and air conditioning system does not work and I have been told that the gang of workmen who are in my flat right now may have to take one of my ceilings down. The feature glass wall and glass wardrobe doors in both the main bedroom and guest bedroom are see-through and I specifically requested mint coloured opaque panels. God only knows what else I will find, I have only been in the apartment for ten minutes! I am fuming. You get Mr Robertson to call me immediately," Barlow snapped.

"I am sorry, but Mr Robertson does not speak to purchasers."

Barlow could not believe what he had just heard. "Pardon me?" he retorted.

The personal assistant repeated, "I am afraid that it is Mr Robertson's policy that he does not speak directly with purchasers. I will get one of the sales ladies to call you. Can you give me your number, please, Mr Barlow?"

Tony wanted to chew the phone; he could not believe what he had just been told.

"If Mr Robertson does not call me within the next hour, I will be calling in to his office. I have never heard such arrogance in my life. He was happy to take my money off me...." Tony ended the call abruptly.

"Who was that?" Fraser enquired.

"Mr Barlow, he is extremely unhappy. He has moved in today and there are problems with his heating and air conditioning system and the glass panels and wardrobe doors are all wrong. He wants you to call him in the next hour, otherwise he said he will call round to see you."

"Teething problems, what does he expect? Get one of the sales girls to deal with it, I have enough issues of my own right now with a missing son and an expectant daughter-in-law."

The sun shone through the dining room window, bouncing off the polished mahogany floor. Tony Barlow sat cross-legged surveying the breathtaking views that lay before him. The Anglican Cathedral stood proud amongst the city skyline, along with Radio City Tower, St George's Hall, and Lime Street Station, one of the many gateways to this once proud city. The view was truly stunning. His peaceful state of mind was disturbed as his mobile rang.

"Hello?"

"Oh hi, Mr Barlow, it's Annie Evans, Head of Sales at Robertson Holdings. I just wanted to check that you were settling in OK and wandered if you would be interested in investing in our latest planned development."

"You obviously have not spoken with Fraser Robertson's PA," Barlow replied.

"No, is there a problem?" Annie asked.

"You could say that, no – make that I have a number of problems. I suggest that you speak with her and get Fraser Robertson to call me."

"He does not speak with clients, I am afraid. I will ensure that your issues are resolved, Mr Barlow," she replied confidently.

For the next few minutes, Tony recounted all the issues. Annie Evans committed to meeting him "on site" within the hour. "On site" was a term used for "at your apartment" although to be fair it was probably far more accurate, as *Robertson Heights* was still very much a building site and would be for some months to come.

During the next hour, Tony inspected the penthouse, adding several items to his growing "snagging list". Amongst major pieces of work was replacing the transparent glass bathroom cabinet double doors with opaque glass as requested. The ceiling in the en-suite also came down to provide access to the air conditioning unit, which the engineers continued to work tirelessly on without any degree of success.

"You would think when you have spent the best part of a million pounds on a luxury penthouse that they would get it right, wouldn't you?" Tony said to himself, fearing that he would relapse into a state of negativity and depression.

His train of thoughts were interrupted by the arrival of Annie Evans, clutching a blue clipboard and a large manila folder.

"Mr Barlow, Annie Evans, Head of Sales." She offered her hand as a greeting, but Barlow declined, preferring to go straight on the offensive. He uttered his disgust at the state of the apartment and the building relative to the money he had paid.

"I am absolutely appalled that you can get it so wrong and your arrogant boss won't even return my call."

His protest was met with the standard response: Fraser Robertson has a strict policy of not talking to clients.

He was reassured that everything would be taken care of. The glass would probably take at least a few weeks, because it would have to go back to the factory to be treated.

The temperature continued to rise inside the apartment. This was caused in the main by the sun beating through the floor to ceiling windows, although Tony Barlow's current state of stress was also probably a contributory factor. He opened a couple of windows to let what air there was outside in an attempt to cool the environment. He simply could not imagine living at this height in a glass tower, having no air conditioning or blinds to cool the oppressive atmosphere.

"I am far from impressed with the finish to my apartment and for that matter the building itself," he continued. "The doors and skirting boards are really poorly finished, rough cuts with a lick of paint – hardly what you would expect. The paint job looks like one coat and will no doubt rub off if you have to wipe the surface. If Mr Robertson won't speak to me, then he will speak with my solicitors."

"I am sure there is no need for that," said Annie. "Please just give me a chance to put things right."

"OK, but I will be writing to Mr Robertson."

"I will advise him," she acknowledged.

"In the interim, I will ensure that we get underway with resolving all your issues without any unnecessary delay."

"One other thing before you go: how the hell am I supposed to get my furniture up here, as it's obvious the lifts are way too small to carry any large pieces?"

"You can either dismantle the furniture or it's up the stairs, I'm afraid," Annie sighed.

"You must be joking. Thirty-nine storeys up carrying expensive suites, dining room furniture, beds. We are talking delivery men here, not highly trained Olympic athletes, although it would no doubt be a challenge for them," Barlow fumed. "Who the bloody hell designed the building with two tiny lifts that you would struggle to swing a cat in?"

"I was told that there were two large express passenger lifts when I bought the property. This is turning into a bloody nightmare!" Barlow ranted.

Annie Evans offered no comfort through her silence and left him to stew.

As he contemplated the events of the morning, his thoughts were interrupted by one of the workmen.

"Your air conditioning is back on, guv, although we think there is an intermittent fault on the system so we will leave the ceiling down for a few days just in case we have to get at the control unit again."

Tony just nodded, his mental energy levels depleted from the morning's events.

"We will be back in the morning to check on it." The engineer and his accomplices packed up their toolboxes and left.

A whirring noise broke the silence. It resembled a hair dryer being switched on. It was the air conditioning unit in the lounge springing to life. As the air began to chill through the unit's ugly steel ventilator panel, the noise of the motor and fan that were driving it grew ever louder.

Tony barely heard his phone ring – it flashed "Robertson Developments" as he accepted the call.

"Hello, Mr Barlow, it's Jenny Sinclair from Robertson Developments' sales office. I was wondering if you would be interested in investing our latest planned development, *Western Heights*?

"To be honest, I am already regretting spending the best part of a million pounds with an organisation who clearly say one thing and then deliver another. I've moved in today and in fact Annie Evans has just left my apartment with a list of snagging that is as long as your arm. Furthermore, I feel extremely uncomfortable dealing with any organisation whose chairman will not speak to his paying customers."

"I am sorry to hear that you are not happy and I am confident that all your issues will be resolved. This development is a rare off plan investment opportunity that we are initially only offering to our existing clients."

"Out of interest, where is this development – Manchester, Leeds, London?" Barlow asked.

"No, it's in Liverpool. Are you in your apartment now?" Jenny enquired.

"Yes, why do you ask?"

"Well, if you go to your lounge window and look down to your left, there is a small piece of land in front of the brand new offices – you should see some cars parked on it. That is the site for what will house Liverpool's tallest building, a whopping fifty storeys," she said enthusiastically as if she was reading from sort of script, utterly unaware of the effect she was having on his mood.

"Pardon me," uttered Barlow, who could not believe what he had just heard.

Before the sales lady could repeat her pitch, Tony played it back to her.

"So you are telling me that Robertson Developments have acquired the tiny car park that I am looking at and are planning on putting a fifty-storey residential tower on it, which will not only take away my views of the Liver Buildings and the River Mersey, it will devalue my property greatly and force me to live on a building site for three years! Is this a bloody wind up?"

"No, err, no," she replied nervously. "I am sorry you feel angry. I had no intention of upsetting you."

"Tell your boss he will be hearing from my solicitors!" He threw the phone across the apartment. His blood had reached boiling point and he was baying for blood.

Chapter Eighteen

Tony Barlow sat cross-legged on the floor with his head bowed in cupped hands, recalling the shocking events of the day.

The ceiling was down in the en-suite, the air conditioning and heating had an intermittent fault, the build quality was cheap and nasty, and all the glass wardrobe doors, as well as the feature wall panels and bathroom cabinets would have to be replaced because they were clear glass.

He had just had a call from Robertson's sales lady asking if he wanted to invest in their latest development, a fifty-storey tower that is going right outside his window and to make matters even worse, Fraser Robertson would not speak with him as he had a policy of not talking with his clients, especially when he has been paid out.

"Fucking cowboy, fucking cowboy organisation! I'll fucking kill the bastard!"

Tony was finding it difficult to think straight. His world, his empire, was collapsing around him and he was coming apart at the seams.

"The first thing I need to do is speak with my solicitor to understand my legal position. What have I got myself into? Christ, all my money is tied up in this dump."

Questions and self-doubt whizzed around his head. The inner rage rose like a torrent inside him.

Barlow eventually calmed himself and called his solicitor. He recited the events that had unfolded and registered his concern as to what there may yet to be disclosed. His solicitor listened attentively, confirming that a letter would go out by registered post to Fraser Robertson that evening. It would seek clarification as to whether or not Robertson Holdings or any of its subsidiaries were in fact planning to build a fifty-storey residential development on the car park in Gartner Street and if so, why had they not declared this prior to completion of sale.

Barlow's lawyers were also going to look to seek damages from Robertson Holdings in the event that the land was developed and subsequently negatively affected the value of their client's investment.

The correspondence would conclude with reference to Barlow's total dissatisfaction with the finish of the apartment, detailing all the issues he had been subjected to.

This should have been a joyous day in the life of Tony Barlow. Instead, it was rapidly descending into one of the worst days of his life. Once more he felt the inner rage, a sure sign that depression was looming.

There was a knock on the front door. It was one of the removal men.

"We're just going to grab a sandwich, then we'll start to unload. It looks like we will have to use the stairs for the larger items of furniture which will mean putting another two men on the job". "We'll also need some covers, as the stairs are pretty tight. Mike is seeing who is available. I can't believe they've built a place like this and put ridiculously small lifts in."

"I know … it beggars belief."

Within the next three hours or so, things were beginning to take shape. The removal men worked tirelessly. Their distinctive red bib and brace overalls were soaked with sweat, a result of their repetitive toils up and down up and down. They were kept well fed and watered with a variety of drinks and refreshments whilst Tony multi-tasked, supervising the placement of the various pieces of furniture as well as unpacking endless boxes of possessions, finding new homes for them.

By six o'clock, they had broken the back of moving him into his new apartment. The removals men had completed their work and returned to their respective homes for a much needed, well-earned rest.

The new red leather sofas were placed in the lounge, although the larger of the two sofas was damaged trying to get it up the stairs. The Bang & Olufsen fifty-inch plasma TV, complete with two pairs of state of the art speakers, looked superb as the centrepiece of the room.

The boat-shaped glass dining table and six white leather chairs took pride of place in the centre of the dining room, which boasted superb views of downtown. Tony looked forward to entertaining his friends in his new apartment.

He busied himself unpacking boxes and hanging clothes in the wardrobes. He hated it as he could see all the clothes through the clear glass doors.

Following a quick shower, he decided to take a short walk into town to one of the fashionable bars. He ordered himself a pint of lager to start the process of drowning his sorrows. It tasted rather bitter and slightly flat, which summed up his day.

"You need to sign for this one," the postman told the young receptionist at Robertson Developments. "It's for your boss, Fraser Robertson – recorded delivery."

She duly signed and took it through to Fraser's PA. The A4 plain white envelope was clearly marked with the sender's name – Kinsey & James Solicitors, Tony Barlow's legal representatives. Fraser's assistant had permission to open all of Fraser's mail. She duly removed the letter, placing it in a burgundy leather-bound file along with the rest of the mail and the morning papers. It was taken into Fraser with his pot of tea. She closed the door behind her, returning to her desk.

Whilst Fraser Robertson sipped his tea, he began to go through the mail. The registered letter from Kinsey & James Solicitors sat on the top of the pile and so received his earliest attention. His concentration was disturbed by the arrival of his son and business partner Simon, closely followed by Fraser's assistant, armed with a cup and saucer and some biscuits.

"Morning, Dad, what's happening … you don't mind if I pour myself a cuppa, do you?"

Without looking up, Fraser acknowledged Simon's request by nodding and motioning his right hand.

The silence was broken with his outburst. "Shit, fucking shit."

"What's up, Dad?"

"We've received a solicitor's letter from one of our clients who bought into *Robertson Heights*. He is seeking clarification as to whether we, or any of our associate companies, have plans to build a high-rise residential development on the council-owned car park at Gartner Street. They are requesting confirmation or absolute denial. They are seeking compensation for their client's potential loss of value if we do build, as the sweeping views of the River Mersey and the Liver Buildings that we marketed in our sales brochure, that their client had relied upon in making his purchasing decision, will be compromised, not to mention he will be inconvenienced by being forced to live on a building site during its construction."

"That's bad news, but it won't be the last one we get. We lied, Dad – we kept vital information from all our purchasers. Who is it, anyway?"

"Tony Barlow."

"Shit, Dad, he bought one of the penthouses on the west side – he will be totally compromised. He's a smart guy; I think we will have a fight on our hands, He's spent the best part of a million pounds – you would not be happy."

"He is pissed off!" "We have problems with his air conditioning and heating system, and had to take the ceiling down in the bathroom. The glass wall and glass wardrobe doors were not the right glass and we need to change them. He has also complained about the quality of fit and standard of workmanship."

"How did he find out about our plans to build " *Western Heights?*" Simon enquired.

"Cold call from one of the sales girls. I won't reply, I'll let his legal team chase me. If push comes to shove, I will get my PA to tell them that we have no plans at this time."

"But Dad, you can't, the planning permission notices are due out any day, despite the fact that we have already been granted it thanks to our friends in the council."

"We have no choice anyway, he has not got a leg to stand on, he has completed and we have his money – that's all that matters. Get the planning notices put back – he's just another sucker that bought the dream we sold him. Tony Barlow is certainly not the first and he won't be the last. I also have something on him – he won't cause us any problems."

"How are things at The Factory?" Fraser continued.

"Good, another shipment of 'Snow Drift' is due on Thursday; it's unbelievable how it has taken off."

"At least that's good news. How's Gina doing?"

"She's doing great. We are off to the hospital for a check-up later today. I don't suppose you have any news on James, Dad?"

"Unfortunately, no. You know how things work; the police have given up looking for him now they have bigger fish to fry down there. I have sent Joe Deech to see if he can uncover any new leads. You do understand that unless he is dead in a gutter somewhere then he is an absolute liability to The Firm."

"I know, Dad. Joe Deech is a top man, he will leave no stone unturned and you never know what he might find."

"Never a truer word said, Son," Fraser sarcastically replied.

CHAPTER NINETEEN

Barlow awakened following a disturbed first night's sleep. The bedroom felt uncomfortably warm. He looked at the air conditioning control panel on the bedroom wall. It was flashing, and the LED screen displayed System Failure Zone 1 and Zone 3.

"Fuck me, the system has failed again."

He was talking to himself as he awoke. Tony had taken a few days off to get settled into his new pad, although the way things had started, it would probably have been less stressful if he had gone into work.

It was not long after he had enjoyed a bowl of cereal accompanied by some fresh mixed berries and semi-skimmed milk that a knock at the door signalled the arrival of the air conditioning engineers.

"Morning, Guv'nor," the taller of the two men barked.

"Morning," Tony replied.

"We've come to check on the system."

"It failed in the night. If you go into my bedroom, the control panel is flashing an error message."

"We'll start in there."

No sooner had the engineers made their way into the bedroom to inspect the fault than there was another knock at the door – this time, two men in hard hats wearing high visibility jackets. Tony greeted them rather unenthusiastically. They explained that they were there to start to dismantle the glass panelled walls and wardrobe doors. He left them to it, after handing both men a pair of bright blue overshoes to protect his flooring and cream carpets that were laid in both bedrooms.

Tony decided that he could not bear to stay in the apartment to witness it being dismantled – the constant procession of sweaty, smelly workmen marching in and out of his penthouse, most of them showing no respect whatsoever for his new abode, treating it as a building site. He decided that it would be in his best interest to go into town and buy some new bedding and hope that they did not cause too much damage.

* * *

The tall, gaunt-looking young man parked his black Jaguar XKR in the multi-storey car park in Clayton Square. He grabbed his brown holdall from the passenger foot well and made his way to City Residences, one of a growing band of Liverpool estate agents. He had an appointment with Lauren Marsh, sales manager, to discuss a number of luxury apartments that were on the market.

Miss Marsh, looking smart in a navy blue single-breasted trouser suit, was expecting him. Let's face it – it was not every day that she met with new clients from out of town who were looking at spending a million pounds on a property.

Liverpool had lagged behind its near-neighbour Manchester for years, mainly thanks to all the bad press that the militant labour politicians and completely useless bent council officials had brought to the region, driving away any potential investors.

Hundreds of millions of pounds had been invested in Manchester's infrastructure, international airport, luxury hotels, concert arenas, restaurants, and bars. Brands like Harvey Nichols, Selfridges, Armani, Prada, and D & G had flocked to Manchester, giving Liverpool the thumbs down because of its poor reputation.

What was quite ironic, though, were the tens of millions of pounds that had gone out of the collective coffers of the people of Liverpool and neighbouring districts into Manchester's economy, with people travelling down the East Lancs, M62 and M56 in search of entertainment, nice clothes, good food and flying off to the sun. Liverpool had helped Manchester thrive to its own cost and detriment.

Liverpool was very poor compared to Manchester – extremely poor, and yet unscrupulous developers were laundering their dirty money by jumping on the band wagon, trying to take advantage of a short-term opportunity that had been boosted by the recently announced "Capital of Culture" status. What had happened – or rather, not happened in Liverpool over the past forty years was absolutely disgraceful.

Having greeted her client, Miss Marsh ushered him through to her rather sparse office that consisted of a small walnut-looking desk, a couple of upright chairs and a coat stand. A whiteboard hung on the wall behind her, covered in what looked like sales figures or projections and graphs.

"How's business?" enquired her client.

"Excellent, can I offer you a coffee, tea?"

"Water would be great, thanks."

She excused herself but soon returned with two glasses of water.

"So what do you have in mind?" she asked.

"I'm looking for a penthouse, probably three bedrooms; a dining room – at least two and a half thousand square feet, 24-hour concierge service and it must have excellent security."

"When are you looking to move in?"

"Is that important?"

"The reason I ask is that there are a number of new high-rise developments that are currently work in progress. They're not due for completion for a number of months. Some are a year off, but fit the bill."

"No good, I'm looking to move in as soon as possible."

"OK, but that really limits it to a couple of developments – *The Colonnades* and *Robertson Heights*. Are you familiar with either of those?"

"No," he replied.

Lauren showed her client both developments. She started with *The Colonnades* on the waterfront, which he discounted primarily because of the development's age – it was dark and depressing, in his view. He really warmed to his father's development, *Robertson Heights*. The penthouse on the fortieth floor was available, as a local footballer that had reserved it had pulled out of the sale.

A viewing was arranged for later that day. He left the estate agents feeling satisfied.

Following a double espresso at the new Costa coffee, he walked around town taking in the massive transformation that was well underway. He counted twenty-three cranes that were suspended across the city skyline, and he noticed lots of young people clutching designer shopping bags from places like Cricket and Wade Smith. He couldn't help thinking how many of them would soon become his customers.

Meanwhile, across town, Simon Robertson sat patiently with his lovely wife Gina in a private waiting room of The Royal Liverpool Women's Maternity Hospital.

Gina had just about kept herself going following the disappearance and slaying of her lover on a concoction of anti-depressants and inner strength. Her nerves were shredded living each day as a continuing lie, never knowing if and when the police were going to knock on her door or Brian's torturers rear their ugly heads once more. She was deeply concerned about the effect the medication may have on her unborn child. She was beside herself as to the true identity of the child's father, but for now she knew that she just had to keep going and hope that Simon was the father. His mobile rang. It was his office calling.

"Simon, I'm really, sorry to disturb you, but we have a viewing on the main penthouse this afternoon at three p.m., cash buyer, non-sale dependent. The agency has requested your presence if at all possible."

"I can't make it – I'm at the hospital with my wife. Can you please send my apologies?"

As he ended the call, his wife was beckoned into the consulting room for her check up and ultrasound scan. Simon followed her into the room. The staff nurse took her blood pressure whilst enquiring about her general well being. Gina told her that she felt fine and so far, so good.

"Your blood pressure is fine. You obviously look after yourself."

The nurse pulled up Gina's hospital gown in preparation for the ultrasound scan.

"I'm going to rub some gel on to your stomach – it will feel quite cold."

She moved the machine to the head of the bed. Gina grimaced as the gel was applied.

"Sorry."

"It's OK. How's my baby?"

Simon pulled his chair to the bed so he could see the screen on the machine that was scanning his wife's womb. "Wow, is that our baby?" he asked the nurse, pointing enthusiastically to the black and white image that appeared on the small TV screen.

"That is your little baby," replied the nurse as she moved the scanner around the circumference of Gina's tummy. "Everything seems fine – your baby has a strong heartbeat. Would you like to know the sex?"

"No, thank you," the Robertson's replied in unison. "As long as there is only one in there and he or she is healthy, then it will be a nice surprise for us, won't it, darling," Simon said confidently.

Gina was dying to ask the staff nurse some critical questions about the baby, but did not get a chance, given the close attention of her doting husband.

"So we will see you in four weeks, any problems in the interim, then please call us immediately."

The happy couple left. Gina drove back home whilst Simon jumped in a black cab to his office.

The prospective purchaser took lunch at the hotel adjoining *Robertson Heights* – a smoked salmon sandwich washed down with a bottle of sparkling water; he paid his bill and proceeded to the entrance of the residential tower. He pressed the weather-beaten-looking intercom that was already showing early signs of rust from the sea salt off the nearby River Mersey.

"Can I help you?" echoed through the speaker unit of the intercom.

"Oh hi – I'm here to meet Lauren Marsh of City Residences to view the penthouse suite."

The entrance door unlocked and he was met by Lauren, who had already arrived.

The gaunt man looked the part, immaculate in his tailored grey and white pinstripe suit, crisp white shirt and grey silk tie. Shiny black brogues completed the appearance of a city high-flyer; a man with a mission.

The party advanced into the lift, accompanied by a couple of workmen in hard hats. Lauren pressed button 40 and then inserted a plastic security card that allowed access to the penthouse floors.

"You'll have to excuse the appearance of the lift" – it resembled the inside of a wooden box – "it protects the lift whilst we are applying the finishing touches to the building, not to mention people moving in."

"Your boss told me that the penthouse was finished and ready for occupancy."

"Well, it's about two weeks away, does that meet with your timescales, Mr...?"

"Harris, Robert Harris. Yes, that would be acceptable."

"So what brings you to Liverpool, Mr Harris?" Lauren enquired

"Oh, please call me Robert. Business lures me here."

"What line of business are you in?"

"I'm an entrepreneur. I see great opportunity in a number of diverse businesses in this city over the next few years, so I need a base."

"Where's home?"

"London," he replied becoming a little exasperated by the barrage of questions.

The penthouse suite was vast, boasting over three thousand square feet, all on one level. The views were breathtaking, even through the dirty windows that had gathered dust from the building work. They stood nine feet tall from floor to ceiling, wrapped around the entire frontage of the building. The Mersey moved quite graciously beneath them, and the famous Liverpool Ferry bobbed up and down resembling a child's toy in a bath. The Wirral peninsula and the Welsh mountains looked like an artist's canvas: alive, magnificent, colourful and tranquil.

The apartment was largely open plan and boasted three bedrooms, all en suite, a huge L-shaped lounge and dining room, and a family kitchen all fitted with the latest toys. Two secure parking spaces below the building were thrown in for an asking price of one point one million pounds.

He thought it was perfect for what he had in mind, overpriced but in terms of location, views and potential impact, just perfect.

"It's fairly impressive, definitely overpriced – let's face it, this is Liverpool, not London. I will offer you nine hundred and twenty five thousand pounds cash. I can complete inside a month providing that there are no legal hold-ups or unforeseen obstacles that get in the way."

"That's well below asking price. I will have to discuss this with the developer."

"Fine, I am viewing a number of other properties in the area, so will need an answer, say within 48 hours."

"I will hopefully get back to you tomorrow."

"Excellent."

Lauren made a couple of notes and confirmed Robert Harris's contact details as they made their way back down in the lift. Following the customary handshakes, they went their separate ways. On his way out, Harris bumped into a very unhappy Tony Barlow, who was berating some poor girl about taking personal responsibility to getting his apartment up to scratch.

After Tony had finished unloading, he felt temporarily unburdened, stopping briefly to collect his mail in the small, unimpressive reception area that was manned by a security guard dressed in a pale blue short-sleeved shirt that showed off his tattooed forearms. Hardly a concierge as advertised in Robertson Developments' glossy brochure as 24-hour concierge services. Needless to say, the marketed "Impressive marbled entrance and reception area" was yet another complete untruth that he put on his growing list of issues with Fraser Robertson's cowboy organisation. He wanted to kill Fraser Robertson.

There was nothing too exciting or harrowing in Tony's letterbox. Amongst a few flyers for local takeaways and cleaning services were a couple of letters from Liverpool City Council, one to register on the electoral role and the other related to council tax banding assessment.

Over the next few days, it was business as usual for him: the air conditioning was still not fixed, so he was having to sleep with the windows open, which was fine, apart from the traffic noise below and the fact that you really don't expect these kind of issues when you spend so much money on a supposedly luxury penthouse.

Tony had cancelled a number of flat-warming engagements that he had planned with his friends, much to his annoyance. The apartment did not look as he had imagined, what with the ceilings down and open wardrobes where you could see all his threads. The workmen, who dismantled the glass-partitioned wall, had damaged the carpet in the master bedroom.

He was back to work today. No doubt he would return to at least a couple of hundred e-mails, of which probably one hundred and ninety-seven had zero value to him. He would switch his attention to stresses of a different kind. He never really understood why life was so difficult. Almost every day seemed ridiculously challenging.

CHAPTER TWENTY

Joe Deech had drawn a blank so far in his search for the missing James Robertson. He had started his investigations at first base, The Priory Clinic, where he questioned all the staff nurses and doctors, but to no avail. He moved onto London, in particular the Soho area. A mate of his living on Edgware Road who worked in the same line of business had pointed him in the direction of some haunts where jobless druggies and down and outs congregated. Again, he drew a blank. He had called in a favour with an old pal who was working with the Metropolitan force, but again, no positive news was forthcoming. Joe had no idea how far off the scent he was.

A purchase price of nine hundred and fifty thousand pounds for the penthouse suite on the basis that a few extras would be thrown in and that it would be legally completed within a month was agreed. All parties felt pretty pleased with themselves at this stage. The cost of the apartment broke new ground for the city's housing market as the most expensive apartment ever sold, a fact that the purchaser did not want any publicity or connection with. His immediate objectives were to set up his business and maintain a low profile whilst he hatched his plan.

To celebrate his purchase, he decided that some female company was in order. He scrolled through the directory on his mobile to find an old number.

He dialled the number. It went through to her message service. She was probably servicing a client, but he decided to leave her a message.

"Oh, hi … I am staying at The Crowne Plaza Hotel, Suite 705. I would like some company this evening if you are free – you have been strongly recommended to me. Could you call me back on 07867-980564 or at the hotel? Thanks."

He lay on his king-sized bed and began flicking through the TV channels in search of something that would capture his imagination. The local news channel was doing a feature on how drugs and prostitution were threatening to further tarnish the city's image as they worked towards "Capital of Culture year". Liverpool reputedly had one of the worst drug problems on a per capita basis of any of the other major UK cities. Prostitution was also rife in the area with the influx of hundreds of migrant workers who had rolled into town, causing great tension amongst the local working girls by undercutting their price for services by at least thirty-five per cent. He giggled like a school kid as he listened intently to the newscast.

"They ain't seen nothing yet."

The bedside phone ringing interrupted his amusement. He leaned across and picked up the receiver.

"Hello."

"Hi … it's Mercedez; you left me a message earlier."

"I certainly did … funnily enough, I have just been watching a report on the local news channel about tension on the streets between you local ladies and some Eastern European babes."

"Don't start me on that subject. Anyway, would you like some company? I can be with you in an hour or so."

"Absolutely, I will not be moving out of my room."

"It's three hundred pounds for the first hour then one hundred and fifty each hour after, is that OK?"

"I bet the Polish girls are a lot less expensive."

"In this life, you get what you pay for honey …oh, by the way, what's your name?"

"Robert … Robert Harris."

"OK Robert, I will see you in an hour."

"I'm looking forward to it."

He decided to shave, after which he enjoyed a hot shower. He was getting excited just at the thought of what was ahead – he had not had a shag for months. He towelled himself down with one of the white fluffy towels that had been warming itself on the chrome ladder radiator, threw on a pair of denim jeans and a white Prada T-shirt, and added a couple of dabs of Marc Jacobs limited edition aftershave to finish off.

He felt a bit peckish, so decided to order a burger and fries from room service. A bottle of Krug and two bottles of Heineken saw the cost escalate, but he wasn't bothered – he was loaded and looking to have a good time. By the time he had consumed his snack and got the best part of the way through his second bottle of Heineken a knock on his hotel door signalled the arrival of his escort.

Mercedez was wearing a distinctive black and white check coat. She had her hair up, which showed off her high cheekbones and big brown eyes. An unfortunate scar on her neck from her near-death experience with Victor Knight detracted from her real beauty. Her olive-coloured skin glowed, a huge smile revealed Hollywood white teeth, and killer five-inch heeled black peep toe patent leather stilettos exaggerated her height but enhanced her calves and stunning legs. She looked Hot!

"Come in ... you look fab, even better than your photos on the website. Can I take your coat?"

"Sure." She slipped off her coat to reveal a skimpy, figure-hugging black dress.

"Wow... a figure to die for, too". "Now who's a lucky boy?" He could feel his cock growing in his skin-tight jeans.

"Champagne?" he queried as he took the chilled bottle of Krug from the ice- bucket.

"That would be nice, thank you. So what brings a good-looking guy like you to Liverpool?"

"Business."

"Business? In this city?" "Now, let me see, it must be drugs, racketeering or prostitution. You look way to clean for it to be drugs, you wouldn't have called little old me if you were involved in prostitution, so what kind of racketeering you involved in?" The African roots in her accent came through as she howled with delirious laughter at her own question.

"So tell me," he said, "aren't there any decent, honest, law-abiding folk left in this town?"

"Nobody I know, honey. If you don't play football for one of the big clubs, then the only people that I know with money in this city are the dealers and gangsters. All the politicians, the councillors, the police – they're all bent, totally corrupt – they are all on one of the bad guy's payroll."

"See this on my neck? I'm lucky to be alive. Some local scumbag punter, off his head on heroin, tried to kill me. The police were involved and he got shot. We both ended up in hospital. No charges were ever brought against him, even though the police witnessed the whole thing. Mr Big, Victor's employer, bailed him out; paid them off. Within two weeks of the attack, he was walking the streets again, dealing."

"No way... Who is Mr Big?"

"A guy called Fraser Robertson. He masquerades as a respectable local businessman but he is a low-life evil bastard. He controls most of the drug trade here. One of his boys used to be a client way back, nice guy."

"So how come you know so much?"

"Come on ...I'm a working girl struggling to bring up my little princess. I make it my business to know who's who and what's going on, streetwise. That is the most important qualification that you can have in the School of Life. Anyway, I have had some personal dealings with the scumbag."

"Really? Tell me more...."

"Listen, honey you are on the clock and all this negative stuff may affect your performance, so let's get down to business and get you warmed up."

He gave her three hundred pounds in fifties.

Taking a good mouthful of chilled Champagne, she took the remote control off the bed and switched to the adult movie channel. A couple of pretty blonde chicks were playing with each other whilst a black guy looking on was enjoying a wank.

He began to feel hard as he snuggled up to his escort and they watched on intently. She sat on the edge of the bed and pulled him towards her. Looking into his eyes, she kissed her client, at first gently on the lips and then, as their passions stirred with greater intensity, their tongues became entwined, contorting inside each other's mouths. His right hand moved from stroking her face and neck to caressing her boob. She in turn slid her hand down and started rubbing his crotch.

The threesome that beamed from the TV was now being paid little attention as the couple began to devour each other. His palm was now exploring the warmth of her inner thighs. She sighed, moving his hand away to allow her to unbutton his jeans, releasing his erection from its restricted state.

She stood up and took a position at the bottom of the bed, where she knelt between his legs, removing his jeans and boxers. Like a true pro in one move, she raised herself up, removing her little black number to reveal a magnificent athletic torso. Her nipples stood erect like well-drilled soldiers to attention. Her shaven pussy glistened as she inserted her index finger, groaning as her finger slipped in and out of her pussy.

He could not contain himself he began wanking himself off. As he stroked his cock, he felt her warm, moist lips wrapping themselves around his bell end. She started gently nipping his helmet and sucking his shaft whilst she continued to play with herself.

The Viagra had certainly done the trick – he was as hard as a rock. He wished that he had pulled himself off earlier because this felt so good and he feared he would not last much longer. It had been a long time since he had come.

Merecedez took a condom out of her bag and slipped it over his stiff cock with her mouth whilst continuing to give him a blowjob. She pushed him back onto the bed and climbed on top of him. His penis entered her wet pussy and she began to ride him like a jockey would ride a racehorse – no whip but lots of changes of pace and intensity. His cock felt amazing. He was managing to hold on by thinking about ugly women, his father ... indeed, anything that distracted him from his beautiful, sexy companion.

Mercedez decided it was time to change position. She got on all fours and instructed her client to take her from behind. He duly obliged, his cock penetrating deep inside her. She moaned and screamed as he fucked her for all he was worth, her peach-shaped arse bobbing up and down. He felt a hot gush as she came, sinking her painted fingernails deep into the pillowcase as she enjoyed her orgasm. He pulled himself out, ripping off the condom, starting to masturbate furiously as she lay prostrate until he came all over her back.

"Awesome ... absolutely awesome, babe, that was so good."

"I should be thanking you. You made me come and believe me there are not too many people who can do that. I need to take a quick shower if that's OK, then I must make tracks."

Still tingling from the experience, he acknowledged her request by pointing to the bathroom. As she showered, he drank some more Champagne.

He could not contain himself as he said goodbye to Mercedez. His smile was as wide as the ocean. Not only had he just enjoyed momentous sex, but he had passed another of his self-tests: James Robertson was well and truly dead.

✳ ✳ ✳

Tony Barlow had not slept well. He was a man with a lot on his mind. He needed some answers, and quickly. As another day dawned, his mind shifted to his new abode – that was the most important matter. It had taken a monumental fiscal effort to procure it – he had to ensure that not only was his investment protected above all else, but his living experience became more enjoyable, and that meant getting Robertson Developments to show greater urgency and respect. He picked up his mobile to call Simon Robertson, but was interrupted with an incoming call.

"Tony Barlow."

"Good morning Mr Barlow, it's Monica Rule from Kinsey & James, is it convenient for you to talk?"

"Certainly."

"We have received a response back from Robertson Developments. I have written to them again stating our basis of concern and claim. I have put a copy of it in today's post for you; however, I thought that you would appreciate knowing the headlines as soon as possible."

"Definitely."

"The company from which you have purchased your apartment have stated that they have no plans at this time to build a high-rise residential development on what they refer to as land at Gartner Street. From the plans, it is highlighted as a council-owned car park next door to *Robertson Heights*. Unfortunately this has come by way of a third-party conversation with Fraser Robertson's PA."

"So you don't have this in writing."

"No, we had to chase them up several times to get this much out of them; they seem to be a very unscrupulous bunch. That's why I have replayed everything back to them in my letter today."

"So if they go ahead and build – bearing in mind it must have been planned for some time – that would mean that they have withheld vital information from me to make the sale, misrepresenting the facts. What is my legal position?"

"To be honest, it's not great. You've already completed and whilst there is no doubt that they have been economical with the truth, the law is not necessarily in your favour."

"You must be joking!"

"Sadly, no. Let's not get ahead of ourselves at this point. Take a look at the letter I have sent to them and let me have any sales particulars and marketing information that you have relating to the original sale. It would also be useful to have a site plan; you may find this with your legal pack."

A rather subdued and perturbed Tony Barlow sighed and agreed to send on any relevant documents.

"Let's keep in touch, Mr Barlow."

"Indeed."

He could not believe what he had just heard. It was moments like this when he hated his hometown and hated the UK. Nothing really made any sense. How can you have laws that are so antiquated and assist the bad guys? How can the good guys, the honest, decent folk of the country, not be protected by being subjected to Victorian laws that just don't stand up to scrutiny in today's modern world? In fact, worse still, be exploited by calculating conmen through the deficiencies of law?

Tony Barlow knew that he was in a fight. It was not just about the money – it was a matter of pride. He was not going to be conned by some low-life and get trampled underfoot, no way. And what about the poor bastards who were first-time buyers? They had been conned into buying one of his pokey one-bedroom apartments.

The sales information pack lay at the bottom of the wardrobe amongst some other documents and binders.

Tony picked it up and began to flick through the sales brochure. The penthouse suite section boasted, "The penthouses will benefit from unrivalled, sweeping views across the Mersey to the Welsh Hills and beyond." It continued; "Enjoy spectacular views of the infamous Royal Liver Buildings from the comfort of your dining room."

The floor plan of the penthouse, along with a bunch of architectural drawings, was in one of the ring binders. Right now, this was Tony's number one priority. He called into the office saying that he had been up all night vomiting and was going to work from home today so he could dedicate some time to sending the documents over to his solicitors and conducting some research on Robertson Holdings in an attempt to really understand what he was going to have to deal with.

The first port of call was the stationers in India Buildings, where he purchased a large brown jiffy bag in which he placed all the documentation that his solicitors had requested. Next stop was the post office, where he sent the package first class, registered mail. He decided to call into Starbucks in Castle Street, where he could call some old pals whilst getting his caffeine intake, in a bid to find out more about Fraser Robertson and his sons.

The coffee shop was busy as usual; full of suits mingling with students, some of whom would conduct revision or meet business colleagues there, using the place as an unpaid office. This really wound him up because it was difficult to get a table. It could hardly be profitable for Starbucks either, if twenty-five per cent of your client base spent under three pounds and took up space for hours on end.

A table in the far corner became available, and Tony took up temporary residence for the next half an hour or so. He called his solicitors to confirm that he had found a number of documents that he had sent to them by registered post. He also called a couple of contacts to do some digging around the Robertson clan, who currently had the potential to cause him great harm, financial loss and anguish.

The information that he received back was not good. An old Jewish pal warned him not to pick a fight with Fraser. He said that he was a very bad man and allegedly had made and continued to make his fortune by supplying most of the city's junkies with their fixes. His property business was only established as a machine in which to assist his drugs trade and move dirty money.

Fraser had disposed of many people who had got in his way or tried to meddle in his affairs over the years. Another Scouse mate who was very well connected in the city told a similar story, adding that one of his sons had been an unfortunate victim of his daddy's drugs business.

Tony was starting to get a good picture of what lay ahead should matters take a turn for the worse. It did not make for a pleasant outcome. Quite innocently, he had become embroiled with one of Liverpool's Mafia families.

He finished his espresso and gazed out of the window. Dozens of thoughts flashed through his mind as two men, who looked like they should not necessarily be in each other's company, interrupted him.

One of the men was in his early thirties: tall, pale complexion and dressed in a smart navy blue and white pinstripe suit. He carried a brown holdall. The other sported a black bushy beard that looked like it needed a trim. His long black hair was greasy, his skin dry and spotty. The donkey jacket he wore had seen better days and a distinct smell of oil filled Tony's nostrils. He was a lot older than the man in the suit. The men had noticed that Tony had finished his coffee and guessed that he was about to leave the crowded Starbucks.

"Are you going?" enquired the man in an Eastern European twang. Tony guessed he was Russian.

"Yes ... Please be my guest." he encouraged them by standing up and offering his seat to the tall, pale-looking man.

"Thank you very much. Have a nice day," the bearded guy said, maybe thinking Tony was an American, although it has to be said that there were very few Americans in Liverpool at this time.

The two men sat down and Tony decided to walk into town.

"My contacts tell me that you are looking to set up business in this town, Mr Harris."

"That is a little bit of an understatement, Alexi; I'm looking at controlling the market."

The Eastern European howled with laughter.

"I'm glad you find that amusing."

"Control the market ... Do you know what is going on this city, Mr Harris? Have you done your homework?"

"Of course. I guess that you're referring to Mr Big, Fraser Robertson and his family, who masquerade as property developers, bringing in their cargo that your firm supply in window and door frames. Yes, I know everything about the marketplace, Mr Broshnov."

"You have done your homework, Mr Harris. So dare I ask how you intend to break into an established marketplace that is controlled by a monopoly?"

"Listen, my friend, the marketplace is expanding and there is room for another player. I have my plans, but right now I am looking for a credible supplier."

"This is not easy, Mr Harris. We have a long relationship with our client, they would not be happy if we started supplying a new competitor. Admittedly our client has been slow with payments recently."

"I'm only asking for an opportunity. You know it doesn't make any sense to have all your eggs in one basket, what if something happened to your client's business?"

"I will pay you in cash, half now; the remainder when the merchandise lands. I need five kilos initially, pure cut with a purity rating of at least 7.0. I have a bedding and soft furnishings business that I run from Crosby, you can bring the shipment in inside pillows and duvets, and my carriers will then pick it up from the docks."

"Seven ... As I am sure you know, Mr Harris, five is at the top of the range, but seven, seven is very ambitious. I do like the plan for shipment, though. You probably know we have an interest in a duvet and pillow manufacturer in St Petersburg."

"Ambitious yet attainable, Alexi. I know that you are supplying your client with this level of purity, so do me a favour and cut the crap – it's the best or nothing."

"OK, you have a deal. We both have a lot to lose as well as gain, so in future no more face-to-face meetings. We will transact our business through secure communications and third parties. You will receive details at your hotel within the next forty-eight hours."

"Fine, I understand." Robert Harris unzipped the holdall and gave Alexi an orange Sainsbury's bag that was stuffed full of cash. "Your down payment."

"Excellent ... we will be in touch."

CHAPTER TWENTY-ONE

The next few weeks seemed to rush by for Tony as he worked on a big tender for BT, which released him from the stresses and strains that he had been subjected to recently.

Apart from receiving a copy of the letter that Kinsey & James had sent him, he had not heard anything from them. Robertson Developments had replaced the glass panels in his master bedroom. The wardrobe doors in all the bedrooms had been refitted and looked more like it. His apartment was taking shape, although the air conditioning and heating system was still playing up with alarming regularity.

Gina Robertson had put on a few more pounds. She was becoming more anxious by the day as her term drew ever closer to reaching its natural conclusion. Peter Swann had text her a few times, desperately wanting to see her. Whilst she had been tempted, she had so far resisted his charms. He was in the frame for being the father of her unborn child. Tony Barlow had also sent numerous texts to which she had not responded, as she had more than enough on her hands.

She was growing to hate her body as each day her stomach grew bigger, her ankles swelled and her beautiful bottom spread. Despite this, she was struggling to contain her sexual desires, having gone from unbelievable active sex with two lovers on a regular basis to a veritable drought. As she let the warm water from the showerhead pour over her, she felt the urge to release some of the pent-up sexual tension that had built up inside her.

Gina picked up the soap and started rubbing her pussy with it. God, it felt good. She closed her eyes, recalling the incredible sex that she had shared with Brian in the changing rooms, moving the soap up and her down her pubic bone with greater intensity. She knew it would not take long for her to come. Slipping her thumb into her vagina and using her fingers to rub herself at the same time, her breathing became more intense as she headed towards her climax, pinching her erect nipple whilst she moved her fingers in and out until she felt her juices release. Her head cleared as she came.

Robert Harris had opened his shop the previous Thursday, a very low-key affair, no ceremony, no advertising, apart from a small ad in the *Echo*, offering 25% off all purchases for the first two weeks. He did not want to attract too much attention to the retail side of his business. It was what was occurring in the back of the shop that would make him his fortune and help him achieve his objective of destroying the man who had almost destroyed him. His father had not only deprived him of his formative years, but had left both huge physical and mental scars that would never heal, and now it was payback time.

The first shipment had arrived without a hitch, pure as the driven snow, really good gear. Harris was now ready to ply his trade.

* * *

"Good morning, Mr Barlow," the security guard said with a distinct Scouse twang – the security guard who was supposed to be a fully trained concierge.

"Morning," Barlow replied as he collected his mail. Amongst the collection of credit card bills, he found his salary slip and a letter from Liverpool City Council. The credit card bills were discarded in favour of the wage slip, which he opened with great enthusiasm to reveal a bumper month: £49,365.82 pence after the dreaded 40% tax – not bad for a month's work. Of course, he did not pick this kind of money up every month. It was significantly inflated by a large contract that he had won with BT's Broadcast Services division. He loved big paydays – sadly money was one of the most important things in his life right now.

The broad smile was quickly wiped from his tanned face when he read the letter from the City Council Planning Office.

"Notice is hereby given of an application made by Robertson Holdings to build a fifty-storey residential tower on the land at Gartner Street. The application, which has been approved by Mr J Barrat, planning officer, will be heard on Tuesday, November 22nd 2004 at the Town Hall, Dale Street, Liverpool, L2 2PP at 11 a.m. All objections to planning consent must be sent in writing to the planning manager Mr J Barrat, to arrive no later than November 15, 2004." Tony's hand began to tremble as he read the notice again and again. November 15 – that was two days ago!

"Bastards ... Fucking low-life lying fucking bastards!"

Tony's blood was boiling, his head banging as the fury unleashed from within. He punched the letterbox, cutting his knuckle in the process. He did not know whom to call first – his solicitor?

"Is everything OK, Mr Barlow?" enquired the Scouse security guard.

"No, everything is not OK, far from it."

The security guard put his head down and looked away, thinking that it was time to show some much-needed discretion.

Tony dialled a pal's number. He just had to share this with someone. He was so wound up; he just had to let go

"Hi To, what's up?"

"I've just received notification of Robertson Holdings being granted planning permission to build a fifty-storey residential tower right outside my fucking window!"

"But I thought...."

Before he had time to finish his sentence, he interjected "So did I! They denied all knowledge of such a plan, albeit verbally, to my solicitor only last month. Lying, fucking cowboy bastards."

"What are you going to do, Tony?"

"Fight! Fight the application, fight the bastards, and sue them – there's absolutely no way they are going to get away with this! I need to go – I must phone my solicitors and advise them of this bombshell."

"OK, I understand. Just try and stay cool if you can."

He hastily ended the call and dialled Kinsey & James. After two short rings, a soothing female voice greeted him. "Kinsey & James Solicitors, how may I direct your call?"

"Lorna Davey, please."

"May I ask who is calling?"

"It's Tony Barlow."

"Will she know what your call is in connection with, Mr Barlow?"

"Yes."

"Putting you through." Another couple of rings and Lorna picked up.

"Mr Barlow, how are things?"

"Things are pretty bloody awful, if you will pardon my language. I am really wound up, having just received notification from Liverpool City Council that planning permission has been granted to Robertson Holdings to build a fifty-storey residential tower right outside my dining room window."

"Can you fax me over the planning notice?"

"Of course, shall I fax it to the main number?"

"Yes, please."

"How does it look from a legal perspective?"

"To be honest, not good. They obviously know what they are doing and my guess is that they have done this before. The site plans that show the legal boundaries of the development have the main boundary line skirting around the outside of the council-owned car park. Therefore, it does not form part of the buying agreement."

"They undoubtedly mislead you by at best being economical with the truth when they sold you the property and at worst completely misrepresenting the sale by withholding vital information. The difficulty we will have is proving it."

The phone went dead as Tony Barlow took in what he had just been told. He was dumbfounded.

"Mr Barlow ... Mr Barlow ... Are you still there?"

"Yes, I'm still here. I just can't believe what you have just told me."

"You need to lodge your protest in writing to the planning manager at the city council and notify them that you will be attending the hearing. Is there a date for it?"

"Yes, it's in five days time. Furthermore I have already missed the deadline for filing my opposition by two days."

"No, that can't be right."

"It is, I have the letter in front of me. November 15th was the final date for lodging opposition to the planning consent and that was two days ago!"

"It sounds like you have a case for late notification – however, you must act immediately. Register your intention to oppose planning consent in writing, outlining the main reasons for this. I would also advise that you call the planning manager and tell him that you have only just received the notice. Keep the envelope; it will show the postmark. Planning notices should go out at least four weeks prior to the council planning committee hearing. Is there a residents' association?"

"No, I don't even know anyone else that is living here with just moving in."

"You need to form a residents' association as quickly as possible. Let's face it, you are not the only owner that will be feeling extremely annoyed right now. Fighting as a group of people will obviously have far more clout than just one or two lone voices in the wilderness."

"I will draft a letter and put it in all the post boxes."

"Good. I think that is about as much as we can do for now. Don't forget to fax me the planning notice. As soon as I receive it, I will write to Mr Robertson and ask why only a few weeks ago he denied all knowledge of this project, which by the way will have been years in the planning – these things do not materialise overnight."

"I will call you if there are any further developments at my end. Thanks for your time. He hung up and immediately set to work by drafting a letter to all owners, in which he attached a copy of the planning consent, advising all those interested parties that an initial meeting had been planned for two days' time, November 19th at the hotel next door, to discuss contending the application.

Tony knew that there was not much time, so he had to get cracking. As well as posting the notices, he thought that he would speak to as many residents that he came into contact with although he had not encountered many in the public areas or lifts during his short tenure.

A tear-off slip was attached to the bottom of the notice asking for name, apartment and contact number, if they would attend and finally if they could not attend, whether they would be willing to join a residents' association to fight the application.

By midday, Tony had deposited two hundred and twenty six notices in the post boxes by reception, one for each apartment owner, all he could now was wait to see what the response was like. He would spend the rest of the day and night preparing an agenda, as well as deciding on exactly what he was going to say to the – hopefully – assembled masses.

"Liverpool Direct, how may I direct your call?"

"Mr Barrat in city planning please," Tony responded.

"Putting you through."

"City planning department, Jim Barrat speaking."

"Ah, Mr Barrat, I believe that you are in charge of the proposed development by Robertson Holdings at land at Gartner Street – planning application number 2089768654."

"Yes, I am, how can I help you?"

"I wish to oppose the application and have only just received notification of the proposal this morning, and yet the hearing is due to take place in two days' time."

"The planning notices went out four weeks ago, so I don't understand why you have only just received notice; I will have to look into it. Do you plan on attending the hearing?"

"Definitely."

The next couple of minutes were taken up with Tony Barlow giving his personal details to the planning manager and registering a formal complaint against the council-planning department for late notification.

Tony did not like the tone or attitude of the planning manager, who came across as arrogant.

Jim Barrat finished the call and dialled Fraser Robertson on his mobile. Fraser picked up.

"What's up, Jim?" he enquired.

"I just wanted to let you know that planning for your fifty-storey tower is being opposed."

"How come, Jim? We paid you a lot of money to get this one through."

"I know, Mr Robertson, and it will not be a problem – everyone that needs to be on board with this is, I have taken care of it. I just wanted to let you know that a resident in your latest development who is obviously affected by this has lodged a formal complaint and will be attending the hearing the day after tomorrow."

"Who is it?"

"Mr Tony Barlow."

"OK, I know the guy. I need you to pull every trick in the book, Jim"

"You know I will, Mr Robertson."

"Thanks for letting me know."

"Who was that?" enquired Simon Robertson, who was conducting a meeting with his father when the call came through.

"It was Jim Barrat; he wanted to make me aware of formal opposition to our planning application."

"But I thought everyone had been paid off, Dad."

"They have, it's cost six hundred thousand so far, not exactly petty cash. Mr Barlow has objected and is going to attend the planning committee hearing."

"Tony Barlow, who bought the penthouse? He's a smart guy, Dad; we will have to be on our guard. He is already completely pissed off with us – this will only add to his motivation."

"He's just a punter, son – just a punter like the rest of the suckers that we take money off by painting a picture of a desired lifestyle. It's like taking candy off a baby; he's nothing. What are your plans for the rest of the week?"

"We have a shipment due in the day after tomorrow with a street value of five million so I will be supervising that, it's our biggest shipment to date. I know that it's the date of the planning application – however, that is how it has worked out."

"Don't worry, James Thirsk and one of his partners are representing us, Barrat and his boss have already approved, three of the planning committee have been paid off and as you know, our significant annual donation to the Liberal Democrat coffers pays handsome dividends. Any plans for the weekend?"

"Yeah, I have invited Peter Swann and his wife around for dinner and drinks; we had to cancel a few weeks ago. Their son goes to the college and is Mark's best friend, so whilst the kids amuse themselves, I thought it would be good for Gina to have some adult company and take her mind off her pregnancy. She has been really down recently – I thought it might cheer her up."

"Sounds like a good idea. Anyway I need to go – I'm meeting Paul Gibson, Head of City Planning. Quite opportune, don't you think?"

"Yeah Dad, take it easy out there."

"Of course, I always do. I am bulletproof, son, fucking bulletproof."

Tony Barlow worked away tirelessly on preparing for the residents' meeting. He was hoping to get maybe fifteen to twenty per cent attendance. That would be a good starting point upon which he could build.

He thought that given the position of the proposed tower, those people who had bought apartments on the western side of the development that were city-facing would be more concerned than those who had bought either in the middle or on the eastern side, whose views would not be compromised by the development. Having said that, their lives would still be inconvenienced, as well as their investments being affected.

The office building and hotel that adjoined *Robertson Heights* would be massively compromised, particularly the offices, as the new tower was literally going up right in front of it some ten metres away, only separated by a small service road. Tony made a note on his actions list to find out who owned the respective buildings and establish contact with them to join the fight.

He took some photographs of the site from his apartment window as well as street level. He tried to visualise the dimensions and how the tower might look if it was completed. It would certainly take away the magnificent views of the Liver Buildings. The sweeping views of the River Mersey would also be massively compromised. The more he looked at the strip of land that currently parked fifteen cars and was full to capacity, the more he disbelieved how anyone could build such a massive structure on it.

The next thirty-six hours seemed like an eternity, Tony hardly ate – his stomach felt leaden and heavy, and his mind raced with a thousand thoughts. He had been checking his post box with alarming regularity, almost willing tear-off slips from concerned residents into his box. Sadly he had only received three – three out of two hundred and twenty six. He could hardly believe it.

He tried to reassure himself that it had only been a day and a half since he posted the letters. *Robertson Heights* was still at best only a third occupied, with purchasers still to move in. Even so, he expected a far greater response than he had got so far. The meeting was now only nine hours away. He started to panic.

The first of the three respondents was a lady named Maureen Elves, who owned one of the penthouses on the western side of the development. She had both registered her interest in forming a residents association and ticked the box that confirmed she would be attending the meeting.

Paula Alexander from apartment 1103 had also ticked both boxes, as had Ivor Davies from 1802. There was nothing more that Tony could do, at least for now. As he had devoted the last couple of days to protecting his personal interests, he had neglected his work. Two hundred and forty-eight e-mails awaited his attention. Most of them, he knew, would be complete bollocks.

CHAPTER TWENTY-TWO

The chill of a bitter north wind blowing off the nearby River Mersey greeted the residents as they made the very short but blustery walk from *Robertson Heights* into the lobby of the adjoining hotel.

Tony Barlow had been the first to arrive. He had made a real effort, as it was important that he made the right impression. He was dressed in a tailored navy blue single-breasted suit complemented by a pale blue shirt with cut-away collar. A navy and sky blue striped tie sported a Windsor knot, and highly polished black brogues completed his outfit.

A glass of sparkling mineral water rested on the table by his folder as he awaited the arrival of the other residents. He sipped from his glass nervously, regularly checking his wristwatch.

An elderly lady wrapped in a heavy camel coat approached his table.

"Mr Barlow?" she enquired.

"Yes."

"Pleased to meet you, I'm Maureen Elves; I own one of the penthouses."

Following her introduction, she headed to the bar to get an orange juice as more people moved over to Tony's table. Paula Alexander and Ivor Davies introduced themselves to Tony, closely followed by John James and his partner Ranjit Singh. By seven-thirty, thirty people were gathered around the table chatting away, waiting for their host to commence proceedings.

"First of all, may I thank you for taking time out to attend this evening, my name is Tony Barlow and I own one of the apartments on the western side of *Robertson Heights*. As you are all aware, Robertson Holdings have been granted permission to build a fifty-storey residential development on the council-owned car park right next door to the Heights.

"The main objective for tonight is to get as many owners as possible on board to form a residents' association and fight this application, which by the way is being heard at the town hall in two days' time. I also wanted to get as much information as possible together ahead of the hearing, so a collective brain dump would be useful. Clearly, we do not have much time – however, I am encouraged by the turnout."

"It's not exactly a great turnout, is it?" The big bearded man in the Welsh Rugby shirt piped up. I thought that everyone would have attended. Must have money to burn."

"I had obviously hoped for a greater attendance," said Tony. "However, it's not bad for starters. I only received the planning application notice two days ago. I posted two hundred and twenty six notices, one for each apartment."

"I see," replied Ivor Davies in a gruff Welsh voice.

"I don't think you will get much more support than this. Do you know what you are dealing with?" said the lady in the camel coat in a broad Liverpool accent.

"Not really, no, but whatever obstacles we may face, the fact is we have all be conned by the developer. The sale of the apartments have been totally misrepresented and grossly exaggerated. People are still in the process of moving in and is it not a coincidence that as soon as the last completion has been transacted, planning notices, which by the way have been withheld, arrive in our post boxes?"

"There are a few things that you need to be aware of, Mr Barlow," Maureen Elves continued. "Fraser Robertson, who owns Robertson Holdings, is a very bad man. He has made his money in the drugs trade and controls the market in this city. I know this because my family has lived in this city for over fifty years. We own a couple of bars and a nightclub in town – we know what goes on and just as importantly, who is who."

"Fraser is extremely well connected to politicians, police; high-ranking council officials ... he is a bad man and yes, you are right, we have all been conned and we have to fight – but I don't think for one minute that it will be a fair fight, Mr Barlow."

Tony Barlow felt shell-shocked as he digested what had just been served up.

"There are a lot of bad men in this town. We can't let that stop us from fighting this all the way."

"I think what you are doing is admirable and would like to propose that you represent us as chairman," a man in the bright red sweater said.

"Well, thank you for your support, Mr James."

"So, are we all in favour that we should fight this as an association?" Barlow asked.

"Me and my boyfriend have been saving up for four years now and have sunk all our life savings into a one-bedroom apartment on the west side not to mention the huge mortgage that we have taken on. We are absolutely devastated," a young girl in the bright orange top said.

The small group were unanimous and Robertson Heights Residents' Association was formed. Tony was elected as chairman. The remaining residents would all make a contribution to the cause; the committee was elected and duly formed. It was agreed that Tony, Maureen, Ivor and Paula would all attend the planning committee hearing and report back to the group the following week.

Paula Alexander supported Maureen Elves' concerns about Fraser Robertson. She had heard that Robertson had sold out to a bunch of Irish investors "off plan" in the hope that they would make a quick bob or two. She told the group that as far as she knew, there were very few owner-occupiers: lots of students on group rentals; a lot of first-time buyers in the one-bed units and a number of empty apartments as Investors waited to cash in.

John James and Ranjit spoke passionately about how the sale of the apartments had been misrepresented. They showed the group the original sales literature that promised quality designer-fitted kitchens, when only cheap budget kitchens had been fitted. They talked about video entry phones that were promised and not delivered, twenty-four-hour concierge services as opposed to security men, under floor heating rather than cold ceramic tiles, a magnificent lobby.... the list was endless.

The group agreed to speak to as many people who were living in the Heights as possible with a view to growing the rank and file.

As the group began to disperse around eight forty-five, a smartly dressed lady in her mid-thirties made her way to the front and introduced herself to Tony.

"Hi, I'm Lisa Farrow, apartment 2601. I am very impressed with the work you are doing here, Tony." She gave him a business card that read, "Lisa Farrow – Personal Banking Division, Coutts."

"I work in private banking. I've been posted to this godforsaken place on a four-year contract. This is not exactly the greatest of starts. Where can a girl get a good time in this town?"

"It really depends what you are looking for. Do you have any plans for the weekend?" Tony asked.

"No. Give me a call – the numbers on the card. You've got a date, Mr Barlow."

Up to this point, Tony had had mixed feelings in terms of how the evening's proceedings had gone. He now felt a whole lot better as he made his way back up to his apartment, encouraged that he had a hot date and was not alone, albeit slightly discouraged by the both the numbers and calibre of the turnout. He was beginning to realise that he was more or less on his own at this juncture.

Tony wasted no time in texting Lisa and she responded almost too quickly. They set the date for Friday night – dinner at *Esto*, a local Italian, followed by drinks and hopefully a late one back at Tony's swanky apartment.

CHAPTER TWENTY-THREE

"What's up, Doc?" asked Bugs Bunny on the giant plasma screen as Gina and her son, Mark, relaxed in the magnificent living room of their family home. Before the cartoon character could utter a response, the screen switched to the security channel interrupting the DVD, it showed Simon driving through the big electric security gates and arriving home.

"Daddy's home!" cried Mark as Gina's heartbeat jumped. She was extremely nervous when the screen switched to the security channel, especially since she received the special delivery.

Mark rushed to the front door to greet his daddy. The lights dimmed and the V12 engine's roar dulled to a silence as Simon got out of his Aston Martin DB9.

"Daddy, Daddy, I came top in my maths set, can I have a present?"

"Top boy in maths, hey? Well done, that is great news!"

Simon entered the hallway with an extremely excited son dangling around his neck. Gina was in the kitchen preparing Simon's dinner as well as pouring him a large glass of wine. She missed the alcohol but realised the short-term sacrifice was in the best interests of the unborn child.

"Hi honey, how have you been today?"

"OK, thanks, we have some good news for Daddy, don't we, Mark?"

"Top in maths and he wants a present."

"You don't waste any time, do you, Markie?" Mark giggled. "Anyway, I must have known because as a special treat I have invited your best friend Gavin over on Saturday to stay."

"Wow, Dad, that is great, thank you, thank you!" Mark launched himself at his father, throwing his arms around his waist and giving him a big hug.

"I have also resurrected our dinner date with his mum and dad, providing you are up to it honey."

Gina felt a hot flush coming on. She paused to collect her thoughts. Her eyes fixed on her little boy's beaming smile. "Of course that would be nice, I'll cook something special."

"Great, it's a date then," Simon enthusiastically replied. "Now, young man, it's time you were in bed... school tomorrow."

As Simon followed his son up the stairs to his bedroom, Gina wondered how she would react when she saw her lover. He had texted her a few times since their regular weekly liaisons had finished. She had often reflected on the great, passionate sex that they had enjoyed. Deep down, she still had feelings for him.

How would he react when he saw that she was pregnant? Would Simon pick up a vibe between them? Did he already have suspicions? Was that why he had invited him over? Her heart started to race as all these thoughts and unanswered questions collided in the deepest recesses of her mind.

She would just have to play the doting wife and mother role, dress accordingly and keep a respectable distance from Peter; certainly not get in a position where she was alone with him for any length of time.

* * *

Despite Gavin Swann finishing twentieth out of a class of twenty-two in his maths set, his father thought that he deserved a treat. Gavin was a spoilt brat, ruined by both his parents and grandparents; the victim of being an only child who was doted upon. He could do no wrong.

Peter Swann broke the news to his son and wife that they had been invited to Simon and Gina Robertson's on Saturday for dinner and drinks, and that Gavin had been invited to stay over. Gavin's response was as enthusiastic as his best friend Mark's had been.

"I can't wait, Dad – Mark is my best friend. They live in a massive house, Mark has a football goal post in his garden – it's really cool."

"How do you know Simon Robertson so well?" Peter's wife enquired.

Quick as a flash, Peter replied, "Through meeting him at the college and the football – Mark plays for Woolton FC."

"And his wife…How do you know her?"

"The same as her husband – I've met her when I've picked Gavin up from school or football. They seem really nice. We'll have a nice evening, I'm sure."

I'm sure we will, Peter's wife thought to herself.

* * *

The rain bounced off the old cobblestone road as Tony Barlow tried to negotiate the driest and quickest route into the town hall. He had passed the impressive-looking building countless times before, but until today had never had cause to enter through its majestic doors. This is where the city council planning committee met every other Thursday to discuss the merits of new applications to build and rubber stamp those that had already been passed in principle by the assigned planning manager.

Tony had been extremely busy and diligent in his preparation as always. He had approached the matter just like he would have prepared for a significant business meeting. Given the circumstances that surrounded the case, this was to be one of the biggest challenges that he had faced to date. He knew he was not playing on a level playing field. He was aware of the reputation of the Robertson family. He would have to be at his absolute sharpest and best.

As he entered the main reception area an usher who asked him the nature of his business greeted him. Tony told the smartly dressed usher that he represented the *Robertson Heights* Residents' Association and he was here to oppose planning permission for Robertson Developments' proposed new scheme. The usher checked his clipboard as Tony tried to dry himself off a bit.

"I believe a number of other residents have already arrived. They're having some refreshments in the waiting area, which is down the corridor, then second door on the right. Your case is listed as number five to be heard, so you may well have a bit of a wait."

"Thank you for your help." Tony picked up his black umbrella that was dripping like a tap that had been left running and a bundle of documents that he would need later on and made his way to the waiting room. Maureen Elves and John James were sitting on a couple of cheap-looking beige plastic chairs, drinking tea in between conversation.

As Tony approached, he was distracted by a text from Lisa. He quickly opened it.

"Black or white French knickers for our date?"

He quickly texted back, "Black sounds great." He put his phone away and approached the other residents.

"Good morning, and how are we on this rather wet day?" Tony enquired.

"We have only just arrived ourselves. I'm trying to dry out – I got absolutely soaked," Maureen Elves responded.

"Any further news from anyone?" Tony asked.

"Yes, we are not the only ones objecting to the application, there are four other objectors," John James continued. "F.S. Gaskill, who own the office building, the Labour councillor for the area, Mick Hall, a group of lobbyists who have named themselves Save our Heritage and a gentleman called Dave Hensbury, who apparently owns a couple of units in *Robertson Heights*.

"Great stuff, good work, John," commented Barlow enthusiastically. He felt slightly relieved that they were not alone in their fight - at this juncture, the more objectors there were, then the more impact they would have. He knew that they needed all the help that they could get.

"Do you know if they are planning on attending?" Barlow asked.

"Not sure, the clerk will know when he arrives."

Tony placed his umbrella – which continued to drip, but with less intensity – and his bundle of documents on a chair next to his fellow residents and headed over to the large table opposite to pour himself a much-needed black coffee. He had not been sleeping well. The events that lay before him had taken their toll. He needed a shot of caffeine. His spirits had been lifted by Lisa's text.

A lady in a black cloak carrying a clipboard came into his sight. It must be one of the clerks, he thought to himself.

"Excuse me."

"Hi, can I help you?" the clerk replied.

"Sure, my name is Tony Barlow, I am representing *Robertson Heights* Residents' Association and we are appealing against planning permission at land at Gartner Street. I believe that there are several other objectors to the development. Can you tell me if they are here or have confirmed attendance but are yet to arrive?"

The clerk referred to her listings, flicking over the pages. "Let me see now ... Yes, here it is, a Mr Hensbury is scheduled to attend and a Miss Cook, representing F.S. Gaskill. Oh Mick Hall, the Labour councillor and the lunatic fringe otherwise known as Save our Heritage are also listed as objectors but I am unsure if they will appear. To be honest, you are probably better without them." she said sarcastically. "I would not want them in my corner."

"Have you any idea what time the case will be heard?"

"It is listed as number five out of fifteen. The first three are formalities, no objections have been registered, the fourth case is an objection to a mobile phone mast, then you. My guess is within the hour. You can go through and sit in the public gallery, you will be called to speak."

Tony thanked the clerk and took a mouthful of coffee – hardly Starbucks, but at least it was lukewarm and reasonably strong. He rejoined the rest of the group who had now assembled with Maureen and John. He was introduced to Dave Hensbury, who had arrived whilst he was talking to the clerk.

Dave Hensbury was a small-time property developer, a big man – probably around one hundred and forty kilos. Tony guessed he was in his fifties as he studied his heavily wrinkled face. His nose looked like it had been broken several times. His dark eyebrows had overgrown some years previously and were in dire need of attention.

Hensbury breathed deeply. A smoker, no doubt: the stale smell of tobacco on his work clothes was a dead giveaway. His teeth, like his eyebrows, were crying out for attention: a mixture of yellow, brown and black radiated from his open mouth.

The small-time property developer proceeded to tell Tony that he had bought two apartments "off plan" from Fraser Robertson, whom he knew of old. Like the rest of the buyers that Barlow had met, Hensbury had been painted this wonderful picture of exclusivity: luxury accommodation at Liverpool's premier address, and an investment opportunity not to be missed. No mention of the new development had been made and like the rest of the unfortunate people who had purchased "off plan" in the Heights, he had been lied to and deceived.

As Hensbury continued to relay his war stories that involved Fraser Robertson, Barlow began to warm to him. He told him of Fraser Robertson's connections to drugs and the underworld in Liverpool, and how he was known as "Mr Big." He told him about some of his dodgy dealings in the past. Barlow had heard similar stories from a variety of different sources now; there was no doubt that he was taking on a bad man.

Hensbury began to explain the basis of his complaint against the planned development. It was on the basis of building and planning regulations that Tony was unfamiliar with – something to do with it being illegal to build within one hundred metres of the boundary line from *Robertson Heights*, he was also going to try and get them on another irregularity.

Barlow explained that the basis of their objection was that the site quite simply was not 'fit for purpose' to house a fifty-storey residential tower. He also wanted to understand more about the piece of land and the nature of the transaction.

He wanted to be able to articulate on what basis planning permission had been granted, to highlight the misrepresentation of the initial sale and how they had all be conned by this unscrupulous developer.

Tony was in full flow when the usher interrupted by ringing a bell and calling all those parties with an interest in planning application number 2089768654, land at Gartner Street, Robertson Developments, through to the public gallery.

She led a veritable procession into what could only be described as a magnificent, opulent circular room featuring a splendid domed ceiling that at its peak must have reached a hundred feet. The ceiling coving had been hand-plastered and painted in gold leaf by master craftsmen. The thick red carpets beneath their feet had lost both pile and colour over the years, but still felt good.

High back polished oak benched seats that were padded with red leatherbacks and seats were arranged in arched semi-circles banking down from on high to floor level. Every vantage point was directed to the centre of the room where four men dressed in cheap, ill-fitting suits flanked an elderly lady sporting grey bobbed hair and gold rimmed half-moon glasses, who sat in the middle of a long boat-shaped table.

The group were quickly ushered to their seats and had barely time to sit down as a man on the far left of the planning committee table announced that, "The next application concerns Robertson Holdings development at Gartner Street, a luxurious fifty-storey residential tower that has passed initial planning consent."

He turned to the chairlady, Lady Eileen Grimshaw, "Madam Chair ... there are several objections to this development that need to be heard today."

She peered above her half-moon rimmed glasses, taking a quick look around the chamber before acknowledging the spokesman's address.

"Very well, do we any representation for the development company here that we can hear from first?"

A middle-aged man who was both folically and vertically challenged stood up and made his way to the podium, which was directly in front of where the objectors were sitting. The man did not look in the best of health. He was extremely frail for his years. His posture was appalling as he bent over the podium to introduce himself, positioning the microphone so he could hopefully be heard, if not seen, by the majority of the gathering.

"My name is James Thirsk, I am the chief architect for *Western Heights* and represent Robertson Developments here today," he said.

"Madam Chair, members of the planning committee, this project will break new ground and set new standards in luxurious waterfront residential living. My client's organisation, Robertson Developments, have requested that this application is fast tracked, having already been granted planning consent by Mr Jim Barrat, who is the assigned planning manager."

A huge sigh broke out from just behind James Thirsk as the objectors uttered a collective gasp.

"As you well know, my client has been a significant investor to this city's regeneration programme, with two magnificent buildings completed thus far – *Robertson Plaza* and the ground-breaking *Robertson Heights*, which sold out in a matter of weeks, before ground was even broken. There is huge demand for my client's properties and he desires, with of course your consent, to start work in January next year."

Further gasps and shouts of, "No way" came from the protestors, who were told to restrain themselves by the spokesman.

The chairlady addressed the chief architect "Mr Thirsk, I hear your request and it is duly noted within the minutes. However, there are a number of objections to this development," she paused as she consulted her notes, "four, in fact. We have to listen and give due consideration to the objections prior to granting final permission."

James Thirsk nodded his head, collected his papers and left the podium.

The spokesman called the first objector, a Miss Cook representing F.S. Gaskill.

A very tall, young, well-dressed girl made her way to the podium. She introduced herself as a representative for the company who owned the brand new six-storey office building that the proposed *Western Heights* was going directly in front of, killing the magnificent view of the River Mersey, not to mention the lack of natural light, privacy and total inconvenience that they would face during the construction period.

She spoke very softly and was obviously nervous as her muted speech strained under the pressure of the situation. Her disposition was not helped by Lady Eileen telling her to speak up, as she could not hear a word she was saying. A number of her colleagues shook their heads looking totally disinterested in proceedings; this was not a great start for the case for the objectors.

Miss Cook asked for a glass of water as her mouth had dried up. Her tongue was in danger of sticking to the roof of her mouth. Quick as a flash, a court aide appeared with a tumbler of water that he passed to the nervous junior company representative. She took a couple of large gulps and started again. Following her introduction, she told the planning committee that the basis of her employers' complaints were on five separate counts, namely, gross misrepresentation of the initial sale of the building – no mention of a planned development directly opposite them had ever been discussed or disclosed; loss of natural daylight – section 8, clause 4.2 of the Health and Safety at Work European Union guidelines would be contravened by allowing the development; loss of view; loss of privacy, and inconvenience and loss of productivity caused by a construction phase that was expected to last up to three years.

Lady Eileen duly noted the nature of the complaints that had already been logged in the transcript.

"Do you have anything further to add?" she asked.

"No, Madam Chair," said Miss Cook. She stepped down, relieved that her role for today had been fulfilled.

The planning committee spokesman called the next objector. "Mr Mick Hall, Labour councillor for Sefton ward." The announcement was met with silence. A scruffy-looking woman shouted from the gallery.

"Ee's not ere ... ad to go on udder council bizness."

"Move on," Lady Eileen instructed the announcer. He duly obliged.

Save our Heritage or "the lunatic fringe", as the clerk had referred to them, were next up. Tony Barlow wriggled uncomfortably in his seat. This was not going according to plan, and things were about to turn a whole lot worse. An elderly lady who resembled the character in Mary Poppins who fed the birds for *tuppence a bag* attempted to make her way to the podium, shuffling one foot in front of the other, aided by a walking stick. A monocle swung around her neck like a metronome setting a very slow pace for her progress.

She must be ninety, thought Tony, as Lady Eileen piped up, "Can we please assist Mirabelle?"

Oh Christ, thought Tony, Mirabelle is known to the chair and no doubt her colleagues, who were looking duly pissed off with proceedings. A court aide sprang to assist her with a view to hastening her arrival so she could address the committee and assembled public.

It was hardly worth the wait. Tony estimated that it would have taken her at least nine minutes to travel to and from the podium for five minutes of utter drivel that would add no weight to the objectors' case. He also thought that they had probably heard her repertoire a hundred times before. So much for *'freedom of speech'*.

Mirabelle went on about the skyline being destroyed, the environment being devastated, and local birds, including sea gulls, blue winged gulls and other rare species, having their natural habitat invaded by the construction of this tower. During her delivery, not one of the five-strong committee looked up. No attention was paid to Mirabelle. She had done more harm than good.

Next up was Dave Hensbury, the small-time property developer. God, we need to start scoring a few points, thought Tony. Following a calm and measured introduction, Hensbury launched straight into a full-frontal attack on both the credibility of Robertson Developments and the planning manager, Mr Jim Barrat. The main thrust was based on building and planning regulations.

"Madam Chair, I would like to ask Mr Barrat where he took his measurement of one hundred metres from. As you are aware, the *Planning Act* of 1999, which was revised last year, clearly states that in regard of inner city high rise development, no building can be within one hundred metres of an existing structure."

"Is Mr Barrat here?" asked Lady Eileen.

"Yes." A rotund man with one of the worst comb-overs Tony had ever seen rose from a few seats in front of him. He was dressed in a cheap black crimplene jacket that had cost no more than a couple of quid many years ago and grey trousers that looked like they had been screwed up in a ball prior to donning them. Flakes of dandruff scattered unevenly across the top of his jacket collar were in evidence for all to see. Before he had chance to speak Tony had taken an instant dislike to the look of him.

"So precisely where did you take your measurements from, Mr Barrat?" Hensbury repeated his question.

"Err ... I didn't," came the response.

"Pardon me?"

"I didn't. I took the distance from the developers' construction plan and the architect's drawings."

"But that is completely irregular practice, Mr Barrat. I can tell you that if you took a hundred-metre measurement, you would be off the proposed site and onto the main thoroughfare into town."

"I haven't visited the site, so I can't comment."

More sighs and gasps were emitted from the public gallery at this revelation.

"So, Mr Barrat, let us be absolutely clear on what you have just said. You have passed planning permission for a fifty-storey residential development on a site that is not fit for purpose without either visiting the site or taking the required measurements, which you have just lifted from the developers' report."

"It is perfectly regular practice," replied a ruffled planning manager.

Hensbury continued to pressure Jim over other planning matters, concluding that planning could not possibly be fast-tracked as requested by the developer until such time as further urgent investigations were launched into the validity of the planning manager's report and subsequent approval.

It was finally Tony's turn. He was feeling considerably more upbeat and optimistic as he responded to the call from the committee's spokesman. "Robertson Heights Residents' Association, Mr Tony Barlow."

Tony made the short journey from his seat to the podium. Heads turned as his presence was acknowledged. He looked immaculate in his navy blue suit, crisp pale blue shirt and striking silk tie. He looked the part and his appearance alone raised the bar on proceedings.

Following a concise, powerful introduction, he launched into a stinging attack on the morality of such a project. He talked passionately about people's hard-earned investments being destroyed by this unscrupulous developer. "This is a tower for profit," he said, "and does absolutely nothing to help the regeneration of our city."

He then moved onto the complete unsuitability of the site: "It's a postage stamp that currently parks no more than fifteen cars, it is simply not fit for purpose. I have no idea how they would even go about constructing it, given the constraints of the boundaries."

Next up was loss of privacy and loss of views. If *Western Heights* was allowed to proceed, then it would have a significant detrimental impact on the owners of apartments in *Robertson Heights*. This was closely followed by market demand, and he used the current low occupancy levels at the Heights as a point of reference.

He concluded a riveting performance in public speaking by telling the planning committee that he and his fellow owners had only been in receipt of the planning notices for some two days and consequently had very little time to prepare. He asked for an internal investigation to be launched, as he was uncomfortable with the relationship that exists between the planning manager and the developer, especially now he had heard Jim Barrat admit that he had not even visited the site.

He had saved the best for last. "Madam Chair, members of the planning committee, I put it to you that each and everyone of you that you have a public duty and moral obligation to all the owners of *Robertson Heights* to conduct a physical site visit prior to any further authority being granted for this application. Thank you for your time."

Barlow received applause from the public gallery. As he returned to his seat, he got some well-deserved pats on the back from fellow residents and owners.

A stony silence descended on the room. Lady Eileen was in deep conversation with the members of the committee. They deliberated for a couple of minutes before Lady Eileen rose to her feet.

"This planning application is deferred pending a site visit a week on Tuesday at 11:30 a.m. This will be followed by further deliberations where both the developer and objectors can present their respective cases prior to a final decision on this matter."

Cheers preceded handshakes and more backslaps. James Thirsk looked distraught, and Jim Barrat hung his head. For Tony Barlow, this was only a minor win, but a win nonetheless. He now had time to do a lot more digging. Two whole weeks was an eternity – they had to build on the momentum of this victory.

As Tony and his fellow residents collected their personal items and readied themselves to leave, they were approached by a couple of reporters who had been present during the deliberations.

"Mr Barlow, Mr Barlow … Steve Lamb, *Liverpool Daily Post & Echo*. You must be delighted with this result?"

"I speak on behalf of *Robertson Heights'* Residents Association. Clearly we are encouraged by today's outcome, but there is still a long way to go. We are very confident that once the planning committee have seen the actual size of the proposed site, then they will see how ridiculous this project really is."

"Do you suspect any foul play, given the revelation that Mr Barrat has never visited the site?"

"No comment, now if you will please excuse us, I have a job to get to."

Tony injected some pace into his stride to get away from the growing band of reporters. He managed to leave the town hall by a side door and was soon in the clear, making his way back to his apartment, where once again the air conditioning had failed.

"What? What the hell happened?" screamed Fraser Robertson in response to the bad news that James Thirsk had just called him with.

"James, you screwed up! A site visit is the one thing that we wanted to avoid." "I have millions invested in this project already, it better not fail or I will make sure that you go down with it."

"Fraser, calm down."

"Don't you dare tell me to calm down!" Fraser picked up a decorative glass vase from his desk and threw it with all the strength he could muster. On contact with the wall, it exploded with a loud bang and smashed into hundreds of tiny pieces.

"Did you hear that, James, did you hear that?" he screamed as his PA dashed into the room to see what had happened.

"That's how calm I am!" Fraser slammed the phone back into its base station.

"Get the mess cleaned up, don't just stand there," he ordered his PA. He grabbed his coat and headed out for some much-needed fresh air.

CHAPTER TWENTY-FOUR

Robert Harris was really pleased with the initial takings – forty grand, which delivered a thirty thousand pound profit, was not bad for starters. He had enticed a couple of Fraser's traders to work for him, initially in a dual role, maintaining their relationship with Fraser and his organisation. Their incentive was pretty obvious, really – money. Robert had doubled their money. Fraser was known for his miserly ways and he had taken advantage of that.

He knew he needed people on the inside of his father's organisation that he could trust. Whilst it was a gamble, he had carefully selected his traders – people he knew had despised his father over the years, mainly because they took all the risks whilst Fraser was the main benefactor of the profits. A double your money deal was too good to turn down.

Harris was now going to step up his activity as well as unleashing his pent-up hatred in his father's direction. The pieces of the jigsaw were falling nicely into place. With the festive season only a matter of weeks away, Robert knew that it was going to be a very white Christmas.

A flustered Fraser Robertson struggled to get his mobile phone out of his overcoat pocket as it continued to ring.

"Hello," he answered gruffly.

"Sounds like you got out of bed on the wrong side this morning, Boss."

"Joe, I am not in the best of moods right now."

"I'm sorry to hear that, Boss. At the risk of adding to your woes, I've drawn a complete blank down here. I've exhausted all my contacts and their contacts. It's as if your son has just vanished off the face of the Earth. I'm coming home, Boss."

"You are shitting me, Joe!" screamed Fraser. "We must find him, Joe – he is a fucking liability to me if he is alive. He can cause a lot of fucking problems. You put some more men on this, Joe – there's no way you can come home until you find him or he is declared dead. I was confident that you would find the little shit. I can only hope he is dead in the gutter of some back street and been eaten by the rats."

"He's history, Boss, I am absolutely certain of that."

"I need hard facts, Joe, you know how I operate. Leave no fucking stone unturned. Do whatever it takes."

Fraser reflected on the proceedings of the day thus far. It wasn't that he was superstitious, but he was taken with the idea that everything happens in three's. He dialled Simon's mobile.

"Morning, Dad, what's up?"

"You may well ask. "So far today we have had our application for *Western Heights* put on hold, pending a site visit in two weeks' time, And Joe Deech has just called me; he has drawn a blank down south in his search for your brother. I wanted to make sure everything was ok with the shipment, I couldn't handle any further bad news today."

"The shipment arrived as scheduled and has already been transferred to the factory, it went like a dream. Sorry to hear about James and the planning permission, I thought that everyone had been paid off, what happened?"

"No idea, but I need you to find out. Put a call into Paul Gibson; ask him what the hell is going on. I will speak with Lady Eileen."

"OK Dad, catch up later."

Simon dialled Paul Gibson's mobile and he was transferred to his answer service.

"Hi, you are through to Paul Gibson, Head of Liverpool City Planning, sorry I am not able to take your call at the moment, please leave a message and I will get back to you, thanks for calling."

"Paul, it's Simon Robertson, can you please call me urgently regarding *Western Heights*?"

Robert Harris was making his way across town when his second mobile bleeped with an incoming text message. He knew before he read it that it was from Alexi. It read, "Shipment arrived and has been transferred to 'the powder factory', five million pounds at cost."

This was the news that Harris had been waiting for.

Tony Barlow's mobile was hot for the rest of the day with both messages and phone calls from well-wishers congratulating him on his fine performance in front of the city's planning committee. He felt pleased, but knew that this was only the start and that a great deal of work lay ahead. He also had a text from Lisa saying how much she was looking forward to their hot date.

The early edition of *The Liverpool Echo* covered the *Western Heights* ruling on its inside page under the banner headline, "Heights set to fall?" Tony was also praised for his performance.

Fraser Robertson could not get hold of Lady Eileen or her husband. He had left a message on her mobile, as well as her landline. He fumed as he read the report in the early edition. That evening, Fraser was due to attend a celebration dinner for local businessmen to celebrate the city being awarded Capital of Culture. He called his PA.

"Tell them I'm sick. Send my apologies."

"Will do."

He could not stomach celebrating anything – he had had enough for one day.

* * *

Robert Harris, Gina Robertson and Tony Barlow were all preparing for interesting weekends. Harris had set a target of increasing his sales of "Pure White" by fifty per cent. He was undercutting Robertson's "Snow Drift" by half on the street. Word would soon spread, so a fifty per cent increase in sales was not overly ambitious.

Gina Robertson had mixed feelings about her dinner guests. On one hand, she was quite excited at the prospect of being reunited with her lover in a relatively safe environment. However on the other hand, she was dreading the entire occasion. She was unsure how Peter would react to seeing her distinctive lump. What if Simon picked up some vibe about her and Peter? She tried to reassure herself that everything would be fine, but deep down she was far from convinced.

Gina had decided to make an effort. She had booked a hair appointment, a facial and a manicure, and chosen a black loose-fitting dress that revealed her cleavage.

The menu had also been decided. There would be pizza, chips and Coca- Cola for the boys. The adults would feast themselves on queen scallops to start followed by duck confit. A selection of cheeses would follow. A number of fine wines had been chosen to accompany the food.

Peter Swann had already set his plans. He could not wait to see his ex-lover. How he had missed their weekly rendezvous. Peter had conditioned himself to the fact that he had seen the last of the gorgeous Mrs Robertson.

He found it quite amusing that her husband had enabled the reconciliation. He had not made love to his wife for nine months; the strains on his fourteen-year marriage were very evident. The marriage was in meltdown. Gina had definitely contributed to the state of affairs.

Even at the pinnacle of his relationship with Fiona Swann, she had been a bit of a cold fish – never wanting to experiment; just limiting his sexual pleasure to basic intercourse. Of course, she loved all the trappings that came with being married to one of the finest lawyers the city could boast, but her sex drive, even at its peak, well, it resembled a car just ticking over, idling without ever being taken out of the garage, opened up and really driven.

Peter Swann had always had a big sex drive. The gulf between their respective sexual desires had driven him to disloyalty – initially with high-class prostitutes and more recently with a string of local beauties, his most recent being Gina.

Since his relationship with Gina had broken down, he had resumed his sexual activities with a couple of local escorts, neither of whom could compare, God…how he missed her. He was going to look at his absolute best in an attempt to try and win her back, but without giving the game away.

Tony Barlow was just hoping that the build up to his date with the lovely Lisa would not be a massive anti-climax. She had been teasing him with her texts, and he was absolutely gagging for a shag.

Simon Robertson had other things on his mind right now. Paul Gibson had not returned his call, and his father was on his case. He knew he had to get *Western Heights* back on track and find out what had gone wrong. He decided to call James Thirsk, whom he did manage to have a conversation with. James tried to reassure Simon that it was merely a glitch; that he had absolute confidence that if they continued to position the application on planning grounds, then they would win. James believed that there was no way that a few "emotional residents" could possibly derail the project. Simon felt more relieved and asked James to call his father to reiterate what he had just told him.

"He's my next call, Simon, don't you worry."

Following his briefing meeting with his dealers, where they were given their instructions for the lucrative weekend's trade, Robert Harris decided to try out the gym facilities that were located in the hotel next door to his new palatial home in *Robertson Heights*.

Robert was determined to get himself back in shape physically as well as he had done mentally. After thirty minutes on various pieces of aerobic equipment, he decided that was enough for one day and headed for the pool to cool off. After several lengths, the sauna beckoned. He hoisted himself out, grabbing his towel off one of the hooks. As he turned to walk across to the sauna, his heart sank as he heard a man's voice utter the words that he never wanted to hear again for the rest of his natural life.

"Hey James, you old bugger, what the hell have you been up to?"

As he turned towards the man, he instantly recognised that it was Maurice Watkins, an old school buddy who he had known for twenty years on and off.

"Oh, forgive me," Maurice cried. "I was certain that you were a pal of mine that I had not seen for a while. From the back, you are identical, same height and build too, even the birthmark – I'm really sorry."

"No problem," Robert coolly replied his heart still beating like a drum as he entered the sauna. Thankfully, Maurice Watkins was done and headed off towards the changing rooms, hugely embarrassed by his gaff.

Maurice had long gone as Robert finished his session with a nice warm shower and a shave; he headed back to his apartment for a doze prior to the evening's festivities getting underway.

The cheap-looking Christmas decorations flickered and swung in the winter breeze as the late night shoppers trudged up and down Church Street's well-trodden pavements armed with shopping bags full of presents.

Office parties that had started early were in full swing throughout the city. Many casualties had already emerged; with no doubt a host more to follow as the clock wound its way through to the early hours of a bitterly cold Saturday morning.

The weather beaten faces of the loyal servants manning the newsstands looked rather festive as their complexions glowed various shades of red, mainly owing to a mixture of blood pressure, excessive alcohol and of course the temperature.

"*Echo, Echo,*" they rhythmically chimed in an attempt to tempt the passers-by to part with thirty pence. The *Echo* was a typical small town evening newspaper, its pages dominated by local stories that were of no particular interest to anyone outside of the city and its surrounding suburbs. Over the past few months, its pages had been dominated with articles concerning the growing drug culture and the "Big Dig" as commuters continued to face widespread disruption without the council giving their inconvenience so much as a second thought.

Fraser Robertson was making a significant contribution to both issues.

As the evening began to get into full swing, Robert Harris's dealer's started to ply their trade. Fraser Robertson's operatives also readied themselves to take to the streets to begin their rounds of the pubs, clubs and cocktail bars, as well as the more lucrative business of moving large quantities of their goods on through the out of town network. A dozen or so distributors who bought their gear from the traders and then sold it on through their network of dealers largely controlled this.

The dealers controlled the surrounding North West markets, supplying users in such diverse towns as St Helens, Runcorn, Widnes, Skelmersdale, Southport and Crosby, to name but a few. Robertson's venerable army was under real pressure to raise their game, as right now he was sitting on a five million pound stash that he needed to move swiftly.

The first port of call for Victor Knight, one of Fraser's loyal servants, was the car park at Burtonwood Services on the eastbound carriageway of the M62. He met Archie White every other Friday, same time, same place at eight o'clock. Archie was a low-life petty criminal who had spent most of his forty years in and out of jail for drug-related crimes. Archie controlled the Warrington, Penketh, Padgate and Birchwood markets. Victor liked Archie – he was punctual and reliable.

As his car clock moved passed 20:15, there was still no sign of Archie. Victor had called him a couple of times on his mobile, but it just went through to his answer service. The second time he called, Victor decided to leave him a message.

"Archie, it's Victor, it's quarter past eight, I don't know what's happened, but I can only wait another few minutes as I am on my rounds, please call me as soon as you get this message."

Victor started up the engine and left the car park, heading for his next meeting with Jimmy Dalzell at Runcorn rail station car park. He texted Jimmy saying he was running about fifteen minutes late but to wait for him in the normal spot. As Victor rejoined the motorway, he put his foot hard to the floor, opening up the accelerator in an attempt to make up some lost time.

By the time he arrived at the station car park, he was only ten minutes behind schedule. Dreary-looking commuters flooded the front of the parking lot as they reunited themselves with their vehicles following time away from their homes and loved ones.

Victor drove towards the south side of the car park that was always quiet, being situated well away from the station and main facilities. As he pulled around into the normal meeting spot, his headlights picked out unoccupied tarmac divided by painted white lines: no parked vehicles; no Jimmy Dalzell. Victor punched the dashboard of his car in anger. He reached for his mobile to call Jimmy. The mobile had not received any text messages and there were no missed calls. As his number rang out, he started to think was this just a coincidence, what with Alfie not showing either, or were the two events unconnected? Had he just missed him?

Jimmy's phone rang and rang. "Come on, pick up, pick up." After what seemed like an eternity of endless ringing, he went through to the answer service where Jimmy's dulcet tones directed callers to leave a short message and he would get back to them.

"Hi Jimmy, It's Victor, hope you got my text, don't know if you have been and gone, I got to the station about ten minutes late, I have to go to my next meeting, so please call me when you get this."

The next six collections were made as normal without so much as a hitch. Victor had still had no word from either Alfie or Jimmy; his earlier suspicions had been banished as the evening began to return to a degree of normality.

Back in Liverpool, unbeknownst to Victor, some fellow traders had been subjected to similar disruptions.

Robert Harris sat in the hotel bar, enjoying a glass of Champagne. Over the past few hours, confirmation had been received that his network of traders and dealers had expanded, to the detriment of his father. He chuckled with self-gratitude as his plan was beginning to become a reality. By the end of the evening, he estimated that his takings had rocketed to well over £200,000 and this was just the start; the best was still to come.

* * *

Tony was certainly not disappointed. Lisa had shown up looking like sex on legs, dressed in a tight-fitting black pencil skirt, black figure-hugging blouse revealing a fair-sized cleavage, black hold-ups and a pair of five-inch stilettos. Her blonde hair was swept back from her pretty face and tied at the back. She looked fantastic.

Following the meal, where they consumed a bottle of Rioja reserve and a couple of glasses of champagne they headed off to The Red Bar at the dock to join the Friday night revellers for cocktails. Lisa ordered a slow screw against the wall and Tony duly obliged, much to his delight, in the unisex washrooms.

CHAPTER TWENTY-FIVE

As people around the city began to arise on a wet and windy Saturday morning, across town the previous evening's takings were being verified at the powder factory. They had already been counted, recounted and then counted again by three of Fraser Robertson's trusted generals, but they simply didn't add up. In one of the busiest times of the year, when the takings should be up by around fifty thousand pounds, the numbers were down by around two hundred thousand pounds in just one night.

At this stage, details of the "no show" dealers had not been reported back to base camp, although over the next few hours, as the traders rose from their beds and reported into Fraser's generals, a disturbing pattern would begin to emerge.

Tony Barlow woke to find the lovely Lisa lying next to him in his bed. With just over a week and a half to go before the site visit and a final decision on *Western Heights*, he knew that he could not waste a minute. However, it was not every day that he awoke to find such beauty besides him. He quickly calculated that he must have fucked her at least three times last night. As she began to awake, he inspected his knob that glowed red from the excesses of the previous evening. She spotted him looking at his cock and immediately sunk under the duvet to have a closer inspection.

"It looks fine to me, a little red ... maybe I will kiss him better." Her luscious lips began to gently lick his helmet and slowly move down the shaft of his extending cock before enveloping the whole of his penis. Lisa began to suck him hard whilst wanking him off at the same time. It did not take long for Tony to cum in her mouth.

Lisa resurfaced with the biggest of grins. "Good morning, big boy."

"Good morning," Tony replied. "Listen, at the risk of sounding extremely ungrateful, I need to get up. I have a load of stuff on today that I need to do for fighting the planning application."

"Of course, babe. You do what you need to do. Hopefully you will be a little less stressed."

Tony quickly showered and threw on his favourite jeans, a loose fitting white T-shirt and a pair of comfy trainers. He said goodbye to Lisa and promised to call her later. Armed with his digital camera, he left his apartment and headed for the council-owned car park, which was the site for the proposed development, *Western Heights*.

He reeled off numerous shots taken from every angle; including a number of photographs of the perimeter, with a view to demonstrating to the planning committee the confines of the space that was going to house a fifty-storey residential tower.

The more Tony looked at the proposed location, the more ludicrous he thought it was.

He continued to click away, taking shots of the main thoroughfare into town that bordered the site to the front of the development, paying particular attention to the paved pedestrian areas that no doubt would be lost during any construction.

His next port of call was to be the council planning offices on Victoria Street to view the scale model of *Western Heights* as well as collect a copy of the actual proposal. During the short, brisk walk, he reflected on the warnings that he had been given about Fraser Robertson. He knew that he was marching into dangerous territory. However, he had no alternative but to continue the fight against this morally appalling proposal.

An elderly man sat hunched behind a cheap-looking reception desk that had seen better days. The city council logo – a purple liver bird set in a black crest – hung precariously behind him in a cloud of dust. As Tony approached the desk, the smell of stale tobacco intensified. The old receptionist's skin was yellow; his index finger stained brown from all the cigarettes that he had held as he pointed at the visitors' register for Tony to sign.

"I'm here to view Robertson Developments' *Western Heights* plans."

The old man's chest wheezed as he gave Tony some directions to annexe room 3, where the project was on display.

"Down the corridor, third door on the left." He coughed to relieve the pressure in his chest that had built up during the short instruction.

"Thanks."

Tony entered the deserted room. In the middle, perched on a trellis table, sat a model of the proposed development. It certainly did not represent reality. It gave a false impression of the distances between Robertson and Western Heights, and the distance from FS Gaskill's offices were grossly exaggerated in the developers' favour. The proximity of the tower to the main road into town also failed to represent any degree of reality.

Tony picked up a document that had been produced by the architects in association with Robertson Developments and the city planners – a brochure entitled "understanding planning rules & regulations". He put a copy in his jacket. He had seen all that he needed to see, so decided that it was a good time to go for a coffee, where he could study the documents and make some copious notes.

He passed the old receptionist – who was puffing away – on the way out.

The coffee shop was deserted. Tony guessed most people were still at home in bed. Many would probably be nursing hangovers from their excesses of the previous evening. A grande vanilla latte accompanied by an almond croissant would do the trick. A large table beckoned in front of a brown sofa. Perfect, thought Tony, as this was to be his office for the next couple of hours.

He swiftly consumed the croissant as he started to the turn the pages of the proposal. Like the model that he had just viewed, the proposal contained some gross exaggerations. The wording was instantly recognisable, having been lifted from the *Robertson Heights* brochure. *Western Heights* was described as "the jewel in the crown" – a collection of luxurious apartments and stunning penthouse suites, many benefiting from unrivalled, sweeping views of the River Mersey and the Royal Liver Buildings, all built and finished to exacting standards.

The dwellings ranged in size from six hundred and fifty square feet up to the largest penthouse suite at two thousand five hundred square feet. More blurb followed relating to what was included in the price – more bravado, almost certainly numerous lies and further misrepresentation. Prices started at two hundred and seventy-five thousand pounds for a smaller, lower floor unit, scaling up to a cool one and a half million pounds for a penthouse suite on the fiftieth floor.

Granite worktops, hand cut Italian marble floors, German hand-built designer kitchens and state of the art bathrooms were all promised, but there was something missing that Tony could not put his finger on.

He read the document again, trying to find the missing elements, and then it hit him right between the eyes: there was absolutely no mention of car parking. He must have missed it. Nobody in their right mind would seriously think of trying to sell city centre apartments for the prices that they were quoting with no parking. He scanned the proposal again and again, but could not find any mention of car parking.

"Result!" he shouted, making a note on his pad highlighting the words "No parking". Surely it couldn't be right. He needed to speak with Mr Barrat, the planning manager, to confirm or deny that this was the case. He would have to wait until Monday to do this. Tony continued to plough his way through the proposal. He also took a brief look at the brochure about understanding planning rules.

Another significant issue that the residents' association wished to contest the application on was that of demand. At best, they believed that *Robertson Heights* was thirty per cent occupied. There were few cars parked in the parking spaces and not much traffic flow around the public areas. To prove this point, he planned to take pictures of the Heights on Sunday evening after dark, so he could show the committee the lack of visible lights on a night that most reasonable people would expect residents to be at home.

Finally, he penned a request under the *Freedom of Information Act* for all documents pertaining to the sale of land at Gartner Street to be released to him. For now, he was reasonably satisfied that he had done all he could, at least for today.

News was starting to come through to the generals at the powder factory that would bring some substance as to why the sales figures from the previous evening had been decimated.

Victor Knight was the first to report two no shows, two fellow traders who worked the East and South sides of the city closely followed him. They brought the running total of no show dealers up to eight. What made matters worse was the dealers had not been in contact with the traders, despite numerous voice mails and texts. An emergency meeting was called for seven o'clock. All traders and generals were to attend, for the time being they had decided not to mention this to "Mr Big" or his son, as they knew Fraser Robertson would want answers and right now, they simply did not have any for him.

* * *

Gina Robertson sat under the drier as a beautician prepared to apply a new set of acrylic nails whilst the hairstylist waited for her recently applied highlights to go off. Her preparations for this evening's dinner and pizza party had gone without so much as a hitch, and she was now putting the finishing touches to her appearance. Gina wanted to look at her best for tonight – after all, her former lover was a dinner guest.

Simon had decided to go into Robertson Holdings' office to catch up on his significant administrative backlog.

He was frustrated, as he had still not heard back from Paul Gibson over the *Western Heights* planning deferral. Unlike his wife, the furthest thing from his mind right now was the dinner party – he had far more pressing matters to attend to. He dialled Paul Gibson's mobile. Once again, it went through to his voicemail and once again, he left him a message.

Simon sent the main contractors of *Robertson Heights* who were still on site, an e-mail giving specific instructions about cleaning the site up prior to the site visit. He knew that the area of land that they were going to build on was at best conservative for such a structure and at worst insufficient. The challenge was to make it look bigger than it actually was. He also knew that the land that they had already built on was earmarked by the previous owners, St Paul's Eye Hospital, for disposal only to a non-profit making scheme, and indeed they specified in the head lease that it should be passed on to any worthwhile care in the community project. His father had seen to it that the special needs school who had tried to secure the land from the council were well and truly trampled on.

Paul Gibson had removed the lease and other documents from the main file. If it ever came to light, what would people think? How would he be able to face his family? For now, he could not think about the consequences.

He sent an e-mail to Jim Barrat requesting an urgent meeting to review the decision of the planning committee, and copied Paul Gibson. As he pressed the send button, his mobile phone rang. "Paul Gibson" flashed on the mobiles screen.

"Paul, how the hell are you?"

"I'm full of flu. I haven't left my bed for over a week now, I feel as weak as a kitten. Apologies, Simon, for not getting back to you earlier."

"Paul, no problem, I fully understand. You sound dreadful."

"Listen, I have spoken with the powers that be and to be honest, we are dealing with a small number of very emotional, pissed off residents who feel that they have been duped by your organisation."

"They have formed a residents' association under the leadership of a Mr Tony Barlow; I believe that he bought one of the penthouses."

"I am aware of all this, Paul. What I need to understand is why Lady Eileen and the planning committee have decided to conduct a site visit and defer any planning consent on what we were told was a done deal. My father has looked after you, Paul, not to mention your peers. We have a lot invested in this project and we need you to pull a few strings and ensure that this is merely a hiccup."

"Simon, please give your father my assurance that I will make this happen."

"Paul, if details of our land deal were ever revealed, then we would all be in trouble. I trust any documentation that relates to this particular transaction is under your control."

"Absolutely, don't worry about it."

"Give my regards to your Dad, Simon."

"Will do, and I hope your dose of flu clears up soon"

Simon felt relatively relieved and called his father to pass on the good news. Fraser was glad that there was an explanation as to Paul Gibson's lack of contact and the reasonably upbeat assurances that he had passed on. At least for now, a certain calm had been restored.

Gina left the salon feeling good about herself; sporting a new hairdo and a sexy natural white set of nails. She had planned to spend the rest of the afternoon preparing the table and doing some preparation in the kitchen – nothing too taxing. This would be followed by a doze on the couch and a warm bath prior to donning her makeup and trying to slip into her little black number. Mark, her son, was already round at Gavin Swann's playing, after football practice. He would return home with their dinner guests, no doubt very excited at the prospect of Gavin staying over.

The remainder of the afternoon absolutely flew by. Gina glanced at the bedside clock as she was putting the finishing touches to her makeup. 19:22 shone brightly in big red numbers. Simon, who had been delayed at the office, was grabbing a quick shower.

"Hurry up, honey, it's nearly seven-thirty," she shouted.

"I'm nearly done, won't be long now and I will give you a hand."

Gina looked radiant, absolutely stunning, although she hated her temporary condition. Her bump was not the worst part for her – it was the fact that it was not just her tummy that was swollen, but nearly every other major body part was suffering from the same dilemma. Her backside, her arms, legs, ankles, and her feet, were all swollen; her feet gave her the most discomfort. She got a sharp reminder, not that she needed one, as she donned a pair of antique brown patent leather stilettos.

Simon towelled himself down whilst Gina headed downstairs to check on the duck. Her pulse began to quicken as the clock moved slowly towards eight o'clock, when their guests were due to arrive. She lit the cluster of tall off-white candles that sat in the centre of the dining table, impressively displayed in a magnificent cut glass candelabrum. Vanilla essence began to fill the air as the candles' fragrance was released.

"Wow, you look gorgeous, are you going anywhere nice?" Simon joked as he walked into the kitchen dressed rather casually in a pair of blue chinos and an open necked pink shirt.

"I thought that I would make a bit of an effort – I don't want to let you down now, do I?"

Simon poured himself a glass of Chablis and turned on the TV to catch up on the news whilst they nervously awaited the arrival of their guests.

No sooner had the newscaster come into vision then the plasma screen switched to the security channel. The cameras picked up a private-hire taxi as it approached the Robertsons' home. Within a few minutes, Peter and Fiona Swann were strolling up the path with the two boys, who were both still dressed in their football kits. Like Simon, Peter had selected the smart casual look, and was dressed in navy trousers, a light blue shirt, navy blue cashmere sweater and mid brown lace up brogues, whilst Fiona had more of a Laura Ashley look in a frumpy, flowery dress.

Gina and her husband greeted them and welcomed them to their home.

"Hi there, you found us OK, then?" Simon said light-heartedly.

"No problem at all, the taxi driver brought us straight here without so much as a wrong turn," Peter responded.

"Mummy, mummy, can Gavin and I go and play in my room?" Mark screeched enthusiastically.

"Of course. Are you boys hungry?" Gina enquired.

"Oh yes, I'm famished." "What about you Gavin?" Mark asked. "I'm hungry too," came the response.

"I've got you pizza, chips and cola. So if it's OK with your mum and dad, Gavin, you and Mark could have a feast in Mark's den."

"It's fine by us, isn't it dear?" said Peter.

The boys rushed up the stairs and into Mark's bedroom. A large television was the first thing to get switched on, hastily followed by a PlayStation.

Nervous laughter broke out amongst the grown ups as Peter passed Simon a couple of bottles of rather expensive-looking wine and the girls exchanged kisses on each other's cheeks. Introductions were made as they made their way into the kitchen dining room.

"Look at you, you look fantastic," raved Peter as he took a good close look at his ex-lover. "I had no idea that you were pregnant, when is the baby due?" he enquired rather sarcastically. Gina picked up the sarcasm, but it eluded Simon and Fiona.

"Well, thank you, Peter, you don't look so bad yourself. Our baby is due in just over three months' time. Now, can I get you both a drink? We have some nice wine, Champagne, beer, spirits, whatever you fancy."

"I think that Champagne would be in order to celebrate your great news," Peter Swann said confidently.

"Well, Champagne it is." Simon made his way over the refrigerator and took out a bottle of chilled Krug whilst Gina took four Stewart crystal Champagne flutes out of one of the display cabinets. Simon popped the cork and the couple's clinked glasses.

"To the next Robertson, may he or she be healthy, happy and prosperous," was the toast proposed by Peter Swann.

Simon, Peter and Fiona sat down at the dinner table sipping their Champagne, chatting away whilst Gina served up the boys' pizza and chips. A bottle of tomato ketchup and two glasses of Coca-Cola sat on a large tray; a couple of cheese and tomato pizzas and a large bowl of fries soon joined them.

"Here honey, I'll take that up to the boys" Simon offered.

"That would be great, thanks."

"I hope you like fish and duck – not on the same plate, of course," Gina said to the Swann's.

"Sounds great. We love most food, to be honest," said Peter acting as a spokesperson on his wife's behalf. So far, Fiona had said very little.

"It's scallops to start, followed by duck confit with a cheeseboard to finish, providing you have any room left."

"So how do you feel about the baby?" enquired Peter. "I mean, were you and Simon planning for another child?"

"Peter, don't be so personal!" yelled his wife.

"No, it's OK ... we are both extremely happy, thanks."

Gina felt very uncomfortable with Peter's line of questioning. She was just glad that Simon had been out of the room. She hoped that he would not persist over dinner.

Simon, having delivered the grub to the boys' room transitioned from room service porter to wine waiter, pouring three glasses of Chablis Grand Cru and a glass of sparkling mineral water for his expectant wife.

The scallops were served with small pieces of crispy bacon and mixed leaves; they were quickly devoured and met with unanimous appreciation.

Peter and Simon talked business and world affairs whilst Gina struggled with Fiona on any subject. Boy, she was hard work. Gina could now understand why Peter had strayed – they simply did not go together in any form, be it looks, interests, intellectually or emotionally.

The duck received even greater plaudits than the scallop starter. The triumvirate washed it down with a couple of bottles of Nuits St George, while Gina stayed on the water. The boys had made a couple of visits to the kitchen during the meal to recharge their glasses with cola whilst collecting a couple of bags of crisps and an assortment of sweets.

"So, then, Simon, how do you feel about becoming a father again?" pitched Peter Swann.

"You are at it again, Peter, stop being so personal, it's none of your business. Anyway, why are you so interested in how Simon and Gina feel about their unborn child?"

"Sorry, sorry ... my wife's right – it's really none of my business; I was just making conversation. Hey, you have a magnificent home – is there any chance we could get a guided tour?"

"Of course, I will show you round after dinner, replied Gina. Now who's for cheese?"

Peter and Fiona looked at each other before they both declined the cheeseboard as they attempted to digest the rich food that they had just consumed.

Whilst Simon became increasingly relaxed, his father's loyal servants worked tirelessly, trying to make up for the lost ground that the business had suffered last night.

As the last two generals left the powder factory they failed to spot two blue transit vans parked in the lay by opposite.

As the taillights from the general's car began to disappear in the distance the night sky faded back to black. The powder factory was situated on a quiet road. It was well off the beaten track down by the dock area near Bootle. After dark, the only people who ventured anywhere near the place that masqueraded as a builders' yard were either employees who worked on the production line starting or finishing a shift or consenting adults who wanted to exchange bodily fluids but could not afford a cheap hotel room, so they would park up and pleasure each other.

The last shift had begun at nine o'clock – over an hour ago now – so all was perfectly quiet: no courting couples, no sign of life at all, apart from the six hooded men that sat patiently inside the Transit vans.

The driver of the first Transit van texted his boss, "All quiet on the Western front". Within seconds, a reply was deposited in his inbox – "At your discretion, commence Operation Night Sky." The driver flashed his hazard lights to indicate to the van behind him that they had a green light.

The two men all dressed in black with matching balaclavas who had been sitting in the rear of the van got out of the vehicle and began unloading military style jerry cans; their colleagues in the front vehicle performed the same operation. Both teams were immaculately drilled, working with military precision. They unloaded twenty cans in less than ninety seconds. A human chain was now formed to move the jerry cans into the builders' yard. Once again, this was performed quickly. Two of the men stayed in the yard just outside the building. All was quiet, apart from the creaking of the old sign reading "Robertson Developments" that was in dire need of renovation and oiling as it swung above their heads.

The next phase of the operation for the men in the yard was to empty the contents from the cans all around the perimeter of the building without attracting any attention, whilst the other two returned to their vans to remove the temporary roof panels that covered the holes that had been cut out to modify the vehicles for this particular operation.

The walkie-talkie crackled, as the dousing of petrol began with great calm and the precision of a Swiss watch. Because the powder factory was hidden from prying eyes, it was effectively a building within another building, so the hitmen were very confident that they would not be heard. They had plotted their course to their target away from the cameras that were supposed to monitor the premises.

They had allowed themselves five minutes to disperse the entire contents, but completed it in just less than four minutes before setting off back to rejoin their colleagues.

Two of the men were already positioned in the back of the van, diligently assembling the rocket launchers. The vans pulled out of the layby and drove a short distance to a disused warehouse which was not only perfectly placed to mount the attack from but was the exact distance that the military marksmen required. Everything had been planned with painstaking detail; nothing was being left to chance. The Transits pulled up to the markings they had made last week when they had a dummy run, and once again the headlamps were dimmed.

The marksmen made their final preparations, adjusting the sights until they were locked perfectly onto their targets. Three high-powered motor bikes were off loaded from the vans, and the four men who were not involved directly with launching the rocket attacks began to place the chargers and timers under the Transit vans, as well as removing a couple of haversacks from the footwell.

They took three remote detonators out of the canvas sacks and placed one in the middle of each bikes seat; the haversacks were then strapped to their backs. Once they had completed all of their remaining tasks, they put black bell crash helmets over their balaclavas and handed the marksmen theirs. They now sat and waited for the final authority from their paymaster before heading for the nearby docks to make their escape.

Everything was now set; their specialist work almost completed. The final authority came in by text. It read, "Ready when you are to take you home."

The tallest of the men nodded, signalling that it was time to leave. The bikes were brought to life. The rocket launchers donned their helmets and moved towards the motorbikes. They picked up the remote control units as they straddled the bikes, lowering themselves into the waiting pillion seats. Throughout the entire operation, not a single word had been spoken.

The first two motorbikes left the disused warehouse, embarking on the very short journey to the dockside, leaving behind two of their colleagues, who would follow shortly having confirmed the destruction of the target. The riders weaved in and out of the narrow, pitch black, cobblestone streets, maintaining a comfortable speed. The white beams shone from the headlamp units, plotting their course to the waiting speedboats.

The military men who were riding pillion activated their remote control units. Three green LED lights flashed simultaneously before turning to a restful state, indicating they had locked onto the rocket launchers. The first unit's red launch button was depressed quickly, with the second unit following the same procedure. Within seconds, a loud whoosh that resembled a Red Devils flypast could be heard, this signified that the first rocket had been launched then the next whoosh was heard, second rocket launched. The adrenalin began to pump around the launcher's bodies. This is how they got their buzz. This is what they did and they were handsomely rewarded for it.

The rockets covered the short distance to their target in virtually no time at all. The first one struck the exact spot, destroying the back of the building instantly. Flames gushed high into the night sky and the ground moved violently as the foundations contorted and twisted in some last-ditch attempt to support the structure. The second rocket also landed directly on its target. The impact removed the front and remainder of the building immediately. In a matter of seconds, the deathly quiet black sky was lit up like the brightest of summer days.

A third and fourth explosion followed as the vans were blown to smithereens, destroying all forensic evidence and signalling that it was time for the last two military men to high tail it to the docks to reunite themselves with their colleagues, who were already on board the first high-powered speedboat. The bike's engine screamed as it sped through the deserted back streets. As the counter hit seven thousand revs, the driver struggled to keep the front wheel on the road.

The second speedboat awaited their arrival, its engines already primed and raring to go. The third and fourth explosions signalled the departure of the first boat, its passengers work well and truly done as they headed back home to Ireland to be reunited with their loved ones.

The final bike roared onto the deserted dockside and made its way to the waiting boat. The bike was quickly stowed on board, with the two men retreating below decks as the boat powered its way across the Mersey, following the trail of their colleagues' escape transportation. They looked back at the bright orange sky. The flames danced against a black backcloth, almost rhythmically, as they were moved by a light chilled wind.

As the dockside faded from vision, the sound of sirens on land was drowned out by the grunt of the boats' powerful engines cutting through the swell of the filthy water.

The powder factory, its contents and night staff had been wiped off the face of the earth in an instant; they never stood a chance of escaping and were met by a horrendous premature end to their natural life.

Two fire engines were dispatched from the local Bootle fire station; four more would follow from nearby locations, the paths to their currently unknown destination illuminated by the glowing night sky. News of the explosions was spreading fast.

Locals who had been enjoying a drink at nearby pubs had spilled out into the streets to find out what the hell was going on, seeking an explanation for the huge bang. Some of them believed that there had been an earthquake; others thought a tanker may have crashed and exploded. The shudder had been felt as far a field as the city centre, where the glowing fireball hung above what was once Robertson Developments Building Supplies.

Robert Harris could not contain his excitement as he viewed the devastation of a significant part of his Father's empire through the high-powered telescope from the warmth and excellent vantage point of his swanky penthouse.

CHAPTER TWENTY-SIX

A couple of local policeman who had been patrolling the local hotspots were the first to arrive at the raging inferno. They could not get very close due to the intensity of the heat from the flames that soared high above. The stench of fuel and burnt flesh filled the air.

"What the fuck…?" exclaimed one of the policemen.

"Shit the bed, I have never seen anything like it," replied his colleague as he radioed into his headquarters.

"10-33 … repeat 10-33; Emergency need urgent backup all units, location corner of Manning Street and Garmoyle Road, Bootle Docks, major incident."

The sirens from the approaching fire engines grew louder as they rapidly neared their destination; ambulances were hurried to the scene as part of standard emergency services major incident procedure. As news spread of the explosion, reporters were quickly contacted and instructed to high-tail it over to Bootle to find out what the hell was going on.

Within the next thirty minutes, six fire engines, three ambulances and a dozen police vehicles, ranging from special incident vans through to patrol cars and a mobile forensic portakabin, had arrived. The police had moved quickly to set up a security perimeter that spanned six blocks on all sides of the incident site to keep the media and prying eyes well away from the scene. At this point, nobody knew what they were dealing with, other than a mounting state of panic.

Simon Robertson and his guests were none the wiser as they finally decided to take the cheeseboard and open yet another bottle of wine. Fiona Swann decided to pass on the cheese.

"Is it alright if I go and check on the boys?" Fiona enquired.

"Of course ... I'll come with you and give you that guided tour that you requested," responded a rather tipsy Simon. Taking her by the hand, he led her out of the dining room, leaving Peter Swann, who was the worse for wear, and his beautiful, unfaithful wife alone for the first time that evening.

Gina's pulse quickened as she realised her predicament. Peter grabbed her hand and looked deep into her eyes. She turned away. His grip tightened and began to hurt her.

"Look at me, Gina, look at me." Silence greeted his request.

"The baby, why didn't you tell me? It's my baby, isn't it?" More silence followed.

"For God's sake, Gina, you can't ignore me – this is ridiculous." Realising her silence was futile, she decided to launch an attack.

"Listen to me, Peter, you are not the father, it is Simon's baby. We had some great fun, but that's all it was, fun. I love my husband and that's it."

"But Gina, you know that's not true."

"Peter, you are drunk, and I really do not want to discuss this anymore. I knew that it was a bad idea when Simon told me that he had invited you. We had a great time, but I realised the errors of my ways. We need to move on."

Peter Swann relaxed his grip; his shoulders dropped and his head bowed.

The silence was broken by the house phone ringing, closely followed by her husband's mobile, which he had left on the dining room table. It was late for anybody to be ringing, she thought as she decided to answer the house phone ahead of the mobile that flashed number "unknown".

"Hello, can you hold for a minute whilst I answer the other phone?"

She picked up the mobile, but it was too late – they had hung up.

"Good evening, I am sorry to call you so late – however, I urgently need to speak with Simon Robertson, please, there has been an incident at Robertson Developments building yard."

"Of course, can I ask who is calling?"

"Merseyside Police."

As if on cue, Simon entered the dining room. Gina passed him the phone.

"Simon Robertson, I believe you need to speak with me."

"It's Merseyside Police, I am really sorry to spoil your Saturday night, Sir, but there has been a major incident at your builders' yard in Bootle. We have tried to contact your father, but to no avail. I need you to come down straight away."

"I'm on my way," said Simon.

"Please prepare yourself for the worst, Mr Robertson; you will have not seen anything like this."

The colour drained from Simon Robertson's face as the reality of what he had been told began to sink in. His mind jumped erratically as what seemed like millions of thoughts rushed through it. A major incident, prepare yourself; you will have not seen anything like this before … all he could think about was the five million pounds worth of "Snow Drift" that was on site, what if something had happened to it?

"Simon, can we help?"

"No thanks, that was the police – there has been a major incident at our supplies depot. You will have to excuse me, but I need to go immediately."

"I'll run you there, honey, would you and Fiona mind staying here with the boys? Help yourself to food and drink."

"No problem," Peter Swann replied.

"We'll call you and let you know what's happening," Gina continued.

"Don't worry, just go."

Simon was desperately trying to reach his father; there was no reply from either his home or his mobile.

"Are you sure you're OK to drive, honey?"

"Yes, I'm fine – what's happened?"

"I don't know anymore than I have told you. The policeman told me to prepare myself for the worst. Whatever that means, it doesn't sound good. Can you put your foot down?"

The 911's tyres smoked as Gina obeyed her husband's instructions and hotfooted it to the Bootle site, completely unaware of what awaited their arrival.

She switched on the radio, which was tuned to one of the local stations; ironically, Elton John's "Rocket Man" filled the airwaves as Simon continually dialled his father's numbers.

"Where can he be?" he asked himself. Fraser had decided to have a dirty weekend in The Cotswolds with Sheila Gibson, who had told her husband that she was going to a health spa with some of the girls. He had promised himself not to switch his mobile on and was sticking to it. Fraser's wife had gone to stay with her parents.

"Rocket Man, burning out his fuels..." Elton John's distinctive vocals were abruptly interrupted by a newsflash. The radio presenter announced "Sorry to interrupt the programme. However, news is just reaching us of a major explosion in the docks area of Bootle. It's claimed that four separate explosions were heard in the area of Manning Street around ten-thirty this evening. All of the emergency services have attended the site, which is believed to be a builder's yard that has been devastated in the blasts. Early indications are that a major gas leak may have caused the explosions."

"Shit ... shit ... shit," screamed Simon, causing Gina to lose temporary control of the car as it briefly veered to the right before correcting itself.

"Bloody hell, Gina, watch what you're doing, will you?"

"I'm sorry, you scared me. I know you're upset, but let's hope it's not as bad as they're making out."

"Not as bad as they are making out!" he screamed, forgetting his wife's current state. She jumped as his scream resonated around the car's interior. Her hands shook as she began to feel very uncomfortable in her husband's presence. She had never seen him in such a state and did not like what she was witnessing. For the rest of the journey, she decided not to speak unless she was spoken to.

* * *

Robert Harris had decided that he should share his great moment of triumph with some female company. The Champagne was on ice and Mercedez was on her way round to his apartment.

The blue and white striped police tape fluttered in the chilly breeze, serving as a marker that nobody without the necessary security access could pass beyond.

The flames continued to scale the black sky as they fed off the fuel that had been laid around the perimeter; thick black smoke had started to billow from the devastated site, engulfing the raging fire.

As Gina's 911 turned onto the dock road, accelerating towards its destination, the view changed dramatically as the high rise buildings gave way to the open road, revealing a giant bonfire in the distance. Simon immediately knew that the dramatic backcloth of bright fire was his father's business going up in flames.

"For fuck's sake, tell me that can't be what I think it is."

She bit her tongue; she knew she had to maintain her silence to avoid a row, which was the last thing either of them wanted right now.

The fire brigade had not been able to get anywhere near – the flames were pinning them back, and the icy wind that was picking up in strength was not helping matters, either. The senior fire officers were in deep conversation. They had set up a base station about one hundred metres from the blaze as they strove to assess what had caused the horrific carnage that lay before them.

Three ambulances with a team of doctors were parked just behind the fire engines, awaiting instructions. At this stage, it was unclear if anyone had been working at the depot. They suspected not, other than maybe some security guards, but were unsure, so they had arrived in numbers just in case. They were also concerned that secondary explosions may occur.

Searchlights were erected around the boundaries, and all access roads within a mile of the site were closed down to the public, with the police erecting manned blockades to control traffic flow in and out. The 911's engine whined as it approached a control point. Gina brought the car to a temporary stop and wound down the window to speak with the policeman. Simon lent across her bump, flashing his business card at the officer.

"Let us through, I own the depot that is involved in the incident. I'm Simon Robertson, one of your senior officers called me before."

The officer took the card and began checking a long list of pre-authorised personnel, moving his torch down the list as he searched for Simon's name."

Simon's frustration was growing. "What are you doing?" he asked the officer.

"I'm checking my list of authorised personnel. There's no Robertson on it."

"Listen, mate ... I know you have a job to do, but this is ridiculous. My business is going up in smoke before my eyes and you won't let me past. What on earth would my pregnant wife and I be doing driving around here in a Porsche 911 at this time of night?"

The officer spoke into his radio to confirm that it was OK to let Simon Robertson through. The message came back as confirmed and to send them to the base station, just under a mile down the road.

"Sorry, to have kept you, Sir, Madam. Please proceed to the base station which is at the bottom of this road, ask for D.I. Peters."

News of the explosions was spreading like wildfire with local, regional and national media beginning to dispatch reporters and camera crews to the disaster site as ambitious news editors got a whiff of a potentially interesting developing story.

Robert Harris and Mercedez enjoyed a glass of Champagne as they surveyed the dramatic scene that was unfolding in Bootle. His fifty-inch plasma television was tuned to Sky News, but as yet there was no word. He knew that it would only be a matter of time before they started reporting the story.

Merecedez was fascinated. The vantage point was unrivalled. At this stage, she had no idea what had happened, unlike her partner, who had engineered the entire event at much cost, offset by deep personal satisfaction.

As his brother, who he thought was missing, presumed dead, took a large sip of Champagne, Simon pulled up to the base station on the edge of the disaster area. As he stepped out of the car the searing heat hit him, he felt like he had just disembarked from an aircraft that had recently landed in a very hot climate. Gina stayed in the car whilst her husband stood dumbfounded and motionless, trying to make some sense of what lay before him. The reality hit him hard; he was certainly not expecting to see anything quite like this. What the hell had happened? What on Earth could have caused so much damage?

He could see several large twisted metal stanchions that once supported the building rising from the ground being barbecued by the ferocious flames. There was nothing left apart from them. The stench of fuel filled his nostrils as the commercial loss, not to mention the loss of life, was calculated in his head. He felt a sudden rush from the pit of his stomach. He could not contain the surge and vomited on the pavement.

Simon reckoned that there might have been as many as a dozen staff, plus a couple of irreplaceable generals amongst the victims. He desperately needed to speak with his father prior to engaging with the police and authorities.

The fire would certainly have destroyed the drugs, but would they have left any residue that the highly skilled forensic scientists would pick up? He was certain that the charred carcasses of the night shift would be recovered. How would they explain that a dozen or so staff were working at a rundown building depot late on a Saturday night?

His stomach churned; his mind began to race out of control. He knew that he had to control the emotions that were starting to run away with him.

As he walked towards the base station, a slim, middle-aged, bespectacled man approached him. "Mr Robertson?"

"Yes, Simon Robertson."

"I'm D.I. Peters; I'm in charge of the police investigation."

"Police investigation?" queried Simon.

"Yes, we have no idea at this point what caused the explosions other than clearly it was something fairly substantial to cause so much damage. It could well be a series of gas explosions, although the engineers who have recently arrived on site say that they have never seen anything like it."

"We have a full forensic team here; trouble is until the flames die down, nobody can get anywhere near it. Is that your good lady in the car?"

"Yes, she drove me out here, despite being heavily pregnant. We were entertaining friends at home when

I got the call. I'm a bit worse for wear so Gina offered to bring me."

"Bring her into the cabin – we'll make her some tea. She'll be more comfortable inside. I have a lot of questions to ask you, Mr Robertson – this is going to take some time."

"In that case, she may be better going back home."

Simon and the inspector explained to Gina what was going to happen over the next few hours or so. She was visibly shocked at what she saw and decided to stay with her husband, at least for the time being. A hot cup of sweet tea and the thought of returning to the further advances of Peter Swann offered sufficient incentive for her to make her decision.

D.I. Peters led the couple into the portakabin. Gina was left with a community support police lady whilst Simon sat down with the inspector to start what was going to be an exhaustive round of questioning.

"So, Mr Robertson, first things first." The clock on the wall showed 11:27 p.m. as D.I. Peters began.

"Do you own the building?"

"Not directly, no. It's my father's business, of which I am a director."

"Your father, a Mr Fraser Robertson, is that correct?"

"Yes."

"You also have a brother, James, but he is filed as a missing person."

"That's right."

"Prior to his disappearance, did he have any interest in the business?"

"He was a paid director." Simon wriggled in his seat as he felt himself becoming nervous once more. How the hell did Peters already know about James?

"I believe that you run a successful property development company and this site was used as a building supplies depot."

"Yes, that's correct, Inspector."

"What kind of things did you store on site, Mr Robertson?"

"Oh, all kinds of building materials – everything from doors to window frames, flooring to light fittings, plaster board and paint."

"What was all the petroleum stored for?"

"Petroleum...." Simon stuttered.

"Didn't you smell it as soon as you got out of the car? What do you think is fuelling the flames?"

"We would have some petrol on site to fuel the power tools that we use."

"But not enough to create the mother of all bonfires and bring a 5,000 square foot building to its knees."

"I have no idea, to be honest, but I wouldn't have thought so," replied Simon.

As the questioning continued, the media circus was growing outside. Sky News was setting up their cameras alongside BBC and ITV regional news crews in the designated area. Journalists and radio news teams were primed to start reporting as soon as they were given the all clear. It would not be long now before this intriguing story broke to the watching and listening world.

"So where is your father, Simon?" D.I. Peters asked.

"He must have gone away for the weekend. I've tried both his home and his mobile and had no luck with either."

"Can I check his numbers with you to make sure they are correct?"

"Certainly." The numbers were the right ones.

"We will continue to try and reach him. My guess is that with the media interest in this story, it will only be a matter of time before he hears about it anyway."

Gina had called the Swann's to check on the boys, who were fine. She had told Fiona of the wanton destruction to the building supplies depot. She was feeling tired and emotionally shattered, so had decided to head off back home – she needed her bed. Fiona had told her that they would get a taxi as soon as she got back, which was a relief.

The community liaison officer knocked on the interview room door to let Simon know that his wife was feeling tired and was planning on heading back home. The police were going to drive her back. He was fine with that, as he knew that he would not be leaving D.I. Peters' company for some time yet.

CHAPTER TWENTY-SEVEN

The naked couple quickly inhaled another two lines of charlie. They rolled up fifty-pound notes and snorted the white powder from the glass coffee table in the lounge area of Fraser Robertson's hotel suite. All was quiet in The Cotswolds apart from the romping couple, who had been pleasuring each other for the past couple of hours.

Sheila Gibson sniffed loudly, rubbing her nostrils before taking a mouthful of Champagne. She switched on the adult movie channel and watched studiously. She quickly became aroused as she watched the two blonde girls in their late twenties playing with each other's pussies. Fraser was turned on as he poured himself another glass of fizz. Sheila made him sit on the armchair so she could suck him off whilst continuing to watch the two blondes that were really making her hot.

"I want to do it with another woman, Frase... God, I am so turned on, this is really good stuff."

"How about your friend Jenny?"

"Oh yes, she is gorgeous. I would love to play with her – you could watch us. You could fuck us both." she stroked and licked his cock. Her talk and the thought of watching Sheila and her gorgeous friend Jenny having sex proved too much for Fraser as he quickly came.

"Oh my God, that was so good. Life is great!" he exclaimed, blissfully unaware of what was happening back home. They decided to retire for the night – both of them sexually satisfied; both of them ready for bed.

As the news channels were getting ready to broadcast at midnight, Fraser fell into a deep sleep.

* * *

Initial reports swept the airwaves of a massive series of explosions that destroyed a builder's supplies depot in Manning Street in the docks area of South Bootle. Sky News was the first to broadcast pictures of the devastated site, which amongst others, Robert Harris watched, much to his amusement and deep personal satisfaction.

Most of the channels reported that it may have been caused by a major gas leak and that British Gas investigators were on site, but owing to the intensity of the flames, had so far not been able to get within one hundred metres of the ruins.

Fraser slept whilst his son continued to be questioned by the police.

The two generals who had left the powder factory just before the attack listened in disbelief as the local radio station reported the explosion at Robertson Developments' building supplies depot. They turned the car around abandoning their next meeting to high tale it back to the powder factory to survey the damage first hand.

Gina returned home and invited the policemen in for a cup of tea, not really as a thank you for them taking the trouble to drive her home, but more as a security measure to ensure that Peter and his family left. She was relieved to see a waiting taxi outside the house. Fiona embraced Gina as she entered the house. She had seen the enormity of what Gina had just witnessed first-hand on the television. Peter also gave her a respectful hug as the Swann's said their goodbyes and got in the taxi.

Over the next couple of hours, the flames lost a lot of their intensity. Thick black heavy smoke, accompanied by a nauseating pungent smell filled the cold night air. The fire crews, dressed in special protective clothing and breathing apparatus, had been working remotely using enormous ladders and powerful jet driven foam to contain the inferno. They could now finally move in and begin to quell the flames. The emergency services boundary line was also advanced.

Inside the base station portakabin, policemen and women mingled with forensic scientists drinking copious amounts of coffee, tea and water – all of them waiting to play their parts. The chat was incessant, mainly exchanging opinions and speculating on what could have caused such a catastrophe.

Simon Robertson sat in the waiting room, having been subjected to two hours of questioning from D.I. Peters.

He tried his father's mobile once more, but it just went through to the answer service, where he had already left a number of messages.

The generals who had abandoned their evening's round in favour of returning to Manning Street had been and gone, both of them struggling to comprehend what they had seen. They too had tried to raise Mr Big without success. Like Simon, they knew that lives had been lost. Friends and colleagues in a sordid business whom they had known for years had undoubtedly perished, and it was only a matter of time before this came to light. Furthermore, was it coincidence that the previous evening's takings had been down some £200,000? They decided to leave town and had no plans on returning for the foreseeable future.

By dawn, the fire had been put out and the ground beneath where it had raged resembled that under an active volcano that had become dormant. Ashes glowed red, and footprints from the firemen and emergency service workers who had been working on the site for the past few hours were clearly visible in the black and charcoal soot that they had trampled underfoot.

As dawn broke, the daylight revealed two huge craters that covered the entirety of where Robertson Developments' building supplies depot once stood. Nothing, absolutely nothing from the original structure remained. During the next few hours, the inspectors from British Gas and the highly skilled forensic scientists would try and piece together a jigsaw whose pieces had been destroyed.

Cameras clicked and whirred, reporters advanced, and TV crews began to transmit as the first shafts of daylight descended like giant spotlights illuminating what had been a black canvas.

Fraser Robertson and Sheila awoke early on Sunday morning feeling pretty lousy from the excesses of the night before. Sheila pointed the remote control at the plasma screen that was hung on the wall opposite and began channel hopping. Fraser decided to take a shower in a bid to liven himself up, his mobile remained by the bedside switched off.

As the warm water descended from the showerhead, engulfing Fraser's large frame, Sheila had settled on Sky News. The newscaster was reporting on an earthquake measuring 7.8 on the Richter scale that had hit Osaka overnight, causing widespread damage and disruption to the area as well as a significant loss of life.

The news pictures showed overpasses that had once carried thousands of vehicles and commuters into town all now devastated, crushed beyond all recognition by the forces of Mother Nature. Black body bags neatly arranged along the roadside, awaiting collection and identification added to the harrowing scenes.

Fraser, dressed in a fluffy white towelling robe, walked back into the bedroom, refreshed by his early morning shower.

Sheila lay motionless, clearly disturbed by what she had been watching.

"Would you like a cup of tea?"

"That would be nice" "There has been an earthquake in Japan that has killed hundreds of people, the pictures are really upsetting Fraser."

"Then don't watch them," came the arrogant reply. "Here, give me the channel changer," he demanded.

Sheila threw the remote control to him. As it landed, he clasped his hands. The news report from Japan ended and the broadcaster returned to the studio for some breaking news in Liverpool.

"Hey Frase ... let's watch this."

Fraser's grip began to tighten around the remote control as the pictures changed in an instant from the calamity in Osaka to an emerging tragedy in Bootle. The screen was filled with the charred remains of what appeared to have been a large industrial unit. The reporter stood in the foreground of the picture surrounded by thick black smoke.

"At around ten past ten last night, two massive explosions were heard shortly before two further blasts completely destroyed a local property developer's building supplies depot.

"Emergency services were rushed to the Manning Street unit that is owned by Robertson Developments. However, they were beaten back by the massive inferno that greeted them." Footage was then shown from the previous evening with the flames rising high into the night sky.

As Fraser and his lover watched in total disbelief, his pulse quickened. The recorded footage continued to roll as some locals who had been enjoying a few beers at their local pub, which was a mile away from the explosion, were interviewed relating what they had heard and seen the previous evening. Fraser and Sheila were oblivious to the whistling from the kettle, signifying that it had boiled.

The reporter told the watching audience that at this stage it was unknown what had caused the blasts, although a major gas leak was being investigated as a possible cause.

As the newscast faded, Fraser threw the remote with all the strength that he could muster. As it hit the bedroom door, it smashed into several pieces.

After saying how sorry she was and offering her support, Sheila decided that silence was the probably the best form of diplomacy at this stage.

Fraser continued on a three-minute rant, picking up anything and everything that he could lay his hands on and throwing it with all his might in an effort to get the inner rage out. He picked up his mobile and switched it on. As it connected with the outside world, his answer service rang. "You have fifteen messages." He played the first two, the first of which was from his son, Simon, sounding very distraught and asking his father to call him urgently. The message had been left at seventeen minutes past two. The next message was from Detective Inspector Peters of Merseyside Police, asking Fraser to get in touch with him as soon as he picked the message up.

Simon was on his third black coffee of the morning; he felt shit, hung over, tired and massively stressed as he sat in his wife's 911 listening to the local radio station. His mobile rang; thank God it was his father.

"Dad, I am so relieved to hear from you, where are you? I have been trying...."

His father interrupted him. "Listen, son, I've seen what has happened, it's all over the news. I need you to listen to me carefully. I'm away in The Cotswolds, I will be back within three hours, depending on the traffic. What I need to understand is what has happened since the explosions last night, specifically with the police.

"Looking at the pictures on the news, the place is completely devastated. Everything will have been lost, which is nothing short of a disaster. Lives will have been lost, too. The most important thing right now is that we have our stories straight."

Simon spent the next ten minutes or so relaying "chapter and verse" of what had happened, the questions that D.I. Peters had asked him and the responses that he had given. He assured Fraser that at this stage, they suspected a major gas explosion and explained that due to the intensity of the flames, the inspectors and forensic teams had only just managed to get on site.

They discussed at length what they may find, agreeing that they had to come up with some plausible answers, particularly if they found human remains or any traces of illegal substances. Simon mentioned the vast amounts of fuel that D.I. Peters had asked him about. This baffled Fraser, as they did not keep significant amounts of petroleum at the site.

They agreed that the most plausible explanation for why people would be on site was that they were working a weekend shift for a high-rise development that was in the final fitting stage in Manchester, spray-painting hundreds of interior doors that were due for shipment and fitting the following week.

The development was already running two months behind completion and a bunch of angry investors were threatening legal action against Robertson Developments. In an attempt to avoid this, they were working around the clock. This was unknown to Simon, as his father who was in sole charge of the Manchester project, had arranged for the work to be carried out prior to him leaving for a weekend break.

The other piece of reasonable news was that all the workers who worked in the powder factory were single and unattached – that was part of the criteria for employment. Simon was convinced, having witnessed the devastation first-hand, that nothing would have survived the ferocity and intensity of the flames.

Fraser told his son that his next call would be to the generals who were on duty the night before, who would undoubtedly know how many were working the night shift – working on cutting their five million pound investment that had gone up in flames. He would then call Peters and head straight for the site.

At this stage, neither Fraser nor his son suspected any foul play, but were desperate to get some answers. The absolute priority right now was to stay out of jail and for them to continue to uphold the good family name. This was a disaster that they could recover from, given time; however, the next twenty-four hours would be crucial.

There was no reply from either of Fraser's trusted generals phones, which frustrated, angered and concerned him.

D.I. Peters was relieved to hear from Fraser Robertson, who confirmed that he was heading back from his weekend break and coming straight to the site to meet him.

As the morning rolled by, more equipment arrived at Manning Street to assist the investigating teams as they tried to find some answers. Simon Robertson was allowed to return home for a much-needed shower and change of clothes. He was told to return within two hours, by which time his father should have arrived.

Tony Barlow was opening the mail and enjoying a healthy breakfast of bran flakes, fresh fruit and skimmed milk as he learnt of the Robertson Developments disaster. Not knowing the full extent of the catastrophe, he felt pleasantly amused "There is a God!" he shouted. The A4 envelope that had arrived from the city council's planning department contained a relatively short covering letter stating that the file that he had requested, relating to the sale of land at Gartner Street, had been lost. There were a couple of documents attached, probably to appease Tony. Upon inspection, it was clear that they had not been scrutinised prior to dispatch. Meanwhile, Robert Harris was resting a couple of floors above him, delighted with his evening's work.

CHAPTER TWENTY-EIGHT

As the investigators continued their detailed work, Fraser's Bentley powered ever closer to the outskirts of Liverpool. He placed a call to Julian Wilberforce, Chief Constable of Merseyside.

"Sorry to trouble you on a Sunday, Julian, it's Fraser Robertson."

"Fraser, I was going to call you. I am so sorry about what's happened. I saw it on the news – terrible, absolutely terrible. If there's anything I can do, then just ask."

"I appreciate that, Julian, I'm just on my way to the site. I've been away in The Cotswolds. I am meeting with Detective Inspector Peters; he has already spoken with my son."

"Ron Peters ... he's a good man, one of the best."

"We might need some strings pulling, Julian, some favours. There may well have been casualties, not to mention what residues or evidence they may find."

"Of course Fraser, no problem. I will speak with Ron Peters."

"Thanks Julian, let's keep in touch."

Fraser Robertson felt slightly better for making the call. He called his son to let him know that he would be there in about twenty minutes.

The first shift was coming to an end. The white plastic boots and matching paper overalls were covered in a mixture of mud, soot and dirt from the morning's search for evidence. Numerous sacks had been filled and taken away for forensic testing. The utility companies had started work on fixing the burst mains water pipe that had fractured during the explosions; electricity and gas supplies had been cut off. The gas inspectors had escalated their investigation to their senior management, requesting further expert resources to be dispatched to Manning Street.

Teams of reporters waited patiently for further news. Hundreds of people had gathered at the police boundaries – having seen or heard about the explosions, they decided to come and have a closer look. Dozens of extra police officers had been dispatched to help with controlling the growing inquisitive masses.

Sheila Gibson and her overnight bag were put in a taxi just outside the city boundaries. Fraser continued the short journey alone. Heads turned as the Bentley's V12 engine became audible to the gathered crowd, making its way up to the first control point – the registration plate FR 1 acting as the necessary authority to be quickly waved through the barrier onto the base station, away from prying eyes. Tongues wagged as the locals speculated on who was piloting the luxurious vehicle.

A refreshed Simon greeted his father outside the main entrance to the base station. Fraser Robertson was struggling to come to terms with the sheer scale of the operation and the enormity of the destruction. Father and son embraced, holding onto each other in a reassuring hug. D.I. Peters, having been notified of Fraser Robertson's arrival, descended the small aluminium steps from the portakabin to greet him.

"Mr Robertson ... Detective Inspector Peters. I am really sorry that you had to cut short your weekend break. However, under the circumstances, I'm glad that you are here." The detective held out his arm to indicate that it was time for them to go inside and start the lengthy round of questioning. Simon Robertson was asked to join them. Fraser declined the offer of a hot drink and immediately took up the initiative.

"So Inspector, what the bloody hell has happened here?"

"I'm hoping that you can help us provide you with that answer, Mr Robertson. Right now, as you are probably already aware, the speculation is on a major gas leak. We have specialist investigators on site, working closely with a team of top forensic scientists. Unfortunately, they have only been able to spend about four hours on the site thus far – we had to wait for the flames to lose their intensity so the fires could be extinguished before they could start their work. Rest assured, they will find the cause of this."

"That's reassuring, Inspector."

"It was one hell of a fire, Mr Robertson. The senior fire officer said that he had never seen anything like it in twenty-five years' service."

"Why were you storing so much fuel at the depot?"

"We always keep a fair amount of fuel on site, Inspector. This weekend, we had an exceptionally large holding as we are starting a major fit out of our Manchester development on Monday. A gang of at least seventy men all armed with petrol-driven power tools." Fraser decided to play his trump card. "We had over three hundred litres of paint in the depot, which won't have helped matters."

Fraser paused, hanging his head. "Oh no, what about my workers? Please tell me that they managed to survive. Please tell me that they are all OK."

The inspector gave him a concerned look. "Your workers, Mr Robertson? "You are saying that there were people inside the building at the time of the explosion."

"Yes, probably a dozen or so?"

"A dozen or so ... I need you to be more specific."

"Let me see, now." Fraser pretended to calculate the employees in his head. Simon and the inspector sat in silence, watching this immaculately enacted performance.

"Provided they all showed up for the shift, then it is twelve people. I can give you all the personal details."

"This indeed is news to me, Mr Robertson. Your own son and partner had no idea that people were working inside the building and yet he is a director of Robertson Developments.

"That is correct. Simon had no knowledge as he is not involved with the Manchester development, I run that exclusively."

Simon nodded his head in confirmation of what his father had just said.

"What were they doing on the shift?" queried Peters.

"Spraying interior doors in readiness of the fit out in Manchester on Monday."

"I will need a full inventory from you."

"No problem."

After a further forty-five minutes of questioning, it was decided to give the Robertson's a thirty-minute break. This gave the inspector the opportunity to brief his team and all the onsite investigators with the latest news. The fact that people were present during the explosions changed the landscape dramatically.

Fraser used the time to call his PA, instructing her to contact the insurance company advising them of the disaster as well as preparing a schedule of employees who were scheduled to be working that night. He also tried the generals again, but they were not taking his calls.

Julian Wilberforce was as good as his word. He called Detective Inspector Peters, giving him explicit instructions to make him personally aware of any significant developments. He told Peters it was absolutely critical not to let anybody else know of them prior to speaking with him.

* * *

The duck down quilt was tossed in the air for the umpteenth time as a troubled Gina Robertson tried to find a comfortable position so she could get some much-needed sleep. She had not slept well, tossing and turning for most of the night. Her thoughts shifted between the events of the previous evening, the explosion, Peter Swann and his advances; her pregnancy. How her life had been turned upside down in recent months. She thought of poor old Brian and what had become of him – his terrible premature end, and still she did not know who was responsible for his vile execution. However, they clearly knew all about her tryst with the personal trainer.

Gina loved her son deeply, but she could not feel the same strength of emotions for her husband, despite what she had told Peter. She knew that now. Simon was a good father and provider, but what passion that had existed between them had dried up a few years ago. Gina needed passion in her life; she craved the love and affection that both Peter and Brian had bestowed on her. She began to sink into a deep depression as the reality of her current situation resurfaced.

She gave up on trying to fall asleep; her mind was way too active. She got up and took a nice warm shower before checking on Mark, who was in a deep sleep following the excitement of the night before.

Even after their much-needed thirty-minute break, Simon Robertson was undergoing a relapse, having previously perked up for a couple of hours. The lack of sleep, coupled with the sheer enormity of what had happened, let alone what may be revealed, was taking its toll. His belligerent father, meanwhile, was continuing to punch above his own weight and was more than holding his own with the seemingly endless rounds of questions that were being thrown at him by D.I. Peters and his team.

During the break, Peters had briefed his entire team, as well as all the onsite inspectors and investigators with the news that there may well have been human fatalities. It was decided to deploy more search teams and increase the area of the search, mainly owing to the ferocity of the blast – it was thought that any human remains that may have survived the explosions could well have been jettisoned into adjoining streets. Sniffer dogs were also being sent to the site to assist with the search for bodies and evidence.

It did not take long before the latest development was leaked to the media and began to be broadcast to the nation. Shocked locals were gripped by what was emerging from Manning Street, with some of them deciding to go and have a look at what was going on. Many decided to stay in the warmth and comfort of their own homes, glued to the television or listening intently to the local radio station's regular news bulletins.

Fraser Robertson had not really had any time to even contemplate what might have occurred. He was too consumed with the thought of self-preservation to even think about what had caused the explosions.

It was a shade past four o'clock when the first breakthrough came to light. A team of local officers who had been deployed to work on the southern side of the boundary had come across a large crater in the grounds of a rundown, disused warehouse not far from the devastated site. The crater, which resembled the size of a small swimming pool in dimensions, was still smouldering; whatever may have stood above ground had been destroyed, leaving only a huge hole surrounded by large mounds of earth.

Within thirty minutes of the discovery, the area had been sealed off, searchlights erected and teams of specialists deployed to start the painstaking search for clues. The initial thoughts were that the crater could have been created by the first gas leak as the main gas supply travelled directly from the crater to where Robertson Developments once stood. The specialist from the gas board had recently arrived on site and was immediately dispatched.

Fraser Robertson's PA had done a sterling job. She was the model of efficiency, compiling a schedule of contents as well as assembling all the personnel files that were given to D.I. Peters.

It had been agreed with Julian Wilberforce that both Fraser and his son would be allowed to return home and continue trying to run their fractured business whilst the investigation continued. There was little point in detaining them at this point.

The Robertson's left the site in the back of a police van, away from the watching and waiting hoards. They would be reunited with their cars later that evening.

Fraser and Simon knew that for the time being, they had to let the authorities do their thing whilst they attempted to pick up the remains of the business, and hope that all traces of the actual stockpile in Manning Street had evaporated into the cold night air.

Chapter Twenty-Nine

The combination of torrential rain and fifty mile per hour winds hampered the work at Manning Street during the course of the week. Several times, they managed to erect giant tarpaulins to protect the site, only for them to be savaged by the inclement weather. Frustration, stress and despair started to set in amongst the dispirited investigators. The forensic teams were particularly concerned as potential evidence was washed and blown away.

Fraser and Simon attempted to return to some degree of normality. They were relieved that there had been no major developments and prayed that the horrendous weather would continue for some time yet.

Victor Knight and a number of other loyal servants had finally managed to speak with "Mr Big" and his boy. They had relayed the news that traders had failed to turn up for business on the Friday evening prior to the explosions and that takings had been down by around two hundred thousand pounds at a time when they expected to see them rise.

Fraser had discussed the missing generals and wondered if they had perished in the explosion or whether their disappearance was something more sinister. Victor was instructed to do some digging and report back. They were all beginning to smell a rat.

Fraser and Simon knew that they had to prioritise matters, deciding to focus on ensuring that the *Western Heights* site visit – which was only a few days away now – went without a glitch.

The site had been tidied up. Old trees that had stood in the car park for hundreds of years were illegally uprooted and removed in an attempt to make the space look larger than it actually was.

More palms had been greased, with a view to making sure that those in authority who needed to be on board were actually on board. Given the Manning Street disaster, the consequences of losing out to an objection to planning from a bunch of what Fraser saw as "emotional punters" could bring his empire crashing down around him.

Robertson Holdings stood to make a cool twenty million pounds from the development. They would leave no stone unturned in their pursuit of this bounty.

Tony Barlow had done all he felt that he could in preparation for the site visit and subsequent planning committee meeting, where they would reveal the outcome of their findings. His solicitor had not had any response back from Fraser Robertson to her latest enquiry, querying why he had denied all knowledge of *Western Heights* just a matter of weeks ago.

Barlow had also had a couple of letters from Liverpool City Council planning department. The first of which stated that the council had found no fault in his complaint of receiving the planning notices late for *Western Heights*. Whilst he was disappointed, he was certainly not surprised by their claim of innocence. He knew what they were up against.

The second letter was from Jim Barrat; the planning manager for the proposed development, confirming that there was no parking planned at the residential tower. At least this was some encouraging news. Tony hoped that the Robertson's had other priorities following the events of the weekend.

Despite a further push from Tony and his residents' association members, the number of complainants had failed to rise. It had come to light that there were only six owner-occupiers in *Robertson Heights*. Fraser Robertson had sold out "off plan" to a bunch of mainly Irish Investors, all looking to make a quick buck by selling on to local buyers who wanted to live in city centre luxury. Their plans had failed to materialise, and instead they had rented their expensive pads to an assortment of low lifes and students, the majority of whom were regular drug takers. This just served to make the owner-occupiers' lives even more stressful.

Barlow had not managed to find any information about the disposal of the land at Gartner Street from the city council to Robertson Holdings. He knew this was another significant part of the puzzle. He had made an application to the city council under the *Freedom of*

Information Act. He was also working with Mick Hall, the local Labour councillor who had failed to show for the initial hearing. Hall had committed to finding out about the transaction that took place. So far, Barlow had heard nothing of substance from either source.

Despite living at the top of the tower, Robert Harris had absolutely no interest in registering any protest. He had far bigger fish to fry, not to mention that he needed to keep a relatively low profile. Tony and his fellow campaigners were baffled by the exclusion of the man who lived at the top of the shop – surely he would want to take a stance?

Harris had been contacted earlier in the week by Alexi, who asked if he had anything to do with the explosions at Robertson Developments' Manning Street depot. His suspicions deepened as Harris ordered and paid for, half up front, a million pounds' worth of his finest charlie for immediate shipment. Needless to say Harris denied any involvement, citing the lucrative Christmas period for the substantial order.

Harris's growing legion of traders profited from Fraser Robertson's misfortune by posting record business over the busy weekend, as users craved their manufactured high to ease the stress of the week's burdens. On the street, news was spreading fast amongst revellers of the new wonder drug "Pure White", attracting both new users who had yet to try it as well as those who had already experienced it.

Despite destroying a large part of his father's business and drawing record profits of a cool quarter of a million pounds from two nights' work, all was not right in the world of Robert Harris. He did not feel himself. He felt unwell. The symptoms that his body was displaying were very similar to the flu. Maybe he was getting a cold, or had caught a chill from the bitterly cold winds that greeted him every time he walked out of or returned to *Robertson Heights*. He decided to take to his bed, feeling devoid of energy. His body ached and his head banged.

The following morning, Harris awoke around eight. The bedding was wet; the pillow damp. Whatever it was that he was suffering from, his body was rejecting it by sweating it out. He felt awful: his mouth was as dry as a bone, and he needed a drink of water.

As he got out of the bed, his legs felt weak and struggled to support his body. He began to wonder if maybe he was experiencing a bout of cold turkey – bad withdrawal symptoms from his years of abuse.

His hands shook as he poured himself a glass of water that he gulped down in a matter of seconds. He poured another glass and took a couple of paracetemol tablets. After changing the bedding, he decided to get back under the duvet, where he slept for the next twelve hours, awakening to feel a whole lot better.

Monday was a relatively uneventful day, with the rain finally subsiding only for the winds to intensify, causing minor damage to homes and some added disruption to road traffic as trees that had been blown down caused obstructions to drivers.

Robert Harris felt something like his new self again, putting the events of the past twenty-four hours down to a bad dose of withdrawal symptoms.

Fraser and Simon Robertson had conducted a series of meetings with key decision makers from both the council and the ruling Liberal Democrat party, all of who were on their payroll, ahead of tomorrow's vital proceedings. The site was looking as good as it could. It had been decided that Fraser would not attend the site visit or the follow on meeting at the town hall. His presence would signify concern, and that would not be a good thing to show either the objectors or the city council planning committee.

Tony Barlow had done all he could. He had devoted an enormous amount of time to ensuring that he and the handful of fellow owner-occupiers were as prepared as they possibly could be to fight this appalling project.

He had taken dozens of photographs to support his case – pictures of *Robertson Heights*, showing the views from all of the west side apartments being at best impaired and at worst completely lost by the planned development. Learning of the fact that no parking was planned for *Western Heights*, he had done a great deal of research on nearby parking facilities. The nearest was a good three-quarters of a mile away. Who in their right mind was going to pay almost three hundred thousand pounds for a pad with no parking? He had photographs of endless stationary traffic attempting to make its way into town and getting nowhere because of the "big dig". This would be further compromised if they were allowed to build, by access and delivery of building supplies to the site.

The pictures had been meticulously arranged on a number of large storyboards that he would show at the hearing.

Across town, Detective Inspector Peters and his team continued with their painstaking work in the hope that they could unravel what was still a great mystery. Julian Wilberforce had called Peters several times for updates. Peters failed to understand his obsession with the incident. He believed it bordered paranoia. Peters had no idea that it did not really matter what was found on site as Fraser Robertson had more dirt on the paedophile chief constable than you could shake a stick at. Wilberforce was going to pull rank to protect himself, his reputation and his future.

Tuesday was going to prove to be a significant day in more ways than one.

Barlow had not slept well. His sleep was disturbed at regular intervals by a combination of the air conditioning in his apartment switching itself on and off at will, and his concern over the presentation he was going to deliver to Lady Eileen and her committee. His pitch was being repeated in his subconscious over and over again. By six-thirty a.m., he decided to surrender to the malfunctioning air conditioning and his hyperactive mind. He ran a warm bath; a good soak was in order and may help him relax ahead of what was going to be an eventful day.

Simon Robertson and James Thirsk, who were representing Robertson Developments, had both slept well. They had arranged to meet at Thirsk's offices ahead of the site visit to ensure that they were as prepared for what lay ahead as they could be. Neither of them was expecting any issues whatsoever and had passed on this cocky reassurance to Fraser.

The rules of the site visit were both archaic and restrictive, particularly for the objectors. The developer was allowed to have a representative attend, along with the architect, the planning manager who had already approved the development and the five members of the planning committee. The visit would precede the final presentations and objections that would be heard by Lady Eileen and her committee back at the town hall.

Grey, overcast skies combined with low-lying fog sweeping off the banks of the Mersey formed a fairly depressing backcloth for the arrival of the site inspection visitors. First off the people carrier was Lady Eileen, dressed in a heavy, charcoal grey, double-breasted overcoat. A bright red scarf that was double wrapped around her neck with matching red leather gloves added a splash of colour to an otherwise dull palette. She was closely followed by Paul Gibson, Head of planning, and the rest of the cast and crew that would ultimately make the decision that would affect many people's lives.

The people carrier parked on the service road around the back of *Robertson Heights*, opposite the newly constructed offices. The first port of call was to an unoccupied apartment on the western side of the development. The main purpose of this was to demonstrate to the planning committee members the proximity of the planned construction to *Robertson Heights*, which would cause the loss of views, not to mention the impact on privacy.

The small yet quick passenger lift soon reached the twentieth floor, and the delegation was lead into the unoccupied apartment by the security guard who had left his reception post. The apartment smelled musty from its inoccupation.

The delegation was led over to a position in front of the floor-to-ceiling windows that enjoyed spectacular views of the city and the infamous Royal Liver buildings. They were not as dramatic as they could have been, mainly due to the early morning fog and dark grey sky – however, for a first-time experience, they had the desired effect. Lady Eileen was the first to express herself.

"Stunning." Her colleagues nodded in agreement.

"So where is the proposed site?" she asked the architect.

He pointed to the spot, which looked minute from their vantage point. From the expression on her face, which matched the colour of her scarf, he quickly realised the error of his ways.

Unravelling a clutch of architectural drawings, he selected the site plan that he duly laid out on a nearby dining table.

"You will get a far better idea of the proposed site from this drawing."

Her team followed her to the table like an obedient, well-trained flock. James Thirsk took centre stage, trying to recover from his schoolboy error. He pointed out the boundary lines and talked them through how they would manage the construction of the high-rise development, giving due consideration to minimising any disruption to residents of *Robertson Heights* or inbound city centre traffic. His performance was reasonably polished, ably supported by Paul Gibson, who reassured Lady Eileen and her team that his department had worked extremely closely with the developer and architects.

Following further discussion and a number of questions being addressed by Thirsk, it was time for the party to move to the adjoining office development. The security guard led the way across the windswept compound into the offices. The uninterrupted views from the six-storey facility were all river facing. The building had been designed as a glass-domed semi-circle. All the workers' desks pointed out to sea; there simply was not a bad seat in the house. The Mersey was an ever-changing landscape before their eyes, its waves curling and frothing, tossing the numerous forms of transportation that sailed its historic waters as they made progress towards their destinations. What a magnificent canvas.

Western Heights was going to be constructed right in front of the offices on the other side of the service road. The natural daylight and magnificent views of the River

Mersey would be replaced by dark days, glass and concrete. Paul Gibson and James Thirsk fidgeted nervously as the members of the planning committee spoke softly with each other, regularly pointing out of the enormous glass panels in the direction of the site, which was their next and final port of call.

The site had been cleared – no cars filled the spaces that they normally occupied between the painted white lines. A rusty old chain draped around a couple of unpainted metal posts, a combination lock, the type of which you could pick up for a few quid at your local chandlers, secured the entrance to the parking facility from neighbouring Gartner Street.

The *Liverpool Echo* and *Daily Post* offices stood on the other side of the street, bordering Pall Mall on the north side. The *Echo* and *Post* had survived and indeed prospered over the years – however, due to the constraints of their premises, they could not store paper and supplies in bulk, which necessitated numerous daily deliveries from their suppliers. Huge articulated transporters regularly queued to unload during the course of most weekdays, causing congestion and disruption in Gartner Street. This was significant, as Gartner Street was being proposed as the construction site entrance for *Western Heights*.

Barlow had got the powers that be from the newspaper to join forces with him by lodging an objection to the proposed residential development on the grounds that it would cause significant disruption to their business, as well as the local economy.

Lady Eileen and her flock were led onto the actual site. She stood in amazement, surveying what little there was to see.

"Is this it?" she asked Paul Gibson

"No, Madam Chair, the site will extend down to the corner of Pall Mall that will be landscaped once construction has been completed."

"Where we stand is the actual area for the footings of the tower, though, Mr Gibson ... is that correct?" she continued hastily.

"Er – yes; I believe that to be correct."

"I personally have seen quite enough, thank you. Unless anybody else has any reason to extend our stay, then may I suggest that we head back to the town hall?"

With no great surprise, the sheep followed Lady Eileen and got back into the people carrier to make the short journey over to the committee rooms.

Tony Barlow, Lisa, his supporters and the other objectors had been waiting patiently – some sipping tea, others drinking coffee whilst nervously making small talk as they awaited the arrival of the decision-makers. A gathering of local press reporters sat close by, hoping to pick up some snippets from the idle chatter.

Shortly before noon, one of the ushers announced by ringing her bell that the planning committee was now in session and that all parties interested in planning application number 2089768654, land at the corner of Brook Street and Gartner Street, should make their way into the council chambers. Tony accompanied by Lisa and his fellow objectors, took up their seats in the gallery, only a stone's throw from where they had sat previously. The room was packed. As before, Lady Eileen and her planning committee colleagues sat at the long, boat-shaped table on the raised platform in the middle of the room. She sat in the middle, with Paul Gibson on her immediate right.

Lady Eileen opened the proceedings, giving directions as to what would happen during the hearing of this application.

"Ladies and gentlemen, as most of you are aware, the planning committee visited the Gartner Street site earlier today. We will report on our findings at the end of today's hearing. Prior to this, there will be a series of short presentations from the developer, followed by the objectors, of which I believe there will be three representations. Can I please request that all those who will be speaking keep it brief, factual and specific."

"Can we have the first speaker for the developer, please?"

Simon Robertson stepped forward, looking business-like in a slate grey single-breasted suit, white shirt and burgundy silk tie. He was only on his feet for five minutes, talking about the commitment of his father's organisation to continue to invest in Liverpool and its great heritage – their determination to play a significant part in helping the city council achieve its ambitious regeneration objectives.

He talked about their desire to build the best value for money city centre residential and commercial property. He did not give any of the objectors a mention other than to say that in his opinion there was absolutely no valid reasons as to why planning permission should not be granted "This development will set new standards in city centre dwellings. It will be 'The Jewel in The Crown', for this fine City" he concluded.

A rather monotone James Thirsk followed; he was lightweight by comparison to Simon. The architect summarised the salient points of the planning application. He had been doing his homework since the shock decision not to approve his client's application. He reminded the planners that privacy and a view were not entitlements by law. Parking was not a planning requirement in the inner city. The belief that *Robertson Heights* was only thirty per cent occupied was mere folly. He told those assembled that the development had sold out "off plan" in a matter of weeks. The pent-up demand for Robertson's exclusive abodes was one of the key reasons to further develop. He concluded by saying that there was not a single reason as to why consent for planning should not be granted.

Advantage Robertson Developments, thought Barlow, who knew that they were up against a lot more than planning rules and regulations.

Councillor Hall and the old dear from 'Save our Heritage' did little to help tip the scales back in favour of the protestors. Barlow's mouth was drying up. His palms started to sweat as his turn was signified. He marched confidently forward to the speaker's podium, with Lisa following a couple of strides behind him carrying two large black sheets of cardboard that were covered with photographs. They were both immaculately dressed – he wore a plain navy suit whilst she had opted for a black trouser suit. Whilst Barlow began to deliver a powerful and compelling attack against the application, Lisa paraded up and down the line of five, pointing to the relevant picture on the large sheet of cardboard; skilfully using the photographs to corroborate what her new boyfriend had just said.

Barlow referred to the project as "scandalous", "a tower for profit and not for the people", "morally appalling", and "an application that broke every rule in the book". He turned towards the public gallery and asked who in their right mind could afford to spend the best part of three hundred thousand pounds on a tiny flat with no car parking. He both appreciated and was heartened by their response as laughter broke out amongst them.

Order was called for by the chair, which gave Tony an opportunity to take a sip of water. He continued his scathing and relentless attack on Fraser Robertson and his cowboy firm, hinting strongly that he most certainly suspected foul play between people in authority who could grant certain favours and Robertson's company. He told the assembly that he had made an application under the *Freedom of Information Act* to obtain all documentation relating to the sale and disposal of the land at Gartner Street and was awaiting a response.

"It will be extremely interesting to see if I get a reply," he said flippantly, signalling another outbreak of laughter from the gallery, who were obviously enjoying his performance.

He then moved onto the actual site itself. "In my opinion, it is quite simply not fit for purpose. It is a postage stamp and totally unsuitable. How on Earth can such a small footprint support a fifty-storey building?"

Lisa showed the committee members photos of the site taken from various angles – a picture that was becoming all too familiar to them.

"Finally, I would like to address the significant matter of disruption. Disruption to local business, disruption to city centre-based workers, disruption to shoppers and visitors trying to get into town from Pall Mall, and of course the massive disruption to all the owners and residents of *Robertson Heights* during the construction period, which I believe will be in the region of three years. Why on Earth should the good people who have already been duped by this disgusting, unscrupulous bunch of cowboys be subjected to further pain and misery by being forced to live on a building site?"

"Madam Chair, fellow committee members, there is not one single good thing about this application and I ask you to do the right thing by rejecting this contrived project once and for all. Thank you."

Cheers and enthusiastic support greeted the conclusion of Barlow's delivery, much to the annoyance of all those who had an interest in *Western Heights*. The crescendo of noise descended into quiet as Tony gathered up his notes and made his way back to his seat.

Lady Eileen rose, adjusting her microphone, prior to addressing the assembly, a number of whom awaited the verdict that she was about to deliver with bated breath. An eerie silence descended on the enormous room, which was broken only by the spokesperson formally introducing Madam Chair.

"I would like to start my address by thanking all those parties on both sides who have put an enormous amount of work and energy into ensuring that their views on this emotive project have been heard."

"I and my fellow planning committee associates have been particularly impressed with the quality of some of the presentations. As I believe most of you are aware, we visited the site this morning so we could see it first-hand. We have also studied the plans for *Western Heights* in great detail."

"I do have to agree with Mr Barlow that building such an exclusive development with no car parking does seem inappropriate. Car parking is already a major headache for the city council, given the severe lack of facilities within the business district. I am also concerned about all the potential disruptions that have been highlighted."

"The site visit this morning, though, confirmed our decision. To say that the site is tight Mr Thirsk, is one of the biggest understatements that I have ever heard in my life. The site is tiny and is quite simply not fit for purpose. Therefore planning for *Western Heights* is rejected subject to final reports from the planning manager, Mr Barrat."

Lady Eileen sat down to more cheers and spontaneous applause; the spokesman called order several times, but nobody took any notice.

James Thirsk and Simon Robertson looked devastated. Clearly, this was not the outcome that they had been expecting. Tony Barlow and his fellow supporters embraced, hugged and shook hands as the enormity of their success began to sink in. The press core began to advance towards them in search of a few quotes for the early editions and newscasts.

Barlow was not expecting such an outcome; he had already decided to speak with the reporters as he felt that the more bad press that he could bestow on Fraser Robertson and his company, the better it would be. He passionately believed that Fraser was nothing more than a gangster; a walking criminal of the worst kind, an impostor in a suit with a public schoolboy accent. He disliked him and everything that he stood for intensely.

Whilst Barlow spoke with the media, Lady Eileen and her flock left the building by a side door.

Within an hour of the decision, Robertson Developments had lodged an appeal and were threatening to sue Liverpool City Council for costs and damages.

* * *

"Come and have a look at this," shouted one of the forensic investigators to his colleague, who answered his call.

Buried deep into the huge crater on the Manning Street site was all that remained from the left-hand side of a human's face and skull. The right side was missing. Congealed, stinking skin clung to the forehead like a nervous child would cling to its mother.

The powerful searchlights pierced through the eye socket as they were adjusted to provide more light. A solitary tooth that had been filled previously had somehow managed to survive what must have been a horrendous death. The evidence was carefully bagged and taken away for analysis. Just a few feet away was another shattered skull, smaller and even more damaged than the first. It was possibly that of a female who may have been closer to the centre of the blast. A charred, decapitated torso was also recovered.

It did not take long for the news of the discoveries to reach D.I. Peters, who immediately called the Chief Constable, Julian Wilberforce, as he had been instructed to do.

Wilberforce told Peters to follow normal procedures and complete all the relevant paperwork. He was unconcerned with the discoveries, as it was common knowledge that workers had been present during the time of the explosion. The discoveries merely confirmed this. He would have been far more concerned if the sniffer dogs had found traces of cocaine – that would have given him an entirely different set of challenges.

Fraser Robertson was already having a very bad day. The news of the *Western Heights* planning rejection, on top of the explosions at Manning Street, was starting to take its toll. His spirit was low, his unflappable confidence badly dented; his mood unpleasant. Simon, who had returned to his father's offices with James Thirsk following the hearing, had rarely seen his old man in such a state. Fraser's legal team had already lodged an appeal against the decision following a thorough debrief from his son and the architect.

Paul Gibson and Jim Barrat had already had a conference call with Fraser. They had discussed at length the grounds of the appeal that needed to go into the official documentation.

Fundamentally, the appeal would be based purely on planning laws and planning laws alone. The application stood up, as it did not breach any planning regulations. They wanted to strip out all the emotion that had obviously played a significant part in forming the planning committee's decision. They were also going to turn up the heat on Liverpool City Council by suing them for damages against lost revenue and costs that they estimated to be in the region of two million pounds.

They knew that the council's coffers were stretched and simply could not defend such a lawsuit.

Fraser called Alan Grimshaw, as his wife Lady Eileen, had played a critical role in persuading her fellow committee members to turn down the application. Both Gibson and Barrat had witnessed first-hand her powerful influence. It was vital that she was derailed.

Grimshaw took the call, as he always did when Fraser called.

"Fraser ... Don't tell me my good lady wife is giving your company a hard time."

"Got it in one, Alan. I need your help."

"Well, Fraser, you know as I do that Eileen is her own woman. She has always done what she believes is best for this city."

"I can assure you, Alan, that rejecting our application in favour of a bunch of whining punters is not in either her best interest or indeed that of this city!" Fraser fumed.

"I can talk to her about it, but I really don't hold too much hope. My wife is about the only person in authority who is not rotten to the core. She is honest, straight, and has never been on anybody's payroll, Fraser."

"Unlike her husband, then. Well, you better try harder, Sir Alan, hadn't you? I would hate to have to dish the dirt. I could destroy you."

The phone went silent as Alan Grimshaw attempted to resist the rage that was surging inside him.

"Are you threatening me, Fraser?"

"Wake up and smell the coffee, Alan. You know what you have to do."

Fraser hung up and turned his gaze back to Simon, Paul and Jim, who were all looking a little shocked at having witnessed the conversation.

"I think that we are done here, gentlemen. You know what needs to be done – leave no stone unturned." Fraser stood up and escorted his guests to the door.

As they left his plush offices, his PA came in to advise him of a host of messages. She had received a number of calls from the media requesting comments and interviews following the rejection of planning. Julian Wilberforce wanted to speak with him fairly urgently. Joe Deech had left a message that simply said, "no news."

Fraser called Wilberforce, who told him that human remains had been found at the Manning Street site; the probability was that it would make the evening newspapers and news broadcasts.

"Another bottle of Champagne, please," shouted Lisa as Barlow and his supporters celebrated their success at The Newz bar, which was only a stone's throw from the town hall. Lisa assisted the barman in recharging the glasses.

Tony proposed a toast. "Here's to us, thank you Lady Eileen for listening and doing the right thing." Glasses chinked, smiles and laughter spread throughout the bar. Dave Hensbury was deep in conversation with Mick Hall, whilst Maureen Elves and John James were enjoying a conversation with Tony, who was feeling elated for the first time in a long time. Little did they know that their celebrations were premature, as Fraser Robertson and his firm were planning a spectacular comeback.

CHAPTER THIRTY

"Robertson in a Jam" was the bold headline on the front inside page of *The Liverpool Echo*. The report focused on the decision to overturn planning permission by Lady Eileen and the planning committee following their site visit earlier that day. It speculated on an appeal being launched by Robertson Developments on the grounds that their project did not breach any planning laws. It also covered the prospect of damages being sought for recovery of land cost and all expenses that had been dispersed so far.

The most interesting and indeed worrying part of the report for the objectors was the actual process of what happened to the application now it had been declined. According to the reporter, the original document would get passed back to the assigned planning manager, Mr Jim Barrat, for him to come up with legal reasons to protect the city council as to why planning permission was revoked, having initially been granted. He would be charged with spelling out the planning regulations that had been breached.

Barrat would have six weeks to complete this before submitting his report back to his boss, Paul Gibson, Head of Planning. Following approval by Gibson, it would pass back to the planning committee for rubber-stamping. The reporter speculated about a possible claim for damages in the region of a couple of million pounds. His view was that in all probability, the council would fold. Given their poor financial situation, it was highly unlikely that they would want to get into a costly legal battle with Robertson Holdings.

There was obviously no mention of all the brown envelopes that would be distributed to further assist Robertson's appeal.

The celebrations continued long into the night, as did the ongoing search for evidence at Manning Street. Barlow, in anticipation of a bit of a hangover, had booked some time off work, and so had Lisa. Their foresight had paid off as around 11 a.m., they woke with a pair of almighty hangovers; both of them feeling like shit. Following a quick shower, they decided to head into town for a much-needed double espresso.

The *Daily Post* was reporting on a breakthrough at Manning Street, with forensic scientists uncovering some human remains at the site. The failed planning application was covered on page five, confirming that Robertson Developments had already lodged an appeal against the decision and a counter claim for damages against the council, rumoured to be in the region of two million pounds.

"We're not out of the woods yet," Barlow said to Lisa as he read the article.

"What do you mean?"

"Robertson has launched an appeal as well as a counter claim for damages against the council."

"So? The decision has been made. There is no way Lady Eileen will reinstate it. Her comments were absolutely scathing."

"Unfortunately, it doesn't work like that, honey. Money, power and politics will dictate the eventual outcome. Fraser Robertson will not take this decision lying down. Rest assured he will call in every favour, leaving no stone unturned to get this application through."

"I think you are worrying unnecessarily."

"I don't," he replied, as the realisation of what was still ahead began to sink in.

Following another couple of coffees, they decided that no matter how much they discussed and speculated as to the possible outcome, they should enjoy their 'moment of victory', no matter how brief it may be. They knew nothing would happen now until the New Year.

Out on the streets, shoppers jostled with each other as Christmas drew ever nearer. Tony decided to use the rest of the day to do some much-needed Christmas shopping and headed into town.

Robert Harris spent the day in bed nursing another bout of flu-like symptoms. He had been watching developments at Manning Street very closely and was heartened by the obvious lack of progress that the police were making. He knew that he had derailed his father's empire at the busiest time of year, and he stood to profit greatly from it over the next few weeks. However, he still wanted his father to pay for his sins with his life.

Harris also knew that Uncle Julian, who used to babysit when he was growing up, would protect his father from any harm. Uncle Julian was in his dad's pocket and had been on the family payroll for years. Only Harris and Julian Wilberforce knew what had gone on during those nights where his care had been entrusted to his uncle. Robert Harris utterly despised Wilberforce for the abuse that he had suffered at the hands of his uncle during his early teenage years. Uncle Julian was also on his hit list.

The activity at Manning Street had been reduced. The gas inspectors had left the site without any substantial evidence to confirm or deny that a major gas leak was the primary cause for the series of devastating explosions. The forensic scientists had discovered some further fragments of bone and tissue that had been taken back to their laboratories for further testing and analysis. They would be cross-referenced against the list of employees that Fraser Robertson had provided the investigating teams with.

The search dogs had not discovered anything that they shouldn't, with all traces of "Snow Drift" being obliterated during the blasts and subsequent raging inferno.

Detective Inspector Peters' report was inconclusive due to a lack of supporting evidence. At this stage, the likelihood was that a major gas leak in the area had caused the initial explosions. The volume of combustible materials that were in Robertson Developments' supply depot at the time heightened the intense fires that followed. The loss of life was being reported as a direct consequence of the explosions. All in all, nothing more than a tragic accident in which nobody was to blame. D.I. Peters felt very uncomfortable with proceedings.

Harris managed to raise himself from his sick bed. So far, the medication that he was taking was not having the desired effect. He knew that he had a couple of phone calls to make to ensure that everything was in place for what he believed was going to be a bumper weekend's trade. A number of Robertson's traders had defected and joined Harris's team.

As each week passed by, his feet on the street increased significantly. Robertson's business had been temporarily disabled; there was no chance that they would be back trading for at least a few months. The heart of their operation had been ripped out. Alexi was happy with how things were working out. Harris was so far proving to be not only a man of his word but also a punctual payer, unlike his father on both counts. As a consequence, he secured himself an excellent supply line.

After talking with his generals, Robert Harris decided to return to his bed. He felt absolutely lousy: his body ached and shook periodically, his throat was red raw; his temperature through the roof. Whilst his team worked hard, he slept like a baby, awakened only briefly at around 4 a.m. by the sound of a large bird flying into his bedroom window.

That evening, Harris and his men posted record takings, only for them to be surpassed the following night. In just two nights, he had made a net profit in the region of three hundred thousand pounds, without getting out of his pit. Despite this, he still felt like crap. Robert decided that if he did not feel any better by Monday, then he would go to the doctor, as he obviously required something a little bit stronger than the stuff he had got from his chemist.

Chapter Thirty-One

Simon Robertson spent Sunday being a good family man, taking his son to football and making his wife breakfast in bed. He was becoming increasingly concerned with Gina's behaviour. Ever since the night of the explosions at Manning Street, she had been withdrawn. Unbeknownst to him, she had doubled her dose of anti-depressants and started to have the odd vodka or glass of wine or two, in a bid to lift her mood.

The baby was due in a matter of weeks now and Simon did not want any last-minute hitches. They had created a nursery next door to the master bedroom. It had been beautifully decorated with warm cream walls and bright wallpaper featuring famous characters from nursery rhymes on the far wall in front of a magnificent crib. No expense had been spared in creating baby Robertson's space.

Gina had not been in the baby's bedroom for a couple of weeks. She was dreading the birth of her baby, as all would be revealed. The thought of having Brian Wright's child filled her with abject fear. She knew that she would not be able to explain that one away. At least, If her baby was born with white skin then that would make her life a little easier, even if it did turn out to be Peter Swann's, as long as she could continue to deceive her unsuspecting husband. The way she was carrying on served to underline that she really did not want her unborn child to enter the world.

What if whoever was behind sending her the package decided to tell her husband? Gina was in a state of sheer panic. She did not know what to do.

Fraser Robertson was at his desk bright and early on Monday; he had a lot of matters to attend to. He was on the ropes and needed to come out fighting. He had to start winning a few rounds. He had spent the majority of his weekend studying the transcript from the planning committee hearing, addressing all of the salient points that Lady Eileen had given as reasons for refusing planning permission.

In the main, none of them held any merit. He believed that she had got carried along on a wave of emotion without paying due attention to any breach of planning laws or regulations.

He had received some encouraging news from Julian Wilberforce on Sunday evening, when he was told that D.I. Peters' report would show that their findings were inconclusive, citing a probable series of gas explosions interacting with a stockpile of highly inflammable substances on the Manning Street site as the likely cause of the disaster. The subsequent loss of life was a tragic occurrence that simply could not have been avoided due to the immediacy and ferocity of the blasts.

Fraser was relieved. He realised that he had got out of jail, even though it had cost his business a fortune and his operation was temporarily grounded. But at least he still had his freedom – well, at least for now. A payment of five million pounds was overdue to the Russians and he knew he simply could not make it.

Robertson had a conference call scheduled with Jim Barrat and Paul Gibson for eight o'clock. The main objective was to help Jim Barrat compile the report that needed to go back to the planning committee, giving fact-based reasons as to why planning was refused. Robertson's involvement in this process, like most things in his life, was totally illegal, but of course this is how it worked if you were on Mr Big's payroll in the Capital of Culture.

Bang on eight, Fraser's secure line rang. Gibson and Barrat commenced proceedings by talking about strategy. It was felt that the strategy should be a full frontal attack both on the city's planning committee and the city council with the counterclaim for damages. This would immediately put the council on the back foot.

Gibson agreed with Robertson that there were no sound reasons based on planning as to why the application should not be granted. Barrat and Gibson had already prepared responses to address all the points of record that Lady Eileen had given as reasons for refusal. They were confident that if they kept the matter strictly to planning, then they would get the project reinstated. Gibson alluded to the fact that the lawsuit for damages held the key, as not only was the council hard-pressed for cash, they simply did not have the stomach for a fight.

Robertson also wanted to use some PR spin by getting some positive coverage in the local media about how committed his organisation was to playing a central role in the ongoing regeneration and improvement in city centre living. He wanted to highlight that Robertson Developments not only had their roots in Liverpool, but that they employed local craftsmen who would be put to the sword as a result of his company not being allowed to build *Western Heights*. He wanted to be portrayed as a caring, sensitive local businessman who made significant donations to various local charities. His loyal PA, who had joined the call, was taking copious notes as her boss continued to hold centre stage.

Jim Barrat was tasked with including supportive facts for reference in his final report, mainly concentrated around similar projects that had been granted and not refused. Information about local parking facilities were also to be included, despite the fact that parking was not a requirement by law; it was felt that this would show a softer, more compassionate side of the developer.

Gibson concluded by saying that he had spoken at length with the other members of the planning committee, and even without Lady Eileen's vote, he was now sure that he could get a 3 to 2 vote in favour of reinstatement of the project. The cost to Fraser Robertson would be a further million pounds – half a million going to Gibson; two hundred thousand a piece going to his Liberal Democrat colleagues, who had a vote each, and the remaining hundred being split amongst Jim Barrat and some of his fellow cronies.

"A million pounds and you absolutely guarantee reinstatement?" asked Fraser.

"Guaranteed Fraser," came the confident reply back. "I will need half of it up front and half on delivery of the result, as usual cash."

"What will happen when Tony Barlow and his supporters find out about the land deal?"

"Not a problem. We are going to reply saying that unfortunately the file has gone missing, stating that we are doing everything we can to locate it. By the time we find it and indeed if we find it, then it will be too late anyway, and of course it will have been sanitised."

"I want to see the final report before it is submitted and before any cash changes hands," said Fraser. "I also want a guarantee that details of the land deal will not be revealed. In principal, you have a deal, Mr Gibson." Fraser hung up feeling satisfied with himself. A further million pounds was a small price to pay on a project that would net him in the region of twenty million pounds' profit.

* * *

The GP's surgery was a hive of activity as an impatient Robert Harris waited his turn. The silence was broken by coughs and splutters, interspersed with babies crying and mothers cooing at their prized possessions in an attempt to bring them some comfort. Harris had managed to drag himself to the local family practice where he had registered when he first moved back to Liverpool. He sat on a threadbare chair in the corner of the waiting room, flicking through an old copy of *Cheshire Life*.

Harris was feeling lousy, and his condition was not being helped by the long wait. He had arrived at the surgery shortly after 8:30 and it was now approaching 9:45. Just as he was about to leave, his name was called over the tannoy.

"Mister Arris. Mister Arris, room 3, Doctor Brady."

He was greeted by a diminutive figure dressed in an old tweed sports coat and cavalry twill trousers that looked like they had seen at least thirty years of service. An old pair of tan-coloured Oxford brogues were competing in the age stakes with his trousers. They looked like they had never been polished.

"Now what seems to be the problem, Mr Harris?"

Harris explained that he had been experiencing what he described as "flu-like symptoms" for some time now, and that he had bought medication from the chemist, but it simply was not working.

The doc checked his blood pressure, his ears and listened to his chest – all of which were relatively normal.

"You obviously have a temperature and an infected throat; you are showing signs of typical symptoms that you would associate with the flu," he said. "I am concerned about the shaking that you describe.

"You are very slim, Mr Harris. Have you lost any weight recently?"

"Not that I am really aware of, maybe a few pounds."

The doctor put him on the scales, recording his weight on his personal file.

Following a couple more minutes of questions and diagnosis, the doctor concluded that Robert Harris needed to rest for a few days, taking lots of fluids and regular food.

"I want you to continue with the paracetemol. If you don't feel any better in the next 48 hours, then please come back and see me. I think we will find that it is a viral infection and heavy cold; nothing too serious."

"Thanks, Doc." Harris shook the practitioner's frail-looking hand and left the surgery, really none the wiser about his condition but willing to follow the doctor's orders.

CHAPTER THIRTY-TWO

Following his success at the town hall, Tony Barlow returned to work to find 206 e-mails sitting in his inbox. He knew before he looked at them that most would be trash that had absolutely no value or bearing on his job.

He hated working in the IT industry. He was trapped and desperately wanted to escape from it, but for now he had to continue to go through the processes and play the game.

Buried in the middle of the continuous lines of e-mails was one from Paul Gibson at Liverpool City Council explaining the formal process of what would happen with the application now that Robertson Holdings had lodged an appeal and a counter-claim against the council. Tony was staggered to read that because litigation was now underway, he had no right or entitlement to any further input in the matter. Gibson concluded his mail by stating that the outcome would be decided behind closed doors sometime during the first two weeks of January, Barlow would be notified of the final decision by post. There was no legal right of appeal for the objectors in the event that planning was reinstated.

He thumped his desk, causing his coffee cup to jump, and spilling a proportion of its lukewarm contents onto a report that he had just printed off.

"Shit! That is fucking outrageous!" he yelled.

He ducked out of his 10:30 conference call so he could make a few calls to his supporters and legal team. His solicitor managed to raise his blood pressure even further, whilst at the same time dampen his spirits, by telling him that they were following correct procedure and she had no doubt would take advantage of the giant crevasses that existed in the law. "That is what criminals do, Mr Barlow," she said, "and sadly the bigger the criminal, the better they tend to be at it."

"Have you had anything back from your *Freedom of Information* application yet?" she continued.

"No, only an acknowledgement. Let's face it – they are all in it together. They are not going to give me anything that they don't want me to see."

"You could always consider suing them for gross misrepresentation of the sale and apply for an injunction should planning be reinstated until the outcome of your litigation. But apart from the cost that would be involved, if you lost you would then be liable for their costs, and I have no doubt they would seek damages which could run into millions."

"Unbelievable."

"I am sorry, Mr Barlow. Let's hope that the rejection is upheld."

"No chance of that. Robertson will pay whatever it takes to get this through."

"Is there anything else that I can assist you with, Mr Barlow?"

"No, thanks, you have done more than enough," Tony replied flippantly as he hung up.

Tony spent the remainder of the day sharing his pent-up anger with fellow objectors and a few colleagues who would listen to him. This had not been a great start to the week.

Nothing much happened over the next couple of weeks. Robert Harris seemed to be on the mend and back on his feet. Tony Barlow received a letter from the city council planning department advising him that the folder relating to the sale of land at Gartner Street had unfortunately gone missing – however, they were doing everything in their power to find it.

Tony had decided to throw himself into his job, as well as going mad in the gym, in an attempt to deal with his ever-increasing stress levels. He had instructed a local estate agent to market his apartment – it simply held too many bad memories. Every time he returned home, he felt his mood change, becoming depressed and wound up about the dreadful situation that he found himself in. Barlow did not hold out much hope, given the complicated circumstances that surrounded *Robertson Heights*. Surely nobody in his or her right mind would part with £800,000 with all the current uncertainty.

Gina Robertson reflected on the events of the past nine months or so: how her life had been so perfect – too perfect – only to be destroyed at an alarming speed.

She felt awful both physically and mentally. Her recent increase of anti-depressants and booze was only adding to her chaotic and fragile state. She knew that she was harming her baby, but simply did not care. Thoughts of self-harm became increasingly present in her unbalanced mind as the birth of her child drew ever closer.

Robert Harris's business was going from strength to strength, mainly at the expense of Fraser Robertson's demise. Following the devastation of his factory and the subsequent police investigation, he had to scale down his operations at the busiest time of year, much to his annoyance. Even he, the great Fraser Robertson, could not let his arrogance and total disregard for anyone and anything outside his very close circle trip him up. Somehow Harris had managed to keep both his business and as importantly his true identity a secret from "Mr Big". He knew that it was only a matter of time, though – right now Fraser was distracted with other matters.

Peter Swann had failed to recover his senses from seeing Gina again. He was besotted with her natural beauty. Swann had convinced himself that she was carrying his baby. He had dropped her a couple of texts since the ill-fated dinner date, but she had not responded. Peter was keeping a very watchful eye on her, unbeknownst to Gina.

Mercedez had not seen anything of Robert Harris. She had been putting in a couple of extra shifts to ensure that she had enough money to spoil her little princess at Christmas. She had turned down an invitation to a private party that Fraser Robertson threw for his staff at The Radisson Hotel. Mercedez knew that not only would Victor Knight be there, the man who slit her throat, but also the thought of having to shag a load of druggie gangsters filled her with disgust. Sure, she could have done with the fifteen hundred pounds that was on offer for a night's work, but her pride and self-worth had far more value. She would leave this gig to the Eastern European working girls.

Jim Barrat and Paul Gibson had completed the report that needed to go back to the planning committee. They were delighted with it. Not only had they given valid reasons to address each and every point that Lady Eileen had given for refusing planning, but they also had some powerful third-party reference material from previous similar cases, which they included as appendices. Fraser Robertson had given his blessing to their work. He handed over a fat brown envelope containing half a million pounds to Paul Gibson as per their agreement.

Alan Grimshaw had tried on several occasions to persuade his wife that she needed to have a rethink about *Western Heights* and the ramifications of not granting permission to build the development, but she was unmoved. This lady was not for turning. Lady Eileen told her husband that the development was morally appalling.

Simon Robertson was feeling shattered. He had been working long hours with James Thirsk, Paul Gibson and Jim Barrat on the report that he felt sure would now clear the way to reinstatement. The sheer emotional toil of both the Manning Street disaster coupled with his wife's fragile state of mind weighed heavily on him. Black circles had begun to appear under his eyes. He looked drawn and pale, but he knew that he had to remain strong for the next few weeks, as they would be critical both personally and professionally.

* * *

Snow was forecast. The temperature had plummeted to five below. Liverpool felt more like Moscow. Early risers scraped their car windscreens, and pedestrians broke into jogs in an effort to beat the chill. The River Mersey resembled a millpond. All was quiet and cold, bitterly cold, as Christmas drew ever nearer. It was the calm before the storm.

Despite feeling under the weather again, Robert Harris had decided a bit of self indulgence was in order and had booked Mercedez for a couple of hours that evening. She would come over to his apartment for some much-needed female company. Robert had a soft spot for this working girl. She was spirited, honest and decent. He was growing fond of her.

Fraser Robertson's staff arrived early at the hotel to ensure that the evening's extravaganza would go without a hitch. Robertson Holdings had hired a private function room for the party and the entire tenth floor bedrooms and suites for their guest's pleasure. Invitations had gone out to every male on the payroll, which numbered eighty-six in total. High ranking politicians, police officers, councillors, city planners and dealers would be offered everything from Champagne to charlie and prostitutes as a show of gratitude for all the favours that had been granted during the course of the year. Chief Constable Wilberforce had declined the invitation, as it was not his thing.

Robertson's loyal staff – who were virtually unsackable, as they had been privileged to way too much information – worked diligently throughout the day with the caterers, florists and their own security staff. Nothing was left to chance as guest rooms were swept for bugs and hidden cameras.

By six o'clock, the snow had arrived. "Snow Drift" had been placed in goody bags inside the private guest rooms. The gift tag read, "Hope you enjoy your white Christmas", whilst outside on the streets of the city, large pure white snowflakes descended from the cold black skies.

Twenty working girls were briefed thoroughly. Each girl was shown a selection of photographs of the VIPs and assigned to individual rooms and suites on the tenth floor. Fraser personally selected the prettier escorts for his most distinguished partygoers. At eight, the guests had started to arrive, many of them looking like they had a bad case of dandruff as the snowflakes clung to their hair before melting or being shaken or brushed away.

Simon Robertson had agreed with his dad that he would be present for the first couple of hours or so, but would then need to return home to care for his ailing wife.

Jim Barrat, Paul Gibson and James Thirsk all arrived together and were quickly in the swing of things, quaffing vintage Champagne like it was going out of fashion whilst mingling with the female hosts. Apart from Gibson, whose cheating wife Sheila had no doubt attended to her husband, the other two probably had not had a shag since Robertson's last Christmas bash. Boy, they were ugly.

Shortly after nine, all the guests had arrived, security was in place and the buffet was served. Thirsk and Barrat had already made their way up to the tenth floor with a couple of Polish girls. Gibson was in deep conversation with a local blonde girl who had a cracking pair of pins and a stunning-looking brunette. He was organising a threesome for later. Most of the top brass had not shown their faces in the function room. They had been escorted directly to their suites where some high-class ladies awaited to pleasure them and deliver their every desire no matter what.

Next door in *Robertson Heights*, Robert Harris and Mercedez were enjoying each other's company. A bottle of chilled Cristal lay in an ice bucket at the foot of the huge metal bed. A couple of dozen vanilla candles softly lit the room. They lay in each other's arms like a courting couple, staring out of the floor to ceiling glass bedroom window at the snow that was falling heavily. She made him laugh. Laughter had been missing in his short life to date. Mercedez had lifted his spirits.

"You're a lucky guy, Rob."

"Now, what makes you say that?"

"Well for starters, to be lying here with me. You are loaded, young, good-looking."

"Enough – you'll make me blush!"

"I was supposed to be working next door tonight."

"Really?"

"Yeah. It's Fraser Robertson's annual Christmas bash."

"Fraser Robertson, Mr Big."

"Mr Big, that's him."

"So what happens at his Christmas party?"

"He invites all his cronies for a drug and shag fest. You would not believe who is on his guest list."

"Tell me more."

"High-ranking officers of the local constabulary, politicians, councillors, city planners, traders, dealers and a few of his trusted hangers on. It's his reward to them for all the illegal favours that they grant him. It's his way of doing business."

"So why did you turn it down?"

"Because I hate him and all that he stands for. One of his traders, Victor Knight, slit my throat. There was no way I was going to go to that gig, even though it was paying fifteen hundred pounds for the night. He has hired about twenty girls and the entire tenth floor of the hotel."

"Get dressed, honey, we are going to have some fun."

"But Rob ... What are you thinking of doing? He's a bad man, he'll have his security men all over the place."

"Don't worry, I'm not going to do anything daft – just a bit of fun at Mr Big's expense. Now come on, get dressed."

CHAPTER THIRTY-THREE

"Merseyside Police"

"Oh hi, I would like to report an extensive stash of class 'A' drugs being used at a private Christmas party being hosted by Fraser Robertson at The Radisson Hotel at the corner of Brook Street and Gartner Street. There are also about twenty prostitutes present on the tenth floor."

"Whom am I speaking with, please?"

"That does not matter; please pass this on to your drug squad."

"I will, but I need your name." The phone went dead.

"I don't hold out much hope there, but it's worth a shot," Harris said to Mercedez. "Now for the real fun."

The couple entered the hotel lobby and headed for the bar, where a number of residents were enjoying a late-night drink, oblivious to what was going on ten floors above them. He ordered a couple of glasses of Champagne before taking a good vantage point over by the main entrance.

"Rob, what are you doing?"

"Stop worrying, all will be revealed. I need to pay a visit to the boy's room, sit tight."

Harris excused himself. Within a couple of minutes, the deafening, high-pitched screeches of the hotel's fire alarms were ringing out. Panic started to show itself in the guise of hotel management and staff ushering guests and residents out onto the street. This was standard procedure for any fire alarm. Harris knew this; he had been involved in a false alarm at the hotel when he was a resident. Bright blue lights flashed as the alarm sirens intensified.

Mercedez could not contain herself, bursting out in a fit of giggles as she realised that Robert had set the alarm off.

Up on the tenth floor, where the party was in full swing, scantily clad guests were being ushered to the fire escapes. Embarrassed VIPs tried to reason with hotel management that it was probably just a false alarm, refusing to leave the hotel for fear of being spotted. Other guests that were attending the Robertson party were high as a kite, some of them laughing at what was going on, whilst others became aggressive.

Robertson's security guys sprung into action, prioritising their protection by the importance and standing of Fraser's guests. Fraser was knees-deep in the presidential suite when he was instructed to grab a towelling robe and evacuate immediately, much to his disgust.

Down on the street, an ever-growing group of people dressed in an array of attire ranging from virtually nothing to evening dress shivered in the freezing night air. Hotel staff handed out golf umbrellas in a bid to keep their guests relatively dry from the driving snow. The wind had also picked up, turning the brollies inside out whilst blowing the heavy snow around the gathered guests.

Robert and Mercedez were crying with laughter as more half-naked dignitaries were tossed into the worsening weather. Mercedez had recognised some of the girls, but they had not spotted her. Fraser Robertson appeared in a sky blue towelling robe and a pair of the hotel's slippers. His face was like thunder. He looked like he was going to explode with rage. This made Robert laugh even harder. He had never seen his father in such pain.

"For God's sake, this is obscene," Fraser screamed at the hotel's duty manager.

"I am really sorry, Mr Robertson, but this is standard procedure. We have to wait for the fire brigade to give us the all clear."

As Fraser let loose with another volley of abuse, his words were drowned out by the fire engines as they hurtled down the street, coming to an abrupt halt outside the hotel entrance.

The fire chief confirmed with the duty manager that all guests had been accounted for as the snow continued to fall on the high paying guests. The drugs squad did not show. Most of them were now standing wrapped in towels outside The Radisson.

Robert and Mercedez retired to the warmth and comfort of his penthouse, having had a fantastic laugh at his father's expense. They continued to watch the chaos on the street below from his apartment. The guests jumped up and down in an attempt to keep warm. They looked like they were taking part in an aerobics class.

Following another extremely uncomfortable twenty minutes, the fire brigade had given the all clear. They found the broken lens that had set the alarm off just outside the men's toilets.

Fraser Robertson was baying for blood. Somebody was going to pay for this.

The black chauffeur-driven Bentley screeched to a halt at the front of the hotel. A dishevelled, furious Fraser Robertson took up his position in the back of the car, throwing the chauffeur's coat and hat into the foot well.

"Take me home immediately," he barked at the driver.

The snow was beginning to stick as the Bentley made its way down a deserted Pall Mall towards the tunnel. Fraser was fuming. Who the fuck would have the audacity to show him up in front of all his high-ranking friends and dignitaries? He felt shit, too, as the alcohol excesses conspired with the huge amount of charlie that he had snorted.

"Can't this go any fucking faster?" he yelled.

The driver responded by putting his foot down.

Apart from a couple of squirrels who were making their way across the deserted footpath, nobody saw the figure dressed from head to toe in black make its way across the undergrowth at the back of the Caldy mansion.

Small footprints were left in the thickening snow as the sniper crossed to a good vantage point at the back of Fraser Robertson's magnificent dwelling. It took a few minutes to reach the spot from which the attack would be launched.

The Bentley's powerful engine roared as the car sped towards its destination. Its cargo had nodded off and slumped in the back, having expended more than enough energy for one night.

The tripod was assembled in no time at all. The automatic rifle and silencer were quickly pieced together before being secured on the tripod. The laser-guided sights were focused on the living room and then the main bedroom, which were both positioned at the back of the dwelling. The sniper listened to some music whilst waiting for the victim to return home.

Fraser awoke from his unconscious state as the car began to negotiate the twisting lanes that signalled the fact that he was nearing his home.

"Nearly home, Sir."

"I know, I know," replied a frustrated and deeply agitated passenger.

Within a couple of minutes, the Bentley drew up outside the magnificent entrance to Fraser Robertson's home. The snow had stuck to the tall trees that surrounded the entrance. The rooftop was pure white and glistened under the night sky.

The ornate lamps that stood proudly either side of the door beamed reflective light off the snow. The setting was picturesque.

With the help of his chauffeur and an umbrella, Fraser was escorted into his house without getting wet.

"Will that be all for this evening, Sir?"

"I fucking well hope so. I am going to have a nightcap and then retire."

"Very well." The chauffeur departed and Fraser made his way into the living room.

Taking a crystal tumbler from the display cabinet, he swiftly poured himself a very large 15-year-old malt. He hoped that this would calm his current mental state and help him sleep.

As his lips met with the rim of the glass, the bullet entered the back of his skull. By the time that Fraser's body hit the ground, the sniper was making his way back across the footpath to the getaway vehicle. Fraser shook uncontrollably for a few seconds before his body relaxed and his mind shut down. Fragments of bone, skin and blood adorned the wall and cabinet, whose glass had shattered with the impact. Apart from a couple of squirrels and a fox that had recently inhabited the area, nobody heard the bullet, the breaking glass or the heavy fall.

The cold night air sent a shiver down Fraser Robertson's chauffeur's spine as he stood outside the Bentley enjoying a cigarette to calm his nerves following the volley of abuse he had suffered at the hands of his employer. He opened the rear door to get his jacket. Fraser Robertson's mobile phone's screen shone and lit up the dark interior. It must have fallen out of Fraser's pocket when he fell asleep.

The phone showed two missed calls and a text. The chauffeur quickly stubbed out his cigarette, turned the car around and made his way back to his boss's mansion, which was only a few minutes away.

The headlights reflected against the thickening snow as the Bentley ploughed a lonely furrow in the country lane that led to its destination. As the car entered the driveway, much to the chauffeur's relief he could see a couple of lights on inside the house. He pulled up at the front of the house, grabbed the mobile and made his way to the large front door. He rang the bell – nothing. He rang it again and banged the large brass knocker in the middle of the oak door. Still no response... The chauffer thought that maybe he's gone to bed and just left the lights on.

He decided to go around the back of the house to see if there was any sign of life. He felt the sensation of his feet getting wet as he made his way across the snow covered lawn to the side gate and along the path to the rear.

As he neared the French doors of the lounge, the shattered glass from where the bullet had entered crunched beneath his sodden shoes. Within seconds, he saw the broken glass glistening in the setting snow. The plush burgundy curtains swayed in the light breeze as the room lights cascaded onto the patio where the chauffer now stood. His heart raced as he began to process what lay before him.

"Oh my God, Boss, Boss, are you OK?"

He darted across the lounge floor, leaving wet footprints on the carpet behind him. Fraser was lying in a crumpled heap, motionless. An almost perfect circle of blood had oozed from the wound and formed on the cream carpet on which he lay. The chauffeur began to panic as the magnitude of the situation began to sink in.

"Christ, somebody help us here!" he shouted, as he got no response to checking Fraser's pulse.

He grabbed the phone on the nearby table and swiftly dialled 999.

"Emergency services, which service do you require?" enquired the softly spoken female attendant.

"Ambulance immediately to The Cedars, Croft Drive East, Caldy. Please come quickly, there has been a shooting and it looks like the victim is losing his fight for life. Oh and er, send the police."

"The ambulance should be with you inside 5 minutes."

The chauffeur listened to his boss's heartbeat. It was weak, but he convinced himself that at least there was a beat. He phoned Simon Robertson, but there was no reply, so he left a message for him to call him urgently.

The four minutes that it took the ambulance to arrive, swiftly followed by the police, seemed like an eternity.

The paramedics literally burst through the front door, three of them dressed in bright pea green boiler suits. The fourth man was a young Asian man carrying a large doctor's bag.

The ruffled chauffeur guided them through the spacious hallway into the lounge where the victim lay. The medical team wasted no time in getting down to work. They quickly confirmed that Fraser's state was absolutely critical. He had lost a lot of blood, his pulse was desperately weak and he was losing his fight for life.

"We need to get him to the nearest hospital immediately," said the Asian-looking doctor, who was obviously unfamiliar with the area.

"That will be Murrayfield, Doc. It's about fifteen minutes away if we hammer it."

"I will phone ahead and get the medical team briefed. I honestly don't know if he will make it and even if he does I have no idea of what damage the bullet may have done, he has lost a lot of blood."

A shot of adrenaline was injected into Fraser Robertson's main artery prior to moving him into the back of the ambulance. He lay like a statue showing no sign of life as electrodes were being stuck on his chest and legs.

Two of the paramedics worked diligently in the confined space whilst the doctor spoke to the admissions manager, briefing him on what to expect and what resources would be required as soon as they landed.

The ambulance moved violently first to the right then to the left as it hit a patch of icy snow and temporarily lost control. The medics were quick to react and managed to make sure that their ailing patient was not catapulted across the back of the ambulance into the monitors.

The doctor was not as quick to react and his mobile phone was hurled into the opposite wall and the call was abruptly terminated.

"For fuck's sake, can we please keep some control up there and get to Murrayfield in one piece?" the older, balding attendant screamed at the driver through the intercom.

"Sorry guys. I'm doing my best – the driving conditions are worsening."

The ambulance driver managed to negotiate the last stretch of the journey without any further incident.

The monitors had stayed relatively static during that time. An eerie darkness descended as the ambulance reversed up to the large double doors of the emergency suite and then within an instant of the rear doors being flung open, a piercing shaft of light penetrated the back of the emergency vehicle. Was there to be any light at the very dark end of Fraser Robertson's tunnel?

The trolley to which he was strapped was swiftly pushed through the giant plastic doors of the operating suite where a hastily assembled medical team stood awaiting his arrival. The anaesthetist proceeded with the general anaesthetic, as there was no time to lose. Fraser was hooked up to the giant plasma screens that would be watched diligently by the medical staff as the surgeon readied himself to attempt to save the life of Fraser Robertson.

As the doctors went to work, Simon Robertson was unaware of his father's predicament. Back at Fraser's home the forensic team were well underway with their operation. The chauffeur had given the police a witness statement and had provided them contact details of next of kin. He may well have saved Fraser's life.

* * *

"A shoo ... A shoo...." Harris awoke with the start of yet another cold, his nose once again, running like a tap. The exaltation from the night before was long gone, replaced by feeling stiff, sore, weak and miserable. Mercedez had gone home, so he was left to nurse his ailments alone.

He decided to go back to the doctor. He was becoming increasingly concerned and needed some reassurance. He managed to see Dr Brady, who carried out the same routine tests and weighed him. He had lost five pounds.

"I want to run some blood tests, Mr Harris. You are in luck – the district nurse is in the practice. I can arrange for her to do them now."

Harris agreed, and fifteen minutes later, five vials of blood had been taken from his arm. The doctor told him that with the Christmas and New Year closedown, he would not have the results of his tests back until around January 10. He was given the same advice as before – to go home and rest, making sure that he drank plenty of fluids.

Harris heeded his advice, staying in bed throughout Christmas and New Year. Mercedez came round to see him with her little girl. She was concerned with the visible deterioration. His lips were cracked and a couple of cold sores had grown at the side of his mouth. She was all he had in his life; the only person that had shown any affection towards him. Despite the fact that it was paid for, he felt that there was something between them.

Simon Robertson was looking forward to getting back to work. He had enjoyed his extended time off due to the demise of the family drugs business. Simon had spent a lot of time with his son Mark, playing football and computer games with him. Gina had managed to raise her spirits for the sake of her son, but was once again heading back into her world of worry, spiralling into depression.

Paul Gibson had treated himself and his good lady to a two-week break at Sandy Lane in Barbados courtesy of Fraser's latest bung. They had basked in the luxury of one of the world's finest destinations; travelling first class with BA, and rubbing shoulders with celebrities and movie stars.

Tony had made the most of his time off. After the excesses of Christmas, he fancied a bit of sun and relaxation to lift his spirits. Tony jetted off to Miami on December 26, staying in a boutique hotel on South Beach for fourteen nights. The days were filled with nothing more strenuous than stretching out on a sun lounger. At night, he ate in Miami's finest restaurants and partied hard, dating a string of hot ladies. He had a wonderful time and was dreading going back home, although his cock was in need of a well-earned rest.

On January 9, he returned to driving rain, four degrees and a pile of mail. As he turned the key and opened the door to his apartment, the freezing cold air hit him. The air conditioning unit had failed again, setting itself at its coldest setting and distributing bitterly cold recirculated air around his penthouse.

"Shit! Fucking welcome home."

He switched the system off and reported the fault to the security guy on reception.

There were no messages of note on his answer machine. There had been no interest in his apartment during the holiday – his phone had been quiet. He shifted through the stack of envelopes, trying to prioritise the order of opening; searching for anything that looked remotely interesting whilst pushing what looked like bills to the back of the pile.

The purple and black markings around the liver bird stood out on Liverpool City Council's planning department envelope. The postmark was dated January 7, two days previous. He ripped it open with a fear of dread that was soon confirmed.

The succinct note read, "Liverpool City Council and their legal advisors found no grounds for upholding the planning committee's decision to reject the application for *Western Heights*. Therefore the application to build a fifty-storey residential tower at the site on Gartner Street has now been granted. The decision is final and binding and you have no right of appeal." It was signed by, Paul Gibson, Head of Planning.

"Fucking bastards! Shower of bent cunts! *Fuck!*"

Barlow threw the letter on the floor. He knew by his outburst that he had finally lost his long, hard fought battle to a bunch of bent, corrupt individuals. Tony knew that this would kill him; drive him back over the edge.

* * *

Gina Robertson was now a week late. Her husband and son watched the morning news in the kitchen whilst she poured them a bowl each of their favourite cereals. They had been told that she would need to be induced if the baby did not present itself in the next 48 hours. Her hand shook as she poured the milk onto Simon's cereal, spilling it on the worktop. Gina was a broken woman. She felt that she could not go through with the birth.

"I need to go into the office, honey," said Simon. "I will only be a couple of hours at most – I need to sign the contracts for *Western Heights*. I'll have my mobile; so if anything happens at all, call me straight away. I'll drop Markie off at school."

Gina nodded. "OK."

Simon was actually going to the bank to withdraw another half a million pounds. The money was to be taken now that Paul Gibson had delivered the goods. Gibson had been as good as his word, delivering a 3 to 2 verdict as he had predicted. By all accounts, Lady Eileen was completely shattered.

As Simon and Mark ate their breakfasts, the surgical team at Murrayfield were finishing the complex operation that they had been performing on Fraser throughout the night. It was far too early to know if it had been successful.

Simon gave his wife a kiss on the cheek and a reassuring hug before leaving the house. Mark grabbed his satchel and hugged his mum's midriff.

As Gina waved goodbye to them, she heard the sound of an incoming text and made her way back into the kitchen. She picked up her mobile, which was flashing. Gina did not recognise the number; her heart skipped a beat as she opened the message.

"What are you waiting for, Gina? Is the bastard going to be a black sheep or a white Swann?"

She felt her blood supply cut off. Her heart pounded as the seizure struck. She sank to the floor, banging her head on the corner of the granite worktop and lost consciousness instantly. Her mobile smashed on the ceramic floor tiles.

CHAPTER THIRTY-FOUR

Simon got held up in traffic on his way into town – another poor unfortunate victim of "The Big Dig". He became frustrated as he texted his wife on his new phone that he still had not got the hang of, saying that he would probably be delayed by at least half an hour because of it. Her phone vibrated on the kitchen floor as his text came in.

A small pool of blood had gathered around Gina Robertson's head as she lay motionless on the cold kitchen tiles. The colour had started draining from her face. Her pulse weakened as the morning progressed.

Simon had managed to negotiate his way around the gridlock, putting his local knowledge to good use. He abandoned his Aston Martin outside the bank on Dale Street. His private banker, who should have met him, was held up in an internal meeting that had been called at short notice. The receptionist assured him that she would only be a matter of minutes. In a bid to cool himself down, he poured himself a plastic cupful of water from the complimentary drinks machine.

Six minutes passed by with no sign of his private banker. A sizeable queue had formed at the main reception that only added to boost his already desperately high stress levels. He called his private banker's mobile, but it went straight through to answer phone. He hung up.

Simon caught the eye of one of the receptionists. As he was about to shout over the queues, his private banker emerged from the back office, looking flustered.

"Mr Robertson, I am so sorry to have kept you waiting."

"Have you got my money?" he enquired abruptly.

"I need you to sign this declaration, the withdrawal form and complete some security questions."

"Can we be quick, please? I have had to leave my wife, who is due to give birth at any time."

"It should only take a few minutes, Mr Robertson."

Simon duly completed the security questions, signed all the paperwork and left the bank with half a million pounds. His next port of call was to rendezvous with Paul Gibson at Kings Dock. They had arranged to meet in the car park on the waterfront to conduct the exchange. He darted down the bank's steps to find an over-zealous traffic warden writing out a parking ticket.

"Listen, mate, I have literally been in the bank for five minutes."

"Twelve minutes, Sir. You are illegally parked...."

"Just give me the ticket and spare me the lecture."

The warden duly obliged. Simon jumped in his car, throwing the ticket on the passenger seat, and sped off in the direction of Kings Dock. He called Paul Gibson from his car phone to let him know that he was running behind schedule. Paul was fine; he had taken the day off so he could distribute the dirty money to his co-conspirators. The DB9 growled as Simon's foot pushed down hard on the accelerator pedal. The car approached the bottom of Dale Street to join Pall Mall, only to be greeted by a wall of bright red brake lights. The council were laying new drainage and had reduced the four-lane artery to just one lane.

"Shit" Simon yelled.

His car drew to a halt. He banged his hand hard against the dashboard in sheer frustration. He thought he would take the opportunity to check up on his wife. The house phone just rang out, eventually going to the answer machine. He dialled her mobile, which jumped and vibrated on the floor beside where she lay. You could hear the panic in his voice as he left her a message.

"Hi honey, hope you're OK. I guess you must be taking a shower. Anyway, I should be home within the hour. Love you."

The traffic began to move slowly, much to Simon's relief. The V12 engine grunted and spluttered as the car crawled onto Pall Mall, picking up speed as the lights changed to green. It took fifteen minutes to negotiate a smooth passage through the road works onto Kings Dock. Paul Gibson's black Jaguar XKR was parked up, awaiting his arrival. Simon pulled alongside his vehicle, wound down his window and passed the package to Paul. No words were spoken as the DB9 roared off in the direction of home.

Simon called his father and left a message to tell him that the package had been delivered. He dialled Gina again to let her know that he was en route, but she did not pick up. The speedometer showed 90 mph as he tried to make up for lost time. His palms began to perspire and his mouth felt dry as his concern grew for his wife's welfare. At least he was now heading away from the all the congestion of the city centre. He jumped a red light, followed by another and another, repeatedly dialling Gina, but to no avail.

After what seemed like an eternity, Simon pulled into the leafy close through the electronic gates and came to an abrupt halt on his pathway. His heart missed several beats as he saw the police car parked on his driveway. He dashed into the house, calling Gina.

The policeman met him at the door. "Mr Robertson ... Mr Simon Robertson?"

"Yes ... Yes ... Please tell me what's going on. Is my wife OK?" He brushed past the officer.

"Gina, Gina!" he yelled as he darted into the kitchen. He immediately spotted his wife lying prostrate on the cold floor in a pool of congealed blood, being tended to by another officer.

"Oh no. Please God."

He crouched down and lay beside her. As he held her hand, tears began to stream down his cheeks. As he cuddled up to her, the sound of sirens broke the eerie silence.

The ambulance had arrived in no time at all. The two men dressed in bright green overalls, accompanied by a doctor, sprinted into the house to attend to Gina. One of them carried a large medical bag; the other pushed a stretcher into the house. The doctor asked for a pillow to place under Gina's head. She was still unconscious, her skin looked pallid and felt cold. Simon looked on nervously as the medics set to work.

The doctor checked her vitals, shouting out the results to one of the medics, who was noting them down.

"When is baby due?" enquired the doctor.

"It's overdue". "My wife was to be admitted tomorrow to be induced. Are they going to be OK? Oh God, please tell me that they will be OK," sobbed Simon.

"It's too early to say, her pulse is very weak, and the baby's heartbeat is quite erratic. We need to get them to a hospital immediately. Is your wife on any medication, Mr Robertson?"

"Yes, anti-depressants."

"Do you have her tablets and dosage?"

"They should be in the drawer." Simon handed the tablets to the doctor. The medics had managed to move his unconscious wife onto the stretcher and were heading for the ambulance.

"Where are we taking them, Doc?"

"Liverpool Women's Maternity Hospital. Radio for a couple of outriders, we don't have much time. Take her to the emergency suite as fast as you can."

Simon could not focus. His emotions had taken over.

The police officer intervened as Simon was about to get into the back of the ambulance with his wife.

"Mr Robertson, there is no easy way of telling you this. Your father was shot late last night and has undergone life saving surgery at Murrayfield Hospital."

Simon began to shake. The colour drained from his face as what he was dealing with began to sink in.

"Shot ... what do you mean, shot? Life-saving procedure ... oh my God. No – please no."

"The surgeons operated throughout the night, but I'm afraid if your father survives the surgery, then the prognosis is not good. Is there anyone else that can go to your father? What about your brother?"

"No ... er, there is nobody. Look, I have to go with my wife, she needs me and so does Dad, but there is only one of me and I have to go with my wife and my baby. I will go to my father once I know my wife and baby are safe."

"Very well, we will need to take a statement, but given the circumstances, we can defer this until later."

"We have to go. We cannot waste another second," screamed the ambulance driver.

Simon was hurriedly bundled into the back of the ambulance as the medic and doctor wired Gina up to a large colour monitor that constantly displayed her heart rate and pulse. He sat on the bench seat opposite his wife, his head in his hands, sobbing his eyes out.

The driver radioed for two police outriders and put the call into Liverpool Women's Maternity Hospital, instructing them to have a medical team on standby. He estimated that it would take at least fifteen minutes to complete the journey. The siren came back to life as the ambulance driver floored the accelerator pedal. The first part of the journey was completed swiftly and efficiently. The police had confirmed that the bike cops would meet the ambulance at the junction of Allerton Road and Queens Drive to escort them on the rest of the journey.

In the back, Simon continued to sob as his world fell apart before him. He could not think straight. The medical men watched and listened attentively to the monitors and alarms that were connected to his wife and unborn child.

The outriders spotted the ambulance as it weaved its way in and out of the morning's traffic towards them, its sirens blaring. One of the bike cops manoeuvred his bike into the middle of the dual carriageway, raising his right-gloved hand, instructing the oncoming traffic to stop and let the ambulance through; the second outrider switched on his siren and rode in the direction of the ambulance, creating a passage that it could navigate through.

The ambulance picked up speed as it emerged from the stationary traffic. Blue lights flashed and sirens wailed as an outrider took a position at the front of the white emergency vehicle, his black leather-clad colleague taking a position at the rear of the ambulance. The speedometer hit 70 mph as the main road opened up in front of them.

A new unwelcome sound resonated in the back of the ambulance as the unborn baby's alarm went off.

"Quick!" shouted the medic. "We are losing the baby."

The heartbeat had dropped to a critical level. Gina's vitals, although desperately weak, were managing to hold up. Simon was struggling to keep it together. He grabbed a paper bag from the medical supply rack above his head. Simon heaved and balked, depositing the contents of his stomach into it.

Simon sunk to his knees wrapping his arms around the doctor's legs he begged the medical man to save the lives of his wife and baby and began to pray for the life of his father. He was totally delirious.

"We are doing all we can, Mr Robertson, now please control yourself."

The medic buzzed the ambulance driver through the intercom system.

"We are struggling back here – we have a potential fatality. How much longer?"

"Should be there in five minutes, mate."

The doctor heard the driver's response over the loudspeaker as he administered a booster injection to his ailing patient.

"We need to speed up. I really don't think we have five minutes."

Simon became deranged as the doctor's message was passed to the driver and police outriders. The speedometers climbed from 70 mph through 80 and onto 90mph.

There was enough nervous energy flying around the emergency delivery room of Liverpool Women's Maternity Hospital to power the nearby homes. The medical team had been assembled in readiness for the arrival of Mrs Gina Robertson and her unborn baby.

Over the water at Murrayfield Hospital, Fraser Robertson was blissfully unaware of his predicament. The highly skilled surgeons had managed to remove both the bullet and the fragments of skull that had lodged in his brain. The sniper's shot had penetrated an area of his brain that controlled speech and movement.

Little did he or indeed any of his family know that he was going to survive both the attempt on his life and the major procedure that he had been subjected to – albeit he was paralysed from the waist down and was unlikely to ever be able to speak again. Fraser Robertson had run his last run, delivered his last speech; given his last instructions. There would be no more walks in the park.

Gina Robertson's condition had stabilised by the time they finally arrived at their destination. The medical team on board the ambulance had done their job. Following a quick three point turn, the back doors of the ambulance were flung open and Gina, complete with a comprehensive amount of medical equipment and staff, was carefully moved into the receiving area of the hospital, her suffering, faithful husband in tow.

The trolley on which she lay was swiftly manoeuvred down the stark, twisting corridors into the floodlit emergency room. As Simon tried to enter the theatre, he was stopped by one of the nursing staff and taken to a side room. "Try not to worry, Mr Robertson, your wife is going to be OK."

Simon nervously strutted up and down up and down following the well-marked tracks where once a painted floor radiated but now a concrete track was evident. Time seemed to stand still: seconds felt like minutes; minutes felt like hours. He had never felt so helpless and alone in his life.

Next door it had been decided that given Gina's condition an emergency Caesarean section would be performed. Within a matter of moments, the team got down to business and began the procedure. Gina's vitals, whilst weak, remained within the tolerance threshold. With the precision of a Swiss watchmaker, the surgeon wasted no time in making his first incision. This was quickly followed by further cuts through Gina's abdominal wall until the baby was visible to the medical team.

As Gina lay prostrate on the theatre table, her baby was brought into the world – a baby boy, weighing in at 8lb 6oz, with a mop of black curly hair and big hazel eyes. The crisis was finally over, or was it?

One of the midwives left the theatre and went off in search of Gina's husband to break the good news. It wasn't long before she found the pale, forlorn figure of Simon Robertson huddled up against a radiator in the waiting room.

"Congratulations, Mr Robertson, you have a beautiful baby boy. Would you like to see him now?"

Simon looked like a man who had just had the weight of the world removed from him. "Of course, that would be wonderful. Is my wife alright?"

"Yes, she'll be fine when she comes around. She's been through a hell of a lot, both emotionally and physically."

"I understand," replied Simon.

The midwife led Simon along the corridor and into the theatre, where the medical team were tidying up following the procedure. Gina lay motionless as Simon entered the room. It was very brightly lit and quite warm compared to the waiting room in which Simon had spent the past hour or so.

One of the nursing staff beckoned Simon over to an area where there was a small cot. As he approached, his pulse quickened with excitement. Another son, he thought. As he reached his destination, the nurse moved away to allow him some privacy with his newborn baby boy.

Simon peered into the cot with great anticipation. He immediately backed away as his brain quickly deduced what his eyes had just witnessed. He felt a sharp pain in his chest as he stumbled. Simon quickly regained his composure and decided to take a closer look. A second inspection left absolutely no doubt that his wife had just given birth to a black baby boy.

A host of thoughts rushed through Simon's mind, as he stood motionless, staring at the black baby. He beckoned one of the nursing staff over, a young, fresh-faced looking girl with short bright orange hair and a freckly face.

"Excuse me, I just wanted to check that this is the baby that my wife, Gina Robertson, just gave birth to? There hasn't been any mix up? It's just...."

The young nurse assured Mr Robertson that she had been present during the procedure and there was no doubt that this was his wife's baby boy. "I'm sorry, Mr Robertson, I'm really sorry."

As the enormity of the situation began to sink in, he felt the rage inside him build to a crescendo of hatred and disgust that he just had to let out. "Fucking whore, you fucking little tart!" He swept a metal kidney tray of medical instruments off the table in front of him. As they hit the floor, the sound resonated through the theatre, but still Gina lay motionless and barely conscious.

Simon took out his mobile and took a couple of pictures of the baby and left without so much as a second glance at his wife. He made quick progress down the hospital corridors and out of the main reception. He jumped in the back of a black cab that was at the front of a long queue of taxis outside the main entrance of the hospital. Simon instructed the driver to take him home as quickly as possible, as he faced a family emergency.

As the black cab hurtled through traffic to its, destination, Simon's mind began to race again. His stomach tightened with all the events of the past few hours. He struggled to focus; he could not begin to comprehend what had occurred. He knew that his next port of call was Murrayfield private hospital to visit his father. He dialled the hospital but it rang out.

The taxi driver had made excellent progress and he soon rounded the bend that took them up to the private road at the entrance of Simon's residence. Simon pressed the red button on his remote control and the gates began to open.

As they approached the house, what was once Simon's pride and joy sat proudly on the driveway, but his life had been turned upside down in the last few hours – he felt numb. The DB9 gleamed as a shaft of sunlight reflected through the mature trees and onto the bonnet.

The meter in the cab showed £9.50. Simon tossed the driver a twenty-pound note and told him to keep the change. "Thanks, Boss. God bless you."

Simon unlocked the car and pressed the start button, which brought the big six-litre engine to life. It roared like a fighter plane as he sped down the lane and started on his journey to visit his father.

In barely 30 minutes the DB9 pulled up to the tree-lined private hospital where his father was fighting for his life. He abandoned his car near the front entrance and dashed through the main entrance, clutching his mobile phone. He made his way quickly through a maze of corridors, following signs for the high dependency unit. He could feel the sweat start to drip from his forehead. His heart was beating quickly, and he felt sick to the pit of his stomach, both with the uncertainty of his father's condition and the devastating news that he was going to have to break to him.

Simon rounded what he hoped was the final corner to a set of large double doors, above which a brightly illuminated sign reading "High dependency unit". As he approached, the doors flung open and a couple who were giggling, seemingly unaware of his presence, bumped into him, sending his mobile flying.

"Sorry, mate," the man replied as he bent down to pick up the phone and hand it back before hotfooting down the corridor with his lady.

In the recesses of Simon's mind, he knew he had heard this voice before, but struggled to recollect when and where. He couldn't see the man's face clearly as he had his overcoat collar up, but he did think it strange that anyone would be in such good spirits after visiting such a place. Maybe they had had some really good news; an unpopular relative had passed and left them a ton of money ...

His mind turned back to his current predicament. He quickly checked that his phone had not been damaged and recalled the picture that he needed but did not want to show his father. A couple of deep breaths helped him to compose himself before he entered the high dependency unit.

Simon approached a small reception desk and announced himself to the young man. "My name is Simon Robertson. I came as quickly as I could. How is my father?"

The young man scanned his records and called the doctor on duty. "Take a seat, Mr Robertson, Dr Dewar will be with you shortly. Can I get you a drink?"

"No thanks."

Simon sat down. He felt dreadful. He was not used to bad news on any scale. Throughout his life, he had been sheltered, controlled and supported by his father.

He could not come to terms with the events of the past few hours. He had been betrayed. His life was falling apart.

Simon covered his face with cupped hands to shield himself from further bad news. His brief peace was quickly interrupted.

"Mr Robertson."

"Yes."

"I'm Dr Dewar, I have been dealing with your father's case since he was admitted."

The doctor nodded his head and guided Simon into a quiet anteroom. Simon felt his heart race as he sat down opposite the man in the white coat.

"I'm afraid it's bad news. We didn't expect your father to make it through surgery. The bullet penetrated an area of his brain that controls speech and movement. The surgeons managed to remove the bullet and have carried out repairs to both the lobe and skull."

'Oh my God!" Simon shouted.

"Your father has survived emergency surgery, Mr Robertson, but will never speak again. He is in a coma and is paralysed from the waist down. If he comes out of the coma, he will spend the rest of his days in a wheelchair."

Simon wanted to scream but somehow managed to stay calm. He had found some inner strength to deal with this.

"What are the chances of my father coming out of the coma?"

"At this stage, it's impossible to say. We have him under close observation every 15 minutes. Right now, he needs to rest. You can see him briefly."

The doctor stood up and beckoned Simon to follow him. The short journey from the anteroom to the high dependency suite where his father lay took no time at all. The room was dark apart from a solitary light above the bed that was surrounded by medical equipment; it had that hospital smell.

As Simon approached the head of the bed where Fraser lay unconscious, he barely recognised him. His head was wrapped in a swathe of bandages, his eyes closed, his face pale and drawn. A multitude of tubes projected out of various parts of his body and were connected to TV screens, drips, breathing apparatus and numerous machines. Simon could not take it all in. His mind kept straying back to his wife's betrayal. How could this happen?

"I will leave you alone, Mr Robertson."

"Thank you."

Simon pulled up a chair to the bed and sat down. He held his father's hand and looked into his eyes, which remained shut. A tear ran down his cheek and he began to sob.

"Oh Dad…. What on Earth happened? Who could have done this to you? This is the worst day of my life. You must fight, Dad; I need you more than ever. Gina has betrayed me. She's a little tart; a two-timing bitch. She's had a black baby – a black baby, for Christ's sake! She has brought great shame to our family. I want revenge, Dad. I will not rest until I find out who the baby's father is and who pulled the trigger. I don't think I can do this on my own, Dad."

As the tears began to run freely down Simon's cheeks, he felt his father's hand tighten its grip and his fingernails dig into Simon's hand. His father's upper body coiled and twisted, lashing out with his arms. His head momentarily rose from the pillow and the expression on his face turned to rage. Fraser's mouth widened as he attempted to scream, then suddenly he sank. Two of the alarms on the machines he was wired up to wailed in unison. Within seconds, a couple of medical staff had burst through the doors.

"Get a crash team in here immediately!" the doctor yelled at the nurse.

Simon felt numb – he couldn't move or focus. His state was broken by the arrival of the crash team and the doctor ordering him out of the room. His legs felt heavy as he got up from the chair and quickly made his way back to the anteroom that he had left only minutes earlier.

The doctor quickly charged the defibrillator pads to 150 in an attempt to revive Fraser.

"Clear," he shouted as he administered them to Fraser's chest. The TV screens that the medics were focused on remained unchanged, with a flat green line and a 0 registering by the heart symbol.

"Charging, gain to 150. Clear!" The pads were again pushed into the ailing patient's chest. There was still no change. A senior nurse continued heart massage as once again the defibrillator was recharged, but this time to 200.

"Clear!" The smell of singeing hair penetrated the air. There was still no response.

The medic continued to work frantically in a final bid to resuscitate their patient. One final application of the highly charged pads failed to change the outcome.

"Time of death is 2:37 p.m."

Simon paced up and down the small anteroom waiting for some news. It came very quickly. Dr Dewar entered the room stern-faced. Simon knew he was not going to be the bearer of good news.

"I'm afraid your father suffered a massive heart attack. We did everything we could. I'm really sorry, Mr Robertson, but we couldn't save him."

Simon, who had been staring at the floor as the fatal news was delivered, finally raised his head and looked Dr Dewar in the eyes. "Thanks, Doc. I know you and your team did all you could. Right now I need a little time to sort things out. Can I see my father before I go?"

"Of course you can."

As Simon made his way back to the ward, the phone rang on the reception desk.

"Good afternoon, Murrayfield high dependency unit, how can I assist you?"

"I'm phoning up for an update on Fraser Robertson."

"And who may I ask am I talking to?"

"I'm family," came the reply.

"Well, I'm afraid to tell you that Mr Robertson suffered a massive cardiac arrest following his surgery and passed away about fifteen minutes ago."

The caller hung up.

Simon stood over his father's corpse. He brushed his face with the back of his hand and rearranged the front of his hair. Fraser Robertson looked angry. He had a stern look on his face.

"Goodbye, Dad. I won't rest until I find your killer and restore some pride to our family name. This is now my life's mission – nothing more and nothing less."

THE END

Lightning Source UK Ltd.
Milton Keynes UK
UKOW031919270712

196686UK00009B/2/P